OBSCURA

Book 1: The Boy, the Girl and the Wooden Box

SHANE EMMETT

Copyright © 2019 by Shane Emmett

All rights reserved.

No part of this book may be reproduced in any form or by any electronic or mechanical means, including information storage and retrieval systems, without written permission from the author, except for the use of brief quotations in a book review.

Shane Emmett/Tar & Feather Publishing.

www.tarandfeather.com.au

tarandfeathergroup@gmail.com

Images are used courtesy of Pixabay creative commons.

Original cover design by Janice Goudappel

janice.goudappel@hotmail.com

Book Layout ©2019 Vellum

Obscura Book1. Shane Emmett. 1st edition.

ISBN 978-1-68411-981-3

"*The world is an upside down place.*" How often have you heard this phrase spoken and never really stopped to think about its true meaning. Indeed, it seems to infer a sense that the world is unpredictable, unexpected and at times defies logic. But what if the world actually was upside down? Well, it turns out it is. At least through the lens of our eyes that is. It is true that our eyes see the world around us quite literally upside down and send a confused signal to our brain which inverts the image to allow us to see the world the correct way. Or incorrect way for that matter, because after all, the version of the world that we see is only a perspective. And if those same eyes were gouged out of our head and we no longer had any lens to see the world at all then it would be black...pitch black. But in that event our other senses would come to the rescue and give us a renewed perspective of the world, a sharpened perspective of the world. Far sharper than a razored dagger. We would find our ears finely-tuning whispered conversations from far away which would drift silently over the flutter of butterfly wings in the fields. Of all of the machines in industrious creation, far greater than the printing press, or the talbotype is the human machine. There is nothing quite like it, I can assure you.

If you were to take away all the light in the room where you are reading right now, (you would need to close every door, close black curtains on every window and cover every square inch of light that crept silently through cracks and crevices) you would be sitting in total darkness. But suppose you were to cut a small pinhole in one of those black curtains so that a small stream of light stretched its finger to touch your wall, the most peculiar thing would happen. You would start to see the world projected onto that wall. However it would appear upside down! It's a fact. I dare you to try it and see. The mathematician Alhazen did this over a thousand years ago to try and show the world how the human lens works. It is called a camera obscura, which means 'dark room'.

But there is more. If you were to hang upside down on a monkey bar for a very long time (it might take, days, weeks or even years), it is likely that your brain would eventually correct the upside down world so that you begin to see it the right way up. Or if you quickly dropped to the ground the world would still be upside down for a moment. The world is indeed an upside down place. This raises an excellent question. A question that you will ask at the beginning of this story and a question that you will ask at the end. It is also a question that you may ask of the world in which you live.

Can my eyes be trusted?

They cannot. Now having stripped away all certainty it is time to begin the most uncertain journey of all.

Obscura

Latin for 'Dark'.

LA GAZETTE

Member of the Asscoiated Press .

ILLUSTRATED WEEKLY NEWSPAPER

Est. 1823

Wednesdav 17th November 1859

RIVER DROWNING WITH NO BODY

A Parisian man, Charles Chastain was declared drowned today after going missing from the paddle steamer La Rouen on the first of November. The captain of the ship, Captain DeGarcy, informed the Gendarmerie immediately upon discovering that one of the registered passengers was no longer on the ship. After an exhaustive search of the Seine, the Gendarmerie have yet to recover a body. "It is a most unusual occurrence," said General Caron, "we have searched the river for weeks, from Pantin to Meudon but have not found a body. There would usually be some evidence by this stage of the investigation. " The Gendarmerie have officially ruled Chastain as deceased, most likely from drowning but have not yet ruled out foul play.

Member of the
Asscoiated Press .

LA TRIBUNE

ILLUSTRATED PARIS NEWS

Est. 1799   Saturday 14th September 1879

WOLF SHOT IN PARIS HOSPITAL

A large wolf was shot today inside the Hopital Dr La Salpetriere in Paris. Orderlies and nurses were first alerted to the beast by the screams of patients as it chased them up the stairs. One bystander maintained that it attacked a small boy who was only saved by the marksmanship of a Gendarme who happened to be in the hospital at the time. Constable Berger was in the hospital on official duties when he came upon the fracas with the wolf. He shot the beast only once, killing it instantly. While all those who witnessed the event confirmed the presence of the boy and a girl, both fled the scene and neither has been officially identified.

Parisians have raised concerns with authorities that this anomaly could become more common and have called for culling of wolves as the numbers grow in the forests of Meudon.

LE PARISIEN

DAILY PARIS DIGEST

Est. 1854 Saturday 14th September 1879

STRANGE UNIDENTIFIED AIRCRAFT CRASHES IN PANTIN.

Spectators came in droves to the Pantin hillside today to witness what many are describing as a giant flying balloon that crashed into the farmland nearby. Gendarmerie kept onlookers away as they tried to piece together the puzzle that lay before them. "It was like something out of a Jules Verne novel," said one witness, Eloise Thomas. "I saw it falling out of the sky like a giant balloon. It was coming down so fast I did not think it could be real. Thank God there were no people on board."

The unidentified aircraft was believed to be unmanned but it is not yet known how the aircraft took flight and from where it was launched. The investigation is ongoing.

CHAPTER 1
A DEATH

Our story begins in the usual way with a death, a vanishing and a spectacle, all of which you will discover in due course. Deaths are never an easy beginning given that they are the end, but nevertheless that is what took place on the river Seine in Paris in 1859. This was the most peculiar kind of death, the kind without a body.

On the evening in question, that very body- belonging to Charles Chastain- was hurrying itself along the Boulevard De La Gare. The cold winds had begun unseasonably early in Paris that year and although only November, it could easily have been mistaken for January. Charles felt the cold bite through his woollen overcoat and tried to compensate as one does by lifting his coat collar above his neck and holding his arms around his torso. If done in a fashionable way, that is, without the rubbing motion, this form of warming oneself was a most acceptable Parisian etiquette, so Charles was lead to believe. Not that he was concerned with etiquette at that late hour as he had a most timely agenda to keep and a boat to catch, and the La Rouen was not about to wait for a tardy passenger. Charles marched past the Hospital of Dr La Salpetriere, an imposing structure that made one grateful for good health. Charles had often remarked that before admittance to that institution for illness he would rather be drowned in the Seine. Indeed it was the Seine river that he could now see in the murky distance and on it illuminated in the dark was his vessel. And what a vessel indeed! The paddle steamer was covered in a web of lanterns all glowing orange and red against the night sky. A rippled reflection of the steamer mirrored in the waters and Charles felt his heart lift. His moment was coming. He pulled his top hat on firmer as he approached the crew member manning the gangplank at the quay De la Gare.

'Bonjour Monsieur. Do you have your ticket?"

"Oui. Good sir. A brief moment." Charles reached into his pocket with icy fingers, feeling for the paper stub and instead touching the small wooden box carefully wrapped in oilskin; just in case. He delved deeper, producing a well handled ticket which was inspected carefully.

"Merci. Monsieur... Chastain. Welcome aboard." Charles walked up the gangplank as the gate firmly closed behind him. Before him was a scene of champagne and laughter, card decks and dancing. Before him was a new beginning.

No one but Charles could know that it was going to be the last time anyone would see Charles Chastain in this world again. It was not until the following morning when the steamer docked at the quay and all the passengers disembarked and were accounted for that it became apparent that they were one short. There was no need to draw unnecessary attention to the oversight initially. The Captain was no fool and they checked all the usual places for a stowaway. But the cabins were all empty, the galley stores held only grain and wine, and the lavatories were unoccupied. It became one of the engine hands jobs to next examine the steamer paddle which in itself was no easy task. Through a series of ropes and pulleys he was lowered down to the wheel which he inspected above and below the water line to reveal no signs of fouling. Finally, with no other choice, the Captain approached the authorities and explained their loss to the Gendarmerie. There was a lackadaisical attempt to search for the body of the missing man in the Seine, in truth, he could surely not have survived the icy temperatures. The search involved little more than glancing from horseback on the riverside where possible, but to no avail. All that could be done now was wait. It was not unusual for a body to drift into the reeds on the banks of Meudon, or be found stuck in the masonry of a bridge. It was most unusual that a month later there was still nothing, as if the man had vanished into thin air. There was nothing left to do but to inform his family members of his drowning. In the end there was only one. So the gendarme went to his only brother and broke the news to Corantin Chastain of the passing of his older brother.

CHAPTER 2
A VANISHING

The vanishing of Charles Chastain, although a legitimate and interesting vanishing was not the vanishing in question. In fact, the vanishing in question would not occur until a decade later, as these pages will divulge.

Paris in 1879 was a city reborn. It had been a turbulent time for the city earlier in the decade, a violent time, and many still remembered the Paris Commune clashing on the streets with the Gendarmerie. However, the shouts and screams that seemed to reverberate through closed windows and drawn blinds- a city ablaze with violent change- seemed a thing of the past. And as summer spilled over the Parisian walkways, from the charred, burnt remains of a city finding itself grew a wondrous world of possibility. To the naked eye, the city was a vision of progress. Construction sprouted from every corner. Sounds, metallic and industrial played a concerto of the modern age, a concerto to which artists painted and architects dreamed. Gustave Eiffle had only a dream of his tower in his head as he walked across the same plot of vacant earth each day passing the Seine along the Avenue de Suffren. He was a bridges man himself, and a dreamer of possibilities. He could not possibly know that it would only be years before his dream would become synonymous with the city and that his expertise would help complete another statue that would become synonymous with another. But it is not Gustave that this story is concerned with. His time will come soon enough, but rather two other children that passed by Gustave on his walks each day. If his head was anywhere else but in the clouds, he may have noticed them. But he did not notice them, not yet, and so both parties went about their businesses of dreaming uninterrupted.

The youngest of the children was a bright-eyed thirteen-year-old boy named Phillipe. Oblivious to the similarities he shared with the stranger who passed him each day on the Avenue de Suffren, Phillipe had a rare gift for understanding. He got things. He noticed small details others would miss. He had conceived of a device to enable stream crossing from things that he would find thrown out by the Sauvestre workshop. Not just a plank crossing, but rather an adjustable platform that would accommodate the water rising and change in angle of the embankment on either side. Phillipe got things, and like Gustave, his thoughts soared high above the world in which he lived. He was often surprised by a carriage careening towards him in the street or a scaffolding plank swinging precariously close to his head during transit. It was in this sphere that his older counterpart, his fourteen-year-old sister Angelique, found purpose. The purpose of keeping her younger brother alive. Although there was only a year between them in age, their size boasted much larger difference. Phillipe was unnaturally small for his age and his sister unnaturally tall. The chasm between their appearance stood as a formidable deception to the unwary onlooker. If not for the long blonde hair that was loosely tied at her back, one might have mistaken the two for brothers because Angelique dismissed the frocks occasioned by girls of her age, preferring the convenience of trousers and a cap. Like Phillipe, Angelique had dreams, lofty dreams well beyond her station. On occasion she had silently stolen access to the Theatre de la Ville where she watched the ballerinas glide effortlessly across the timber boards and longed to soar among them. However, despite her agility and poise, she lacked the money for the training which was expensive; and so a dream it would remain. Phillipe and Angelique's father was a lowly type-setter at the Qui Vive printing press and despite his long hours and calloused fingers, his meagre returns did not accommodate dreaming. Their mother had been a ballerina...or so the children had been told in quiet whispered snippets out of earshot of Corantin Chastain, who had no ear for stories or memories about his departed wife. For the children, it was therefore more like an unfinished, patchwork quilt memory. Moments sat like dormant fabric waiting to be woven together. The only completed narra-tive they had deciphered so far was that in the Autumn of 1869 their ballerina mother had gone.

In her time, Delphine had been one of the great celebrated ballerinas of Europe. She had soared in the arms of ballerinos on the stages of Paris and she had curtsied beneath a deluge of confetti and applause. Angelique often imagined her as impos-sibly beautiful. A beauty that was reflected in the black and white photographs of her mother that were hidden in quiet chests in the dusty cellar. But beauty was fleeting. No matter how hard Delphine maintained her turnout, alignment and port de bras, age was an incurable rust that ate away at her success. By the tender age of thirty, she was all but washed up. It appeared the void was unfillable. Lord knows she tried. Not even the birth of Angelique, or the following year, Phillipe could abate the desire within her. And so like the swan that she had so often played, she jette'd off the stage without a curtsy and vanished. There was a note and a leaving. This was the vanishing to which we refer. A vanishing of the most painful kind. The kind that requires continual wonder-ing. Like Charles, there would be no body and no more talk of memories. Delphine's scant and piecemeal story was stitched together by the children from overheard whisperings in the washing halls and late night candlelit conversations heard through paper thin bedroom walls. But never from the lips of Corantin. He suffered alone, and in silence would spare his children the pain that he would bear himself.

The early morning sun was hidden, spilling light behind the St Lambert Cathedral spire as Phillipe and Angelique made their way through a familiar hole in the fence to take a short cut through the Lecourbe chocolate factory en route to their father's workplace in Issy. The chocolate factory was a constant source of intrigue for Phillipe. Not only for the irresistible sweet, smokey trail that wafted from the building's chimney stacks but also the labyrinth of pipes that snaked throughout the factory, like chocolate arteries delivering vital blood from the engine at the heart. At times when the sun went down behind the Meudon hills and the workers poured out through the iron gates like the Israelites from Egypt, Phillipe would sneak in. Not alone. He was too small to reach the gap above the grate. But Angelique had the skill of balance and agility that was a marvel to observe. She would leap to the grille above and with one arm holding her steady, produce her rope belt as a means of raising Phillipe to the gap above. It was a team effort and one well worth the trial, as the world inside revealed a maze of girders and copper pipes. But on this particular day they traversed the field behind the factory to get to the print press as quickly as possible. Phillipe had good reason, for breaking into a secret chest was a complex undertaking.

The greatest hindrance to success was time. His father was expecting him to pass by the print shop on his way to school, this was an inevitable ruse he would need to maintain to deflect any unnecessary attention from his endeavour. Further to this was a broader plan to evade school. This longer term plan was neither ill-conceived nor unjustifiable. The schooling that took place in the republic district involved rudimentary arithmetic and grammar for the sons of artisans and craftworkers. It began in the morning, concluded in the afternoon and felt as fruitless as it was uninteresting. Phillipe found he learned so much more by being out and about in the city. Conversations with the compression machine mechanic at the Pneumatic Clock Centre or the farrier at the Royal Stables about the movement of time or reliability of metals was far more interesting to Phillipe. And so he orchestrated his escape. It was a simple plan that had been executed seamlessly. Professor Caron cared little for his appointment as the teacher of local ruffians in the makeshift school house. A fact he often crudely confessed to others. The Professor's indifferent attitude was reflected in every aspect of his practise. Every morning he would call out a roll from his ledger which contained the names of the registered attendees who would respond to him with matched enthusiasm. Phillipe noted that new students were added with a lead pencil and any adjustments were made by rubbing stale bread on the error which was then scrutinised carefully. Phillipe had "borrowed" some rubber from the shoe factory on the Rue de Grenelle, a substance that was soft and gluey in the summer months. However, he had discovered that by adding a little sulphur in a drum and vulcanising the substance it could be rolled into a firm rubber ball. It was with this that he was able to remove his name from the ledger *ad infinitum*. A slight distraction was all it took and with a few deft hand movements he was removed from the school without a trace, free to pursue his own education from the streets of Paris.

Angelique was not so fortunate. Education was not an option to a young girl in Paris yet, and her lot was in the world of domesticity and keeping house. A pursuit which she loathed. It was expected that while Phillipe continued his formal schooling at the republic, Angelique would be indentured to the enslavement of Madame Bernard. Madam Bernard was a large, course woman who revelled in the power entrusted to her to teach her trade to a band of young filles who would complete her day's work for her. Further to this she would be paid. It was only a few francs a week from the working parents of those left to her charge, but if she continued to expand her intake then 'heavens' it could be a lucrative venture after all. It was not uncommon for Angelique to find herself lost in a sea of girls in the washing room, all clamouring for elbow space and suds as they endeavoured to demonstrate their involvement in the hope of "promotion" to the drawing room dusting. Drowning in this sea, Angelique discovered it was easy to be missed. Whether Madame Bernard was aware of her absence or not, there was never any enquiry. While Corantin's funds continued to line Bernard's apron pockets, there was a silent acceptance of the situation. Angelique suspected Corantin knew but he also did not enquire. Corantin was concerned for his daughter's proper education and spent most evenings teaching her by candlelight about mathematics, literature and science, unaware that this would surreptitiously serve as his son's only education also.

Phillipe rapped on the heavy timber door of the old shop which was duly opened by a young man wiping his greasy hands on a leather apron.

"Bonjour, Master Phillipe... Angelique." The young man gestured to his hands apologetically. "You can come in. I'm sorry, I am trying to fix a machine. Your father is at the setter."

"Merci, Monsieur, we will only be here a moment." Phillipe and Angelique made their way across the dusty shop floor. It was only a small space, but they had crammed every square inch with print machinery as is the custom when the owner is not fond of spending money and so the children inched and twisted their way to the typeset machine in the corner. Corantin did not see them arrive and continued to deftly fill the print plate with letters with thick, inky fingers.

"Bonjour Papa." Angelique shouted over the industrious sound of machinery rolling out the afternoon's news.

"Bonjour my Angel." Corantin did not take his eyes off the lettering in his fingers but smiled in acknowledgement of their daily ritual. "You are running late today children, no? Come and kiss your Papa or you will be late to school." Finally catching his smiling eyes, Angelique leaned in and kissed Corantin on his inky brow. Phillipe followed suit, placing a kiss on his father's brow and swatting away the pangs of guilt that raced through his insides. His father was the kindest man he knew. He held no malice, and exuded patience and generosity towards the children as much as could be afforded. Yes, he was uninteresting, which was a predictable bedfellow of reliability. But like the Clydesdale horse in the Royal stable he was surefooted and dependable, both wonderful qualities, Phillipe imagined. Once, the farrier had allowed him to watch the Royal horse trainer breaking in the new stallion, and Phillipe had found himself mesmerised by the beast and its muscles flexing unpredictably beneath the rider's lash. For Phillipe, it was the beginning of a blossoming romance with excitement. Excitement which could not be found at the print shop; as Corantin continued to tediously place letter after letter into the machine. After all, what was there to feel guilty about? Was it a lie? Phillipe had not told his father that he was no longer attending the Republic school, but neither had he uttered that he was. He had silently agreed that he would be late for school. Indeed he would be very late to school. In fact, Phillipe's adventurous pursuits were surely a divine balance to the bland domestic world in which they lived. It was not Corantin's fault he could not provide adventure and so it would be Phillipe's mandate to bring it about for the sake of the family. And so, with a lifted heart, a renewed sense of purpose and a quick wave to his father, Phillipe left the workshop to return the way he had come.

Angelique followed in disapproving pursuit.

"Phillipe, I think you should leave it alone." There had been an unspoken understanding between the children about their educational pursuits. Neither would discuss or acknowledge the abandonment of their respective formal educations, nor would they betray this information to Corantin. They had little concern over the consequences this knowledge would bear, but rather wanted to spare their Papa the fretting and worriment that would accompany the discovery. It felt selfless, even if it was not.

"What harm would it do? I will not take, or move, or break anything. I will just look."

"But it is locked. Does that not tell you anything?"

"It tells me that it is important. It could be about Mama." Angelique paused at this. It was an unfair check mate and Phillipe knew it.

"Very well. But I will have nothing to do with it. If you are caught it is on your head."

"So I will not tell you what the contents are then? Even if it is about Mama?"

"Phillipe, you are impossible." Angelique smiled in spite of herself and tussled her little brother's hair. "I will be a willing ear, but not a willing accomplice okay."

"Very well then. Suit yourself. But if there is treasure in there. I will not say a word."

Phillipe and Angelique parted ways on the Rue de Vanguard. Angelique would spend the morning at the Theatre de Paris where rehearsals were well underway for La Bayadere. There was a young sweeper she had met in passing who worked in the foyer during the day. He was a lad of fourteen or fifteen and was of no particular interest to Angelique. But it appeared he was sweet on her and this was all the leverage she needed to achieve her goal, the greatest education that Paris could afford her, the observation of the prima dancers in Paris.

Phillipe arrived back at the tenement villa without incidence. He immediately made his way to the makeshift tool shop that was set up in the back room under the stairwell and found his tools to be exactly where he had left them the previous evening. Corantin had allowed Phillipe to use the dormant space to tinker and build his projects as long as he completed his studies and chores. While Phillipe had done neither of those things he rationalised that this endeavour represented his new study regime and he would simply need to complete his chores before his Papa got home, which was usually later in the afternoon. The workshop itself was very small and offered only whatever light could be provided by a lantern. The floor consisted of old sandstone which proved invaluable when Phillipe was vulcanising, as this was as fireproof as any substance. Far more fireproof than the remaining timber and daub structure as Corantin often cautioned. Phillipe immediately set to work with his fine metal tools and began to work the copper around the brass shaft he had fashioned the night before. He had been thinking about locks and keys for some time and it had occurred to him that while the collar, throating and pin were consistently the same, it was the key wards that found variation. If he could manufacture an adjustable key ward that would enable the bits to be both lengthened, spaced and then locked then it should mean that the device would be able to pick any lock... theoretically.

The task proved more difficult than Phillipe had originally estimated and although he relished the challenge, the sun continued to move across the Parisian sky while he submerged himself in a world of boring, filing and tightening. As was often the case, by the time Phillipe had completed his task, the afternoon was upon him like an unwelcome houseguest. Phillipe, surrounded by lamplight alone was not cognisant of this fact.

The initial discovery of the concealed chest was stumbled upon by Phillipe while doing something as unremarkable as poking around in the fireplace. It was not uncommon during idle times for Phillipe to take the iron poker and give the fireplace ash a good poke. It served no real purpose but did generate a fine charred aroma and simply felt quite good. It was during this fruitless endeavour that Phillipe accidentally broke a brick. At least he thought he had, and utterly alone on one of his newly found schooling breaks, he panicked. Fearing discovery he tried to rectify the brick's positioning and discovered that it was one of several bricks that were not morticed at all but rather assembled in a way that could be removed.

So they were removed.

Behind them was a small wooden chest with iron straps and a central hasp that was locked. Phillipe had fiddled with the lock unsuccessfully on that day and confessed his discovery to Angelique when she had arrived home. They had agreed that private matters were indeed private and should remain so.

But it had eaten at him. Like a secret that called to him from the brickwork and grew to occupy every waking moment. What secret could Papa possibly have? It appeared that every signal to his brain was re-routed to this new obsession and try as he might, any agreement that he may have made with Angelique was no longer a match for this new disease of curiosity that possessed him night and day. And so here he was. The best compromise he could justify was that he would merely take a look and return everything as it was, as observation after all was not a crime last time he checked.

Although the house was silent he felt the weight of guilty steps on the wide timber flooring of the living room as he heavily made his way to the hearth. His hand that held his adjustable key was shaking with trepidation and excitement. He leaned into the firebox, careful not to disturb the ash all over the living room rug as evidence of his dark investigative deeds. His fingers carefully gripped the first brick which he placed gently on the hearth as though it were a sweating stick of dynamite. He followed this with the second and third and so on, until he could see the hollowed out cavity and in it, the small chest that had so occupied his waking thoughts. He turned it so he could see the locked hasp and taking his key he carefully inserted it in the lock. The key would not initially turn and so with careful adjustment he turned the collar slightly allowing the key ward to move imperceptibly.

Click!

Phillipe's heart was beating so loudly in his chest, that he almost missed the faint sound of footsteps on the landing. By the time he heard the squeak of the apartment door hinges it was too late. He snapped the lock shut and with clumsy fingers tried to return the bricks to their former cloaking purpose, but he had lost all dexterity in his panic. Corantin entered the living room to find Phillipe crouched at the firebox, covered in soot with the loose bricks in either hand. Phillipe had no words and was mute with shame.

"What are you doing Phillipe?"

Silence.

"What are you doing?"

"I...knocked the brick out accidentally."

"What do you mean? The bricks are stacked beside you."

This was true. Try as he might, Phillipe could not think of one earthly reason how he could justify his situation. Dozens of scenarios ran through his head, all of which were both implausible and bordered on ridiculous. He was caught, like a rabbit in the lamplight. There was nothing left to do but confess.

"I'm sorry Papa. I'm sorry." He could feel tears welling behind his eyes and couldn't be sure if he was genuinely upset or if it was an instinctive survival mechanism orchestrated by his body knowing the best way to play the situation. Either way he let it have its head.

"Phillipe. I need to know what you were doing. What did you find?"

" Nothing Papa. I just found the bricks were loose last week and that there was a small chest in there and wanted to take a look at it."

"Son! The contents of that chest are none of your business." Phillipe noticed that Corantin was shouting. It was the first time that he had ever heard his father raise his voice and it frightened him very much. The world suddenly felt abnormal and unsafe and he did not like it.

"Were you going to pick the lock?"

Silence.

"Did you PICK THE LOCK?"

This was finally too much for Phillipe who having never seen his father in such an uncharacteristic rage, dropped the bricks where he sat and ran to his room amidst a cloud of ash.

It was some time later when Corantin quietly entered the children's room, each step an apology in its quiet consideration. Phillipe lay on his bed staring at the blank wall. He had not been staring at the wall until he heard his father's imminent arrival and decided that looking at the wall might illicit the most remorse from Corantin. He was correct. Corantin slowly made his way over to the bed by the wall and thoughtfully sat next to his son.

"I'm sorry I lost my temper Phillipe."

Silence.

"Can you forgive me?" Phillipe turned and nodded contritely.

"I'm sorry I wanted to see what was in the chest Papa."

"I understand you are curious Phillipe. That is natural. But sometimes there are things that are not for a young man's eyes. Not yet. I assume...you did not see Phillipe?"

"I did not see."

"It is all for the best. You will understand. How was school today?" In that moment with a renewed sense of morality, Phillipe decided that although Papa may be able to keep a secret, he could not.

"I did not go today Papa."

"Nor did you go for the last two weeks. Correct?" Corantin smiled like an ember that sparked beneath the ash. Phillipe met this revelation with genuine shock.

"How did you know?"

Corantin laughed and ruffled Phillipe's hair. "I paid a visit to see the Professor at the Republic school this afternoon, to check on your progress. He said he did not have a Phillipe Chastain on his ledger, which was never wrong. I told him that I enrolled you at the beginning of the year and saw him write your name on that same document. He chided me that any changes were only made by him and bore the smudges of the meagre supplies of a republic teacher." Phillipe looked up sheepishly at his father and noticed a glimmer of admiration in Corantin's gaze.

"What will you have me do Papa?"

"Well... I will have you re-enrol for a start. Next week you are to re-enrol at the school and Angelique will accompany you to make sure there are no problems from the professor. Does that sound fair."

"Fair."

Corantin rose to take his leave and get the soup broth on the stove when he noticed that there was something unfinished in the air. "There is more Phillipe. Is there not?"

"Papa. Is there something in that chest about mother?"

Corantin returned to the bedside. "You must have many, many questions my dear boy. I am sorry that I have told you so little about your mother. But the truth is, I find it a most difficult subject. For the most part, I don't know what to say or how to say it. Why don't we start with you asking me a question." This was an invitation that had never been offered before to Phillipe, and like his father, he was not quite sure what to say or how to say it. He had never known his mother and had never really seen her except in a few scant photographs. She felt to him like a character in a fairytale that did not yet have an ending and all he had was questions.

"Why did mother leave?"

"For that part, I do not know Phillipe. I'm not sure if she even knew it herself. But it had nothing to do with you children or how much she loved you. She did love you both, very much. But she was very, very special. She was like a light that shone so brightly that she warmed everyone that saw her. She was a ballerina. Did you know that? She was the most beautiful dancer that Paris has ever known. She had performed for Kings and Queens. I believe she even met the Emperor Napoleon once. She... was made for other things. I think being a light for the world to see was the most important thing for her. It was her calling, her destiny. She had to make some very difficult decisions at times I imagine. But in the end, she had to be true to her calling. She had to go where she would be needed most.

"Do you miss her Papa?"

"Oui. Oui I do. But I still see her. Her eyes, her smile, her hair. I see it in you and Angelique. You both look just like her. You have a curiosity just like her." Corantin ruffled Phillipe's hair for the second time that evening and made his way to the door.

"Soup and bread will be ready shortly. Come out and clean yourself up after your sister has finished washing."

Phillipe looked down at his sooty clothing and hands which he had long forgotten about. He felt in his pocket for his adjustable key. He had agreed to leave the chest alone and he would. Luckily for him, his new key would be suitable for a great range of other locks.

CHAPTER 3
A SPECTACLE

Spectacles come in all manner of shapes and sizes. Some are an extravaganza of the senses; loud explosions and dazzling visuals that makes one hold their breath in disbelief. If you were to watch a spectacle such as the Royal fireworks at the palace at Versailles, you would be expecting crackles, and fizzles and a night sky alight. You would not be at all surprised and you would know you were truly witnessing a spectacle. This is a very safe kind of spectacle.

But there is another.

The quiet spectacle, one which does not draw much attention at first. You are seduced by the subtleties of uncertainty. In fact, you may not even realise it is a spectacle until it is too late. This is the most dangerous kind of spectacle, the kind that tiptoes at dawn into a Parisian street and awaits an unsuspecting audience.

It was an overcast summer morning on the Rue de Vanguard as Phillipe and Angelique, the captive and captor made their way to the republic school as promised. Phillipe was feeling particularly melancholy because he was likely to have to explain to the professor why he looked so familiar for a new enrolment and he was acutely aware that while his run of truancy had come to an end, Angelique would be free to continue in her deception unde-tected. The summer days were finally ending and cool, crisp mornings brought with them subtle winds that heralded the arrival of Autumn.

"What will you do with your day Angelique?" Phillipe felt the pangs of defeat and jealousy all at once, but was genuine in his query.

"I don't know. I will walk. Perhaps a museum. Perhaps the park. Wherever the day takes me. I'm sorry you have to go back to school Phillipe. I truly am. I am also sorry that...the other day...with Papa and the chest. I'm sorry that it didn't work out as you had...Phillipe? What is wrong?"

Her heartfelt words had fallen on deaf ears, for Phillipe's tenuous attention had already been hijacked. While the source of his distraction was unclear, its location was evident as he began to drift towards the Rue de Vouille. Like a hound following the scent of adventure, Phillipe's steps quickened as he caught clear sight of his quarry. Angelique saw no choice but to follow in mute pursuit. In the distance it did not take her long to ascertain the source of her brother's attention. She sighed, and quickened her pace to catch up.

"The Super Subminiature Box Camera- and the Obscura" read the sign. It was painted in bright red and yellow letters on a canvas that was pulled taut with ropes across the old Vanguard theatre. It was too early in the morning to have garnished much attention from the occasional passer by, and so the vendor stood patiently under the signage using his eyes and smile to engage the interest of those nearby; like a hunter steadying his sights. He was a comically short, portly man with a long, luscious moustache that he would periodically twist on the ends as if by habit. He wore his evening tails and top hat which- threadbare in daylight- betrayed their status with signs of dust and age. Yet despite his incon-gruous appearance he was irresistible. Phillipe had seen photogra-phers before on the Champs Ellyse with their large wooden legs, ground glass and film plane. They would herald the picture with flash powder from the lamp while burrowed under a cloak at the rear of the lens. But this was a box. A small black box no more than two inches that the portly man held with a lens so small it could be mistaken for an eye glass.

"I see you have an interest in the lens young man. Come over. Don't be shy. Come, come... What I have in my hands is the miracle of modern photography, the super subminiature box camera." He gave a pause for effect with a cocked eyebrow waiting for the young lad and his female companion to marvel at the device he raised before their eyes. He appeared more a ringmaster than a photographer, more a man of the stage than a man of science.

"Behold, the miracle in a box! No flash powder, no portable legs, this microscopic marvel of a machine is the entire portrait maker. No trickery of any kind. Just using modern science and the miracle of light. Take a look young lad. Look through the lens. What do you see?" There was a brief pause in the ringmaster's sales pitch as he waited for the lad to reply.

"I see the street monsieur. It looks just like it does through my eye. How does it work?"

"How does a miracle work my boy! The magic of nature. What about you young mademoiselle, care for a look into the future?" Angelique politely softened her decline with a smile.

"How does it work you ask? It uses the same science as your eyeball. Think of this as your eye. Here at the front." He pointed to the lens just above the "SuperCamera" logo riveted below the lens.

"Here at the back you slide a small plate into this slot, pull down on the shutter lever which lets in the light and presto, you have a picture. You may find this hard to believe, but the image will be upside down." He again paused for this to sink in. "You see, the world that you see is upside down. Like the lens of this camera, your eye flips it on it's head. It is your brain that tells you, this can't be right, and flips it back again." His free hand turned in scientific gesture. He could see that both children listened wide-eyed. "Do you believe the world is upside down, lad?"

"No, monsieur."

"Then you will need proof. Behold...the Obscura." He made a magnanimous gesture towards the sign above the theatre being very careful with the expensive Super Box Camera in his non-gesturing hand. "For the mere fee of two francs, the two of you will be able to see the world as it really is. You will climb into the lens of your very own eyes." The excitement in Phillipe's face softened.

"We have no money monsieur. But merci for your time."

"Wait lad. I can not turn away a fellow man of Science. You and your friend may enter. But don't tell a soul I let you in for free." The ringmaster made wide eye gestures followed by a wink that seemed incongruous to his intention. Phillipe looked to Angelique in a query of approval to which she gave a little nod as she too was now as curious as he. It would, after all only be a brief deviation from the morning's agenda.

"Merci, monsieur."

"Just remember. When the world is topsy turvy, one must use one's head." With a final nod and wink, he pulled back a heavy black curtain and let the children enter.

It appeared to be the foyer of the old theatre, but it was diffi-cult to tell and the children were instantly disorientated by the darkness as soon as the curtain was again drawn. The former windows had most likely been covered by darkened boards for as they waited patiently their eyes did not adjust to the black. Phillipe reached out to touch Angelique's hand, partly to confirm her presence and partly to allay his discomfort. Then, in the wall outside there was a rattling sound like a handle was being turned and a small aperture began to open before their eyes. It was no larger than an eye glass but a shaft of blinding light instantly spilled into the tiny room. It was Angelique that noticed it first,

Phillipe was too distracted by the shaft of light. But when he turned to see the shaft spill onto its destination, he also saw it. There, projected onto the back wall was a moving image of dazzling colour. The Rue de Voille was there before their very eyes. But it was indeed upside down. It was an optical wonder, like standing in the midst of a dream as Parisians bustled their way across the ceiling and horse drawn carriages defied gravity as they passed by before the children's awestruck eyes. A small pigeon appeared to take off from the ceiling and fly through the floor across the backdrop of clouds sweeping across the flooring like a rolling fog.

"What are you doing, Phillipe?" Angelique had only just noticed that her brother was now doing a headstand on the floor beside her.

"I am using my head like the tubby man said." They both giggled. "You should try it. It feels really strange." Sensible as she was, it did look like a lot of fun and so Angelique found herself planting her head between her hands and raising her legs in the air beside Phillipe. For a moment, both children were aware of the blood rushing to their heads as the spectacle before them, now correct, continued its animated parade. But something shifted. It happened so suddenly that neither had time to register the event in logic, nor the exact sequence of the event. For in that moment, both fell as it were from the floor to the ceiling in a collective tangle of limbs and the scene before them darkened slightly. It was a small room, so neither were injured in the fall and given the darkening of the space, both were disorientated momentarily. But they found themselves on the ceiling all the same.

"Are you alright Phillipe?"

"Yes. I think so. What just happened?...An earthquake?"

"I don't think so. I think I just fell over. Perhaps being upside down made me dizzy."

"Me too." But silently each of them contemplated the quiet

nagging idea that had planted like a small seed in their fertile contemplation, the idea that the world had just turned upside down.

Both slowly picked themselves up in the semidarkness. The featureless room surrounding them gave no clear indicator of orientation. Neither were willing to speak their thoughts but rather breathed in the room about them trying desperately to rationalise their thoughts and find a clue. Then, there it was. Much fainter than before, but in the dim light they could make out the street still projected on the wall. Phillipe could not immediately find his words and instead took hold of Angelique's arm in a bid for her understanding, for the images were no longer upside down. It was difficult to see clearly, but there appeared to be faint orange lights in the hands of the occasional traveller.

"What has happened Angelique?"

"I don't know. Perhaps nothing more than a sideshow trick. That tubby man out the front is probably splitting his breeches with laughter. Come. Let us leave. You'll be late for school." Angelique took several strides towards the door but stopped short staring at it. For the door now stood two feet higher than the floor. She reached for the handle and realised that it was no longer on the left but rather on the right. This was indeed some trick. She took Phillipe by the hand and both stepped up into the doorway and out of the room.

If what was before them was a trick, it was a conjuring worthy of only Merlin himself, for the city of Paris lay before them under the shade of the night sky. It was still the Rue de Voille, that much was recognisable but it was different. Not only because of the moonlight that spilled over the gothic architecture of the Hotel De Ville, but also because there were imperceptible differences. Subtle differences. Gargoyles in the stonework where dignitaries and angels once were, smooth stone was now rough hewn, flags that flew were gone and the signage almost unrecognisable. The theatre at which they stood appeared the same at a glance, but there was no tubby ringmaster to be seen and no makeshift signage above the building. In fact the theatre looked completely deserted as if it had been for some time. Dereliction hung about its facade like a vagabond's threadbare coat. Angelique's instinct was to step back inside through the door, but as she did she was met with the familiar foyer interior that she knew so well. Even by the dim moonlight, she could make out the small ticket booth by the wall and the ornate double doors that led to the theatre itself. She caught Phillipe's eye trying to remain calm.

"I'm afraid Angel."

"So am I Phillipe. Stand close." The two stepped cautiously back out into the street. It was then they saw it. On the high wall of the market hall on the opposite side of the street there was a large graffitied word, red and bold, the varied sized lettering suggesting that it was painted under the cover of darkness. Only lit by the singular gaslamp nearby, it took Phillipe a concentrated moment to decipher the word. Obscura.

CHAPTER 4
OBSCURA

Fear is a peculiar thing. Scientists will tell you that fear begins its journey in a part of the brain called the amygdala. This is the operational centre. It begins a chain reaction by sending urgent messages to all of the parts of the body that need to be on high alert. The heart will start racing as more blood pumps through the arteries. Breathing speed quickens, drawing vital air into the lungs and every muscle tenses in readiness for what may come. Indeed the trigger for this reaction could be that one is lost, one can not see clearly, one feels that they are in imminent danger or that everything in the world that they believed to be true and real is gone. It was this that Phillipe and Angelique feared the most. For instead of light there was darkness and instead of bustle there was silence.

All about them, the only sound that could be heard was the quiet steps of scarce Parisians moving about in the darkness with raised lanterns, as one by one, they disappeared into buildings with the firm closing of heavy doors. Then, only wind. A quiet inconsequential wind that barely moved a shutter, passed cautiously down the street.

Only one man was animated in the distance. In all of Paris he appeared solitary, standing at a wooden door only partially lit by the moonlight. He continued to look behind him with some urgency and looked about the pavement beneath his feet. Momentarily he would fish into his trouser pockets before doing the same with his waistcoat and topcoat. He glanced at his pocket watch and his movements became clearly more agitated. Given that he was the only other person the children could see, Angelique felt she should seek whatever information the man could offer. Grabbing Phillipe firmly by the hand she began a cautious approach, being careful to stay within the shadows of the market building which loomed ominously above. As they neared the man, they could hear him muttering under his breath. It was the keys, he could not find his keys. Phillipe, finding courage born of overwhelming fear stepped into the moonlight to address the man. He was instantly pulled back into the darkness by Angelique whose hand muffled his voice into silence, for there was something utterly wrong. She could not explain or rationalise what it was, but it pulled within her like a taut rope.

Across the street, a lantern appeared. It was bobbing in front of a man, who, seeing the commotion, made his way over to investigate. It was difficult to see the lantern-bearing figure at first as he was obscured by his light's glow. It was not until he moved closer to the street corner in the light of the solitary street lamp that his appearance could be fully realised. Angelique- still with her hand over her brother's mouth- recoiled. If Phillipe was panicking also, it could have only been reflected in his wide eyes, as every sound that emanated from his lips was stifled by tight fingers. For the figure wore a mask. It was a hideous leather covering that enveloped the entire face fastened by a buckle at the back. Two round portholes of green glass enabled vision and at the mouth, the leather connected to a short ribbed hose of sorts that carried a rectangular metal apparatus the size of a snuff box. One would assume it was a filter of sorts and the mask a protection against some unknown assailant. In the dim light it looked monstrous and made the bearer appear a devil from another world.

The man at the door was now aware of the lantern hovering towards him and whispered to himself in panic. "Gaslampers. Gaslampers." A muffled shout emanated from behind the figure's leather mask.

"Halt! Identify yourself and state your business."

"Bonsoir good monsieur. I am sorry. It is my key." He raised his hands in supplication, terror evident in his trembling voice.

"Curfew is at seven o'clock. There are no exceptions by order of the Maire. You are breaking the law man." The exchange was both surreal and quick. The trembling man began to sob loudly and it was then that Phillipe noticed a shadow behind the wall. It crept. It stalked. It made no sound.

"Please monsieur, please have mercy. I am a law-abiding..." The distraught man's sentence was interrupted by a movement so swift, Angelique did not see it until it was finished. Even then, as she saw the large wolf tearing at the man's throat while he lay thrashing on the ground she could not believe what she was witnessing. The snarling, growling sounds of a savagery incomprehensible were both terrifying and quick. In an instant it was over and the man lay silent on the pavement with the masked Gaslamper illuminating the horrid scene with a raised lantern. By his side stood the wolf, eyes searching in the darkness for any other movement.

It was then that the children noticed them. Large shapes moving in the shadows. All around the murky cityscape before them. Wolves, large and silent emerged from obscurity. They sniffed menacingly as they searched, their yellow eyes seeking out the empty streets and alleyways. Slowly, like fireflies in the distance more lanterns came. Gaslampers with wolves at their sides patrolled the streets, all grotesque and otherworldly in their leather masks and apparatus.

In a moment of terrified distraction, Angelique's fingers loosened around Phillipe's mouth. It was unintentional. She was uncertain if it was Phillipe's quick breath, now freed to breathe without interference, or if it was the barely audible whimper that emanated from her own mouth. But a sound was uttered.

"Who's there?" The Gaslamper hovering over the dead man's body raised his lantern towards the children, still camouflaged in the shadows. The wolf nearby, the remnants of its savagery still evident on its snout, bared its teeth and let out a low growl. The Gaslamper had heard the sound but the wolf had smelled the scent. The wolf lowered on its hind legs and slowly moved forward toward the scent of its quarry. There was nothing left to do.

"Run!" Angelique whispered in the dark and both children took flight. It was an explosion of limbs and adrenaline as only those facing imminent death could know. The wolf, still crouched, waited for one word from the Gaslamper.

"Go."

It did.

There was no time to look back and no room for error. Their legs felt like lead as they pounded forward; step by step echoing in the silence around them. Never before had Phillipe's feet felt so heavy, yet they moved. Other senses heightened. Small details came into focus in his vision and thoughts crystallised as his brain relayed this desperate situation to every other part of his body. His eyes were searching... an open window, an ajar door, a stairwell ladder, any escape they could use to their advantage. Behind them, wolves joined the chase from side streets and alleyways moving into a hideous formation. Angelique, several feet in front of her younger brother, glanced back and caught sight of them, for it was now a pack that pursued with one dark purpose. Fast as the children were, they were no match for the slavering beasts that gained ground with every moment as the cacophony of howling and barks grew in volume, echoing off the stonework that lined the Rue du Voile. It was dark, but Phillipe's eyes had sharply adjusted. Nobody knew the side streets of this city better than he. So many days he had spent wandering around the constructions of Haussman's architectural transformation of the city slums, he knew every piece of brick and scaffolding so intimately that he was confident he could navigate it in the dark.

"Turn right." He shouted to Angelique directing her down a narrow alleyway that he knew led to the reconstructed tenements. Angelique heard the direction and in blind trust threw herself into the darkness of the alleyway, into the unknown. All the while, the howling of their wild assailants echoing around them. Closing in... sounds closing in. Phillipe felt as though their breath was huffing on his heels as he approached the rear fence of the alley. Instinctively, Angelique had already leapt the fence and was offering her hand to Phillipe as he scrambled up behind her with the wild dogs snapping at his ankles.

"Follow me." Phillipe led Angelique along a girder spanning two derelict buildings, the inclination taking them fifteen feet above the street below. Wasting no time, the wolves were already below them eyeing their every movement and howling their presence. Several of the Gaslampers had now arrived, their glowing orange lanterns bobbing in pursuit against the dark sky. But where could they go? Forward was the only answer. And so Phillipe and Angelique raced from girder to strut, from strut to stone ledge, scrambling and leaping as their hands and feet would allow. Phillipe leapt through a large hole in the stonework of a condemned building, the immediate black interior causing disorientation and a slowing of pace. Running forward blindly in the darkness he suddenly came upon a hole in the floor where access boards had been removed. Only by gripping a beam that hovered overhead could he prevent himself from careening down the cavernous opening with Angelique blindly running into his back.

Straining against the fall below, Phillipe pushed them both back as a lantern appeared beneath accompanied by the sharp barks of a wolf.

"Come." Angelique shouted as she leapt across the chasm. Phillipe had a sudden moment of self doubt as he witnessed the fluid and skilled movement of his sister. With a deep breath he heaved himself across the gap behind her, managing to only catch the toe of his boot on the other side. He immediately felt his legs go from under him as his arms flailed wildly grabbing the other end of the timber floor. Angelique quickly reached for him and hauled with all of her might, lifting him away from the floor below. It was in that moment that Phillipe felt the sharp pain of teeth on his shin. It was fast and his escape was narrow.

"Are you hurt?"

"I don't think so." This was true. Phillipe had glanced down momentarily and although his trousers were torn and there appeared to be some seeping teeth marks in his shin, it certainly looked manageable. There was no pain. Yet. It would later come... a throbbing heat that would climb skilfully along every limb, making its way to his forehead, but for now it was manageable. "Go!" He urged.

Angelique took flight again racing along the timber corridor. Behind her Phillipe tried desperately to keep pace with her dark shape several feet in front of him. All the while, the terrible sounds of wolves and muffled shouting seemed to reverberate all around them. The source of the sound became apparent as Angelique arrived at the top of a stairwell and could see a lantern and wolf ascending from the floor below.

"In here." Phillipe opened a door to a side room. The damp, musty smell was instantly offensive; they entered and closed the heavy door behind them. Phillipe noticed a large beam resting against the wall and pushed it across the door. A slow pain began to spiral up his leg from the wound, which he tried to disregard. Angelique was already climbing out of the stone window and using her strong, dextrous fingers to grip each bluestone brick and lift herself to the one above. In no time she had hauled herself up to top of the shingled roof and was lowering her rope belt for Phillipe to hold. He could hear the sound of pounding on the door with such ferocity that he breathed deeply and despite the pain, ascended the rope.

The rooftop finally gave them the opportunity to fully survey the extent of their situation. So startled at the scene below was Angelique, that she momentarily could not draw breath. Phillipe found his eyes stinging with dampness as he saw the lanterns and wolves throughout the city, a busy web of moving lights and sound crawling all over Paris. The Gaslampers below were congregating at the entrance to the tenements in muffled discussion, around them wolves prowling in impatient circles. Others were spilling into the building below, drawn to the sound of pounding against the door. Angelique looked from rooftop to rooftop, the gaps appeared to be only five or six feet.

"Phillipe. Can you jump?"

"I think…Yes I can." Phillipe suddenly realised he had no right to be uncertain in a situation which demanded certainty. This certainty planted a seed deep within him. It was a very fast growing certainty and it began pulsing through his veins and into his conscience. Suddenly the embers of pain that had been burning in his leg dissipated in the night sky and his focus became microscopic. He saw the distance and the next rooftop and rooftop beyond that and without waiting for Angelique, plunged ahead with certainty. His legs found their speed and his boots found their grip and with a controlled fluid movement he ran and leapt effortlessly across the rooftop to the next. If he could have shouted he would have roared with the adrenaline that surged through him. If he was aware of it, he would have said it was like an electricity that ran through him. For in another world, in another country on that same day, a thirty-two year old American inventor, Thomas Alva Edison sat before his illuminated lightbulb in his workshop and understood what Phillipe was feeling for the first time. Angelique felt a surge of admiration and if the situation was not what it was, may have been inclined to express this to her brother. But it was what it was and so she did not, and instead followed suit in a desperate bid to save their lives.

"Look there!" Echoed a voice from below as a Gaslamper drew attention to the rooftops and the desperate escapees. Seeing the patterns of lantern lights change below, Phillipe knew that their relentless pursuers had found them and would anticipate their descent. He had to act now. At the rear of the building, away from the street he could see a lead water pipe that appeared to reach the ground. Although its structural integrity could not be guaranteed it was their only chance. He caught Angelique's eye and silently gestured before climbing over the rooftop, swinging under the eaves and gripping the pipe. He slid down where he could and climbed when he came to a fastening. The sound of his descent was lost amidst shouts and barking in the street. Above him he could not hear Angelique but glanced at her shape on the pipe silhouetted against the moon. When he came to end of the pipe where the remainder had rusted through and fallen he estimated he was probably only a few feet from the ground and let go. Estimating in the darkness is always a difficult and dangerous task, for a few feet turned out to be nearly ten, and the uncertainty of the point and time of landing meant that it was done with little flair or skill. Phillipe hit the ground with a searing pain moving up his leg. It didn't feel broken, but it took a moment before he could stand and walk. Thankfully, Angelique who excelled in this area had judged her landing with more skill and landed with little repercussions. Either way, the landing was a sound that echoed through the tenements and within a moment the now familiar sound of the wolves could be heard moving around the rear of the building.

Onwards, back into the street raced Phillipe and Angelique. Slightly disorientated by the fall and the darkness, Phillipe charged down another alleyway. Obscured by shadow and only dimly lit by moonlight, it was not until they were at the end of the alley that it became apparent that a high stone wall blocked their exit. Before them several lanterns appeared around the corner and with it came the snarling of wolves. In the moonlight Phillipe could see the wolves' bared teeth, narrow and razor sharp, he felt sick to depths of his stomach. The children cowered against the wall awaiting their impending end as the wolves, all noise and yellow eyes approached. A few paces behind the wolves they could now clearly see those masks in the lantern light, like the ferrymen of Hades they approached, terrifying and other-worldly. On their arms Phillipe noticed an armband for the first time. It was red, adorned with a black symbol. It appeared to be a circle inside of which was a pattern of curves joined at the centre like an aperture of sorts.

It was in that moment that Phillipe saw something else. His eyes were looking frantically about him for some measure of hope when he saw her. He wasn't certain at first. But just out of arms reach, several feet above them was a small tenement ladder platform and on it stood a figure. A girl. In the darkness he could not be sure, but her size and shape and long, dark hair tied at her back was dimly visible in the dappled moonlight. She had a device in her hand. It appeared a crossbow of sorts. She raised it to her shoulder and in her left hand lit a phosphorus friction match. This was the first moment when Angelique noticed the girl as did the assailants. But it was too late. In one deft movement, the girl raised the match to a glass bottle in her crossbow which instantly ignited the flammable liquid within. She squeezed the trigger and the bottle hurtled towards the closest wolf, exploding into a ball of flames. Instantly the wolf caught fire and began running in wild flaming circles, howling his disapproval. Terrified of the flames, the other wolves backed away, as those too close to the desperate inferno also caught fire. Within a moment there was a wall of fire between the children and the

Gaslampers as the girl dropped effortlessly down from her platform to the children.

Phillipe could now see her clearly for the first time. She appeared a girl of around sixteen. She wore a brown leather jacket over tan coveralls and high leather boots. If he had been at the Royal stables he would have thought her a princess that had just dismounted her horse. Strands of her long, dark hair fell loosely about her narrow face. Peculiarly, she wore a pair of leather goggles with two telescopic lenses mounted over her eyes. Phillipe imagined them to be like Porro's prism binocular lenses that he had heard about. But here she stood before them, confident and fearless, illuminated by a backdrop of flames. She bent down before them into the darkness and lifted a grate that could not be seen earlier.

"Do you know Meudon?"

"Oui, mademoiselle."

"Go to the Rue de Blomet and follow the road into the hills. There is a small cottage by the Meudon bridge. Ask for the Cerf. The Deer."

"Who shall we say has sent us?"

"Tell him Renard Rouge has sent you. He is expecting you." With that the children were ushered down the grate into the sewers. Renard Rouge placed a small wooden box in Phillipe's hand and lowered the grate before leaping back to the ladder from which she came to disappear back into the night. The children clamoured down into the darkness, their hearts full of fear, their minds full of questions. Who was this Red Fox that had saved their lives? And how could they be expected by a man they had never met?

Above them, striding past the remnants of the flames about him, walked a portly little man. He too wore the Gaslampers mask to prevent him from bringing city diseases from the outside into their walls. On his arm he also wore the red band of the Gaslamper, but his aperture symbol was white. This white symbol enabled him the power to command the entire Parisian precinct. Regardless of the risk of infection he needed to survey the scene before him with his own eyes. He undid the leather buckle at his neck and pulled the mask off his head. It appeared the children were indeed gone. This was not what they had planned and would have to be reported to the Maire. With a last look, the ringmaster turned back towards the flames and twisted the ends of his moustache.

CHAPTER 5
THE CERF OF MOUDON

If you have ever lived in a major city in the world, chances are that beneath you on any given day is a labyrinth of tunnels and connections as intricate and connected as the veins of the body. But it is not blood that courses through their capillaries, it is storm water, and on occasion sewerage, and on a rarer occasion escapees. For thousands of years these chambered networks have existed as a subsystem of secrecy. The pedestrian may note a grate in the sidewalk, or the occasional metal covering that implies a subterranean world, but few have ever plunged into its solitary depths. An experience of which darkness is a blessing. For in the darkness, all manner of unsavoury objects pass by unnoticed, like sewer rats the size of cats and the occasional Parisian citizen torn apart by wolves.

Phillipe lead Angelique by the hand as he counted his steps in one direction and then another. His eyes may well have been closed for all he could see but the ground was solid and the walls were damp. When he felt they were far enough away from prying eyes, he opened the small wooden box given to him by Renard Rouge and felt for the phosphorus friction matches that he had assumed were the contents. He was correct. He struck a friction match on the stone wall and for the first time could take in his dank and dark surroundings. It was also the first time that he could look at the wound on his leg. Angelique leaned over and took the hardwood match, crouching for a closer investigation of his wound.

"It's really not too bad," she whispered cautiously. Phillipe looked at Angelique's hard expression, trying to read the honesty in her prognosis. "Truly. It has stopped bleeding and you can see the puncture marks, but there is very little damage. I fear we will need to be careful that it doesn't get diseased, but I think it will heal with rest."

"Merci. Well, let's keep moving." Philippe felt a sense of relief at this news but was anticipating the sounds of wolves in the tunnels at any moment. "We must find out where we are." Angelique, still holding the match, ran her eyes along the brick-work wall until she found the first marking. It appeared they were under the Rue de Fourneaux. This they could follow to the Rue de Plaisance and then hopefully find an exit somewhere in Vanves. Near the wall was an old lantern that was once used by sewer servicemen to navigate the dark labyrinth. Angelique carefully lit the canvas wick with her match and lowered the glass chimney. An amber hue lit the walls around them clearly for the first time.

"Come." Angelique and Phillipe pressed on into the bowels of the city. Above them, wolves and Gaslampers alike searched alley-ways and derelict buildings like ants crawling over the nest. Their orders were clear. The children must be brought in alive, the city of Paris depended on it. And so the children pressed on in the belief that their assailants were only moments behind them in the darkness. This belief alone drove Phillipe and Angelique on despite exhaustion. It was a misguided belief, as the alleyway grate to the depths below had remained unseen in the darkness by the relentless Gaslampers.

It was difficult to know what time Phillipe first placed his hands upon the ladder ascending to the Rue de Plaisance above.

He lifted the manhole with the utmost caution and glanced into the silent street. He was expecting a trap, and waited impatiently for his eyes to adjust.

"What do you see?" Angelique waited nervously at the lowest rung below.

"Nothing. It looks like the streets are empty. There is no movement anywhere."

"Do you think it could be a trap?"

"Yes. It could be. But I don't know what else to do. It is the only way to get to Meudon. Perhaps they didn't see us escape into the sewers." Phillipe slowly lifted the iron covering above him. It made a resounding scraping sound against the pavers on which it rested. Phillipe held his breath, his eyes darting around the empty streets in alarm for any sign of detection. Nothing. He slowly lifted himself into the street as Angelique silently climbed out behind him. All around, the city was clothed in darkness. If there were any observers hidden in the shadows, they would see very little in the grey hue that hung over the surrounding buildings. Keeping close to the walls and shadows, they crept towards the trees that lined the parklands at Vanves. There was only a brief moment when they both darted across the open street. It felt terrifying and reckless and necessary. They arrived at the trees, breathless, hearts pounding, eyes wildly scanning for movement. Phillipe again could feel the throbbing pain in his leg and tried to think of something else. But there was nothing more comforting he could find to think of, and so instead continued to think upon his pulsating pain. Exhausted and alone, they made their way into the darkness of the parklands. The moonlight was just enough to see the outline of the park's border that lead to a narrow road continuing up the hill to Meudon. Angelique was still uncertain of everything and felt an urgency to get to the house in question. But despite her efforts to hasten their pace, she was met instead with diminishing progress. Phillipe was struggling with each step and she was growing increasingly worried for his wellbeing and, as a consequence, for their safety.

It therefore came as a tangible relief when they finally arrived at the foot of the old stone bridge of Meudon and could make out what appeared to be a small cottage in the distance, hemmed in by spruce trees and darkness. No light emanated from any window in the cottage which did not instil confidence in the presence of occupants that were expecting them. Nevertheless they left the cobblestone path and made their way past the thicket to the cottage entrance. They arrived at a heavy wooden door at the rear of the cottage, away from the road and paused. Angelique became aware of the sound of her breath in the silence around them.

"Should we knock?"

Phillipe shrugged, uncertain of the etiquette at this hour. After all, what was etiquette in a situation of desperation? Plus, they still had no idea what the hour actually was.

A deep breath. Angelique knocked. It was a quiet, apologetic knock and was momentarily met with silence, confirming her assumption.

"Who is it?" hissed a quiet voice from inside the door. Phillipe suddenly became aware of a minuscule glass spy hole at the top of the door with what appeared to be an eye looking through. His sharp breath betrayed his surprise.

"I am Angelique and this is Phillipe. We have been sent here by Renard Rouge. We have been told we could find the Cerf here." After a long pause, the door slowly opened. There before them stood an old man, as peculiar as he was cautiously urgent.

"It is I. Come. Come in quickly. I have been expecting you and so may others. Paris is full of eyes. Good or bad it does not matter. Everyone watches. Everyone reports. Come." He had already ushered them into the small cottage and closed the door before lowering an iron arm bracing it. When he was satisfied that all of the curtains were drawn he sparked a phosphorus match and lit a kerosene lantern by the mantle, bringing it to a small wooden table near the kitchen. It was only here that he could be clearly seen in the lamplight for the first time. He wore a singular leather goggle with a telescopic lens, which he had now pushed up on his head so that it sat like a single leathery horn in his silvery long hair. He was tall, thin and stooped, perhaps as the result of years pottering around his tiny cottage. Whether or not he had been working into the night hours at his craft was uncertain, as he still wore a leather apron loosely tied at his neck and waist. His face was creased with age and his eyes- now visible- appeared pink in the light but kind. He had kind eyes. Angelique felt a weight lift that she was previously unaware of. As soon as she and Phillipe were ushered into simple wooden chairs she was betrayed by her emotions and burst into tears. The kind of tears that would not stop, tears of fear, uncertainty, shock and terror, but above all tears of relief. She wept uncontrollably.

"There, there mademoiselle." He offered a small cloth from the table and carefully looked over his guests. "Oui. Oui. You must have many questions. As do I. You are safe for now." He cautiously reached out and touched Angelique's hand. "I have prepared a small room in the basement for you. We will speak later. First you must both rest. And you... I see you have already encountered our police and their dogs. I will dress this. Oui. Oui. Have you fixed in no time..." He rose and walked over to the rustic kitchen bench. On the top shelf was a terracotta pot labelled 'achilee'. The old man took a handful of yellow herb and tossed it into a small mortar which he duly ground into a firm paste. After applying it to the wound he took a clean rag from his shelf and tore it in two. It appeared effortless and suddenly impressive. Phillipe could not help but wonder at the old man's strength. After tying the rags around Phillipe's wound, he rose and stood beside a set of shelves perched against the wall.

"Come." A wry smile appeared on his face. "Follow me." The Cerf proceeded to push the shelves aside to reveal a small dark passage that led down a steep stairwell to a cellar below. Taking the lamp from the table he escorted the children to the simple room beneath. "It is not much no. But it is safe. Tonight, we rest. Tomorrow, we learn." He pointed to the two simple feather mattresses on the floor by way of apology before excusing himself and ascending the staircase, leaving the lamp behind for the guests. Alone, there was nothing more that could really be said. Phillipe reached across and touched his sister's arm as she extinguished the light. They held hands in silence and fell fast asleep.

❦

At that same hour in that same city, only four miles from where the siblings soundly slept. The Ringmaster approached the former Hospital of Dr La Salpetriere. It was a formidable blue stone building in the middle of the city that had become the civic centre. The irony that it was formerly an institution for disease was not lost on him as it was now an institution where diseases of any kind were no longer welcome. It was for this reason that he, and all of the Gaslampers under his command were required to wear their leather anti-infective masks at all times outside the compound. The Maire would not be happy. Fugitives loose in his city were not part of his plan at all. The Ringmaster passed two masked guards at the entrance both standing duty with wolves. They straightened to attention and clicked their boot heels as he quickly passed. He had no time for ceremony, so he pressed on. He strode through the courtyard, passing two more guards with similar formality as they opened the iron door to the compound. Once inside he finally removed his face mask. Beneath it his face was flushed, sweaty and tormented. He twisted the waxy ends of his moustache with his free hand, clutching his mask in the other, and made his way down a series of corridors and stairs until he had finally arrived at an ornate French oak door. A plaque etched in brass hung neatly on the door 'Maire of the Municipality of Paris'. The Ringmaster took a last, deep breath and knocked.

"Enter." The voice echoed through the door. There was nothing left to be done. He pushed open the door to face his fate.

"Bonsoir, Monsieur Maire." He bowed low and waited. The Maire sat at his desk under a veil of dappled moonlight that shone through the solitary window behind him. He did not respond immediately but took a moment to observe his portly servant so that he could adjust his expectations accordingly.

"What news inspector? I hope it is good news at this late hour."

"Not quite monsieur. We are closing in on their whereabouts as we speak." A long silence forced him to continue under nervous duress. "Ah… we had them cornered you see. There was an ambush. It took us completely by surprise. I couldn't be sure of how many rebels there were but they were many. Many. We were under intense attack from fire bombs, among other things."

"What other things?"

"Ahem. Mostly firebombs. Oui, firebombs. In the fracas the targets seemed to vanish monsieur."

"Vanish?"

"Oui…but I did not see this with my own eyes. It was reported to…"

"Are you telling me inspector that you were not there?"

"No. Just after she attacked the wolves and police is when I arrived."

"She?"

"They. I meant they." But it was too late. The inspector's ill conceived word hung in the air like a Verey flare that illuminated all of the lies that fell around it. Silence was now the best course of action. Silence and perhaps honesty. Perhaps.

"Is it possible that the ambush you speak of was from a solitary girl who fired a fiery cocktail at a line of police that you were not in attendance at, because you struggled to move your rotund frame at the necessary pace to keep up.”

“Oui. That is very perceptive monsieur.”

“You are closing in no?”

“Oui.” The inspector eyed the Maire cautiously, trying to gauge his next step. It was the worst poker hand in history and he felt he had played all of his chips.

“How are you closing in inspector? On what intelligence are you... *closing in?*”

“I have no idea monsieur.”

“So it is not your intelligence of which you speak.”

“No monsieur. I have none.”

The Maire lowered his voice to an intimate whisper. “When I drew you into my circle of confidence. Did I not tell you that this mission, these children were necessary? Did I not say that I am trusting you with a task of the *utmost* significance? The future of Paris depends on these children being in my custody. *Children.* Do you see why I am perplexed?...CHILDREN!” A rage throbbed in roped veins in the Maire’s throat as he clenched his hands in frustration. He breathed deeply, composed himself and slowly sat behind his solid oak desk. He pulled open his desk draw and produced a large map of Paris. In doing so he was also momentarily distracted by something in his drawer that quickly caught his eye but was just as quickly dismissed. The inspector stood without movement from his current position near the doorway uncertain to read this action as an invitation.

“Come.”

He did.

“There are only a limited number of roads that lead out of the metropolitan area. They can not have ventured beyond that distance yet. You will need to put sentries at each of these points and have the wolves patrol between them at once so that we will have them contained within the city at least.”

"Oui monsieur. It will be done at once. Is there anything else Monsieur Maire?"

The Maire shook his head and eyed the door. The inspector nodded in ascent, clicked his heels and bowed deeply before taking his leave, closing the door and breathing a sigh of relief. Inside the office, the Maire remained in his seat. He glanced back at the grey weathered photograph in his drawer that had caught his attention unexpectedly. He had quite forgotten it was there. She stood on pointe, her silk, frilled tutu flowing beneath her fitted bodice. Her arms an impossibly graceful extension, delicate and beautiful. He felt a longing stir deep within him and so slammed the drawer closed.

CHAPTER 6
TWILIGHT

Phillipe awoke as if from a dream. A nightmare. He sat bolt upright on his feather mattress, relieved at the quick realisation that it was indeed a dream from which he was awakening. But as he took in his stark surroundings, the dim, sparse basement echoed an emptiness he felt welling up within him. It was the growing understanding that this was in fact real. Beside him, Angelique still slept on her feather mattress. His leg still bore the torn rags of the previous night's remedy, but it did feel significantly better; the throbbing had abated. He rose from his bed and walked over to the solitary small window perched high near the ceiling. He stood on the only small wooden chair in the room and carefully raised himself up to take a look outside. It appeared to be late in the afternoon, for the sun was going down and Phillipe wondered how long he had slept. He climbed back down from the chair, a new cloud of questions hovering in the storm of his thoughts. Angelique stirred, her awakening face betraying the same realisations.

"Are you alright, Phillipe?"

"Oui. I thought perhaps it was a dream."

"We must find Papa. He will know what to do. Today, we find Papa."

"He will be worried we are lost."

"He will fix it. You will see. Come, let us find out what we can." Angelique rose from her bed. Phillipe did not share the same confidence. He thought of his father's thick, dependable fingers that worked with metal lettering all day long and shuddered to think of that quiet man in a world of noise.

The two tidied the clothes they had slept in and pulled on their boots before ascending the stairs in the twilight glow, cautiously tapping on the shelves that blocked the cellar door. There was a scuffling and a murmuring behind the shelves before they were scraped across the floor to reveal the old man who appeared to have slept in his previous night's attire also. The leather apron was still fastened around his waist but he no longer wore the telescopic lens propped upon his head.

"Bonjour les enfants. Please come. Sit." He ushered them into the kitchen for the second time and pushed the shelf back to its former deceptive purpose. The room was easier to see in the twilight that broke through the curtains. There was no longer a burning lamp throwing shadows on the sparse walls, but a pale hue that gently illuminated the three open rooms of the small cottage. The children quietly sat at the table as requested.

"Merci monsieur. Bonjour to you also." Angelique threw in this final nicety as an afterthought as she had been occupied in the act of viewing her surroundings for the first time and did not want to seem rude in her preoccupation.

"Coffee? Petit breakfast?"

"Oui...merci." Phillipe was starving and uttered his agreement too quickly for politeness. "Is it not too late in the day for breakfast monsieur?"

"It is early morning. But not too early for introductions. I am the Cerf but my real name is Enzo Greniere." Phillipe sat perplexed by this information for he knew morning when he saw it and this was not it. He pulled open the curtain near where he sat. The sun seemed fixed in an idle state behind the horizon creating only a subtle glow whose fingers reached across the fields cautiously. The hand of the Cerf was instantly upon it closing the curtain with such force that Phillipe was taken aback.

"There are eyes everywhere. They look for you. I will not mince words, you are in danger and you must be careful." An awkward silence hung momentarily in the room as Phillipe quickly moved from embarrassment to fear.

"I am Angelique, Monsieur Greniere and this is my younger brother Phillipe. We are very grateful for your hospitality. But we need to find our father."

"Indeed. Let us eat, talk and then I shall do what I can to help you. How is your leg, Phillipe?" Philipe's thoughts were still at the window, still lurking in dark, dangerous realisations.

"It feels better Monsieur Greniere. Merci." A thought dropped into Phillipe's head and was out before it had time to process. "Why are you called *the deer?*" This was met with heart-felt laughter from the old man who was now stirring dried oats into a creamy paste while the coffee heated on the stove.

"I was young once, Phillipe. And strong. It was a name given to me by the *Calibrators* in my younger years. A name that I was proud to bear."

"Calibrators?" Angelique and Phillipe enquired in unison.

"There is much to discuss." The Cerf poured three cups of steaming coffee, before spooning porridge into three wooden bowls and placing them before the children. Phillipe immediately started eating.

"Merci, monsieur." Angelique nodded apologetically on behalf of them both. The Cerf nodded in reply, and then began.

"I received a message from Renard Rouge last night that two strangers had appeared in the city outside of curfew hours. We immediately assumed you were from the other side but did not know how or why you were here. We do know you were expected.

Not by us, but by him. There is only one reason that all of the Gaslampers in Paris were nearby the Rue de Voile last night. They were searching. Expecting. Perhaps you do not know why? Perhaps you do."

"But we do not know. We do not even understand where we are." Angelique was perplexed.

"You are in Paris child. You are in the Obscura."

"That is what we saw painted on the wall in the street!" Phillipe piped in.

"It was first called that by two strangers who came from the other side many years ago. One, we named the Aigle. He was a thinker, an extraordinary mind, he built things you could not dream were possible. We were very close. The other, his companion, I do not recall for he was a quiet man I did not know and never met. But they came and they vanished. I assume returned, though I do not know how. That is how we learned of your world, of night and day and the scientific knowledge by which you progress. Here we have only night and halflight. It is beautiful in its own way. The sun for us is but a shadow that lingers on the edge of the fields. But you are here in dangerous times. The most dangerous times. It wasn't always like this." The old man paused finally to drink deeply from his coffee cup, as though it was a necessary ingredient before the continued narrative. "When I was a child, I was free to wander where I pleased. To sing, to dance, to explore in the halflight. It seems so long ago now...days of endless possibilities. This city... it has always been my home, and like any city, there are times of prosperity and times of adversity. In the summer of 1855, there was no rain. The fields of France were barren. No crops, no harvests, no food. It was a drought that would continue for the next four years. Four long, hard years. Impoverished, the field hands flocked into the city where there was no work or food. And so began a season of great poverty and all of the vices that accompany that villain. But of course, a hero enters this story, another stranger from far away who spoke with a velvet tongue and promised real progress. In desperate times, people look to hope. Any hope. After campaigning in the streets for months, he rose to become our Maire. The people rejoiced, we thought we would be saved. It began with a curfew. No Parisian could be outside after nightfall, workers needed their rest after all. It became apparent that other trivial pursuits were taking the place of real productivity... and so one by one, song, dance, art, all creativity, all the frivolous pursuits were banned by order of the Maire. The only creativity that would be celebrated was that associated with Scientific progress. All of the inventors from far and wide were woken in their beds one night and taken by force. There would be no invention outside the civic walls of the Maire, for real progress required careful supervision. The old Hospital of Dr La Salpetriere, the most formidable building in all of Paris became the new civic compound. It would become the lifeblood of the city, and so the health of its occupants would be guaranteed by the restriction of any outside visitation. The police were issued anti-infective masks and their numbers were tripled. Training began immediately of the wild wolves that were rounded up by the thousands. And so, the hero became the villain."

"Who are the calibrators, monsieur?" Phillipe had not forgotten this word that had hung on his thoughts since the moment it was uttered.

"They are us, young Phillipe. It began as a small band of resistance several decades ago. We are artisans by day and revolutionaries by night. We await the return of the Aigle to join our ranks and help us to overthrow this tyranny. We are committed to using scientific invention and creativity, the very thing that has been disallowed to resist this wave of death and destruction. We are few and they are many. "

"Renard Rouge?"

"Oui. Among others. But there is more..." The Cerf's voice lowered to a cautious whisper. "There is another. I will only say his name once and will not speak of it again. It began as a murmur, whisperings upon the wind, truths half told by lamplight in dark corners of noisy taverns. He came from Reykjavik, Iceland. Little is known about him except that his empire is built on terror and torture, an empire of flames and destruction that spreads its wildfire across the continent. He is known as...*gris loup*. The Grey Wolf. One of our number fled across the Scandinavian waters and confirmed that it is true... and it is coming. But for now the dangers are closer to home, you must be careful."

"What about Papa? Will we find him here? Will you help us."

The Cerf was staring at the floor, trying to find his words, avoiding the desperation in Angelique's eyes. It was an inevitable conversation that had now found it's moment.

"You will not...you can not be on both sides at once."

Angelique's eyes began to instantly well with tears, for now the realisation that they were utterly alone in a strange, dangerous world swept over her like a dark wave. She suddenly thought of Corantin, alone in Paris, looking desperately for his children, and her sorrow found a new depth. Phillipe -also feeling this darkness keenly- tried to be strong for Angelique and held her hand tightly. In a moment there was a hand upon her shoulder, strong and comforting.

"Child. I can not bring your father here. But I will do everything in my power to get you back to him. You have my word. I will need time and ask for your patience."

"Oui monsieur." Angelique struggled to get the words out between sobs. She tried to breathe deeply and calm herself, her face tasted of salt, and she felt a red heat deep within her skin, but despite this she found the old man's words were a comfort.

"But for now, you will need to stay out of sight. Here will be the safest place until I can find something better. We just need a little time and we will work this out. You will see." It suddenly occurred to Phillipe that he still did not know the time, and if he were to observe the curfew and pass the time in this cottage it would help if he was aware of the time he had to pass.

"Monsieur, we will wait. Is there a timepiece we might observe?"

A large smile spread across the old man's face and he quietly rose from his chair. "Is there a timepiece? If it is time you seek, then you will each have a personal timepiece." He made his way into a small room behind the kitchen calling back through the open door. "I forgot to tell you. I am a clockmaker."

CHAPTER 7
CORANTIN

I t was late in the afternoon and the sun had begun its slow descent behind the hills of Meudon when Corantin finally wiped his inky hands on a rag by the printing press, removed his leather apron and pulled the heavy door to the work-shop closed. He was the last worker on the floor at the print press that day, which was most unusual in itself, for the ink work was all labour and no love. Corantin had hoped that Phillipe and Angelique would pass through on their way home, he had wanted to hear how Phillipe had fared on his first day back at the Republic school. And if he were honest with himself, he had wanted to allay his internal fears that his curious son had not found opportunity once again to seek his education elsewhere. But the children had not come. Corantin pocketed the large workshop key and began his journey back to the apartment. His home was quite a walk away and he was eager to return before nightfall.

The children had not passed by in the morning either. It was a concern that had grown in Corantin like a seed watered with irra-tional thoughts all day. It was completely reasonable that having not left sufficient time to make the workshop visit, Angelique had decided to take Phillipe straight to school. After all, he had made them promise that Phillipe would not be late. Surely when he arrived home they would be already there. Phillipe would be meddling under the stairs and Angelique would be preparing the stove for supper. They would have a very good reason for missing Corantin, and no doubt it would be tied up in some long winded explanation that involved some silliness and they would all laugh. A sudden chill in the cooling late afternoon air crept into Corantin's awareness. He raised the collar of his outer coat and hastened his pace. He could not shake the sense that there was something wrong, and it troubled him greatly.

By the time he arrived at the apartment block, the street was shrouded in shadows and flickering lamplight. His cold fingers fumbled in his pockets for the front key. His breath was sharp and his heart racing. There was a flight of stairs, a long corridor and another key before he finally opened the apartment door to silence and darkness.

"Angelique! Phillipe!" He was trying to contain the rising panic that was bubbling to the surface, like a boiling pot on the stove-top. He immediately lit a lantern and moved from room to room. "Angel...Phillipe." Each room met his rising echo with silence. Never had this happened before. The children were as reliable as clockwork. Yes Phillipe had absconded from school and sought his education elsewhere, and he was also aware that Angelique had often missed her domestic training from Madame Bernard and spent her hours dreaming in the theatres. This he knew and understood. But they always came home before nightfall, they always checked in with Corantin in the morning to at least keep up the pretence of educational pursuits. Despite his attempts at rationality, Corantin found with each empty room a spiralling panic that swirled within him a terrifying darkness.

He raced down the apartment block corridor rapping loudly on Madame Covin's door. He knew she would be reluctant to open it at this hour but also knew that her eyes, though old, were keen and reliable. "Madame Covin. It is Corantin. Corantin Chastain. Please come to the door, I need your assistance." Slowly, there was a sound on the other side, a murmuring and a slow turning as the old woman cautiously opened the door slightly.

"How do I know it is you?"

"Please Madame. I can not find my children. Angelique and Phillipe have not come home." Madam Covin did not care a great deal for Phillipe who was a considerable and constant bother to her, but found her heart immediately soften at the thought of sweet Angelique in trouble. She opened the door where she could clearly see Corantin's troubled face half lit by his lantern. She too cast a formidable presence as she held her lantern before her.

"They have not come home?"

"They have not."

"There has been no movement in your apartment all day. I can assure you. I saw the children leaving towards the Rue de Voile this morning from my front window and have not seen them since."

"I fear there is something wrong."

"Is there anywhere else they may have gone. Children can be flighty and forgetful."

"Not these Madame." There was an awkward pause where the old woman sensed there was something that she should say or do, but she was never one to understand social niceties.

"Perhaps you should report this to the Gendarmerie?"

"Oui. If they return Madame…"

"I will send a message to you with Garren immediately." Garren was Madam Covin's middle aged son. He had a reputation for slovenly idleness and lived on the charity of his ageing mother. There were few in all of Paris as unreliable as Garren. It did not instil the certainty in Corantin that the old widow had intended. But he gave nothing away as he fled out to the street and deep into the Parisian night on a desperate and unexpected mission to locate his two children.

As quickly as his legs would take him he raced through the streets, now dimly lit by flickering street lamps. It was a landscape immediately alien to him, for he never ventured out into the Parisian streetscape at night and the sounds and smells were strangers to his senses. He blindly raced down streets and alleyways lit by the occasional lamp or burning iron drum, making his way to the Rue de Lutèce and the Prefecture of Police. The sandstone building finally loomed in the distance, two formidable towers flanking the grand archway in the centre. The French flag perched upon that archway, flapping in the night wind, as gusts billowed down the street. Corantin finally arrived breathless at the foot of a Gendarme sentry standing at the doorway to the prefecture. The Gendarme eyed the frantic man before him and sensing no immediate danger, opened the large wooden door.

Inside was equally imposing. Despite the hour, the Gendarmerie were actively engaged in all manner of busyness. A sea of navy blue coats writing in ledgers, polishing leather and brass, and shuffling away undesirables in iron cuffs.

"Can I help you, monsieur?" A voice cut through the commotion and demanded Corantin's attention. Behind him a Gendarme sat expectantly at a heavy wooden desk. His waxed moustache poised politely, his expression betraying impatience. He was awaiting a response.

"Can I help you, monsieur?" His second address had lost all of the warmth and welcome of the first.

"Oui Gendarme. I have lost my children. I fear something has happened to them."

The Gendarme immediately softened and offered the distressed father a seat. "Please. Monsieur, sit. Tell me what has happened." The policeman took an ink quill, dipped it in the well upon his desk, opened a notebook and waited.

"Gendarme, I arrived home this evening and my children were not home. They are always at home at this hour. They did not visit me in the workshop today which they always do. They always do. They are good children. They would never run away. Something has happened."

"How old are your children monsieur?"

"Angelique is fourteen and her brother Phillipe is thirteen."

There was an instant and noticeable shift in the Gendarme with this information. In his mind he had envisioned infants, not youths or ruffians, and his disposition moved from concern to indifference. "Where do you live monsieur?" Corantin could already feel the attention of the officer moving behind him to more citizens that had since come through the door.

"I live near the Rue Montemartre. In the tenement apartments."

At this, the Gendarme almost rolled his eyes with indifference and put his ink quill down beside his notebook.

"Monsieur. I can not help you tonight. It is dark. Your children, they are not young. They are...what shall I say, coming of age. They are learning. Why don't you go home. Get some rest and have a good look for them in the morning in the light of day. You will see. They will not be far."

Corantin drew his breath to protest but saw that the officer was already making gestures to the citizens behind him, ushering them into his chair. His meeting was done and that would be it. He had been afforded the only consideration that his class would be given and so found himself once again alone in the darkness of the Rue de Lutèce. His mind continued to race with trepidation and confusion. Fear and loss were no strangers to him. He had felt it first twenty years ago, when the Gendarme had delivered news of his brother's mysterious drowning in the Seine. He had felt it again ten years later when his wife Delphine had abandoned him with the two children. Disappearing into the night leaving little more that a vague conciliatory note, she had left him. Heartbroken and alone with two infants to raise and no idea of how he would do this. He had walked the same streets, struggling for answers and now he walked them again. Where could they be? Who could he turn to?

In a vague stupor, Corantin ambled back to the Rue Montemartre hoping that there might be some clue he had missed, some obvious error... or perhaps they had since returned. He arrived on the doorstep of the tenements and though exhausted, ran back up to the apartment to investigate once again. He was met with silence and empty rooms for the second time. He returned to the tenement entrance and briefly sat on the stone steps to gather himself and collect his thoughts. It was then, in the dim lamplight of the street that he first noticed it. It was faint. Barely visible in the compact dirt of the street he could see a peculiar footprint. It was a small boot, to be sure, but at the toe if you were to lean in with keen perception, you could just make out the shape of the letter "P". The recollection hit Corantin like a lightening bolt. On his way to school several months earlier Phillipe and Angelique had passed by the print workshop as the routine had dictated. Phillipe had worn a hole in the toe of his boot. It was a small, inconvenient hole that would invite the passage of small stones and seasonal rain. Boots were expensive, as was their repair. Corantin had fossicked around the workshop and found an old worn brass letter "P" typeset that had been unceremoniously discarded. He then creatively hammered the square letter into the leather sole of the boot to prevent any further inconvenience. It was this same footprint that he now observed in the dim lamplight of the street. His heart quickened, for it was followed by another and another.

He crouched low with his lantern extended before him swinging from left to right as his eyes searched for the next print. If one had stood on the Rue de Voile that evening they would have borne witness to a most unusual spectacle. It is a rare occasion when a grown man is crawling down the street in the darkness, scrambling quickly behind a light held aloft. Corantin moved from one print to the next. So focused was he, that he was only narrowly missed by a horse drawn carriage that rolled down the street oblivious to the man scurrying beneath its line of vision. At times the prints had all but disappeared. He would stand and extend his search perimeter. Aware of the direction the steps were heading he managed to pick up the trail once again, taking care not to foul the prints behind him in case he would lose the trail again. Indeed it lead to the Rue de Vanguard and came to a grinding halt at the oddest of places. The old Vanguard Theatre. It would make sense that Angelique would venture here, but why Phillipe?

The street was eerily quiet for the time of evening and Corantin felt as though he had reached a dead end. The wind again whistled down the street and he looked for inspiration. Anywhere. The only other inhabitant nearby was a vagabond propped against the alleyway wall like a bookend. He was covered in the tatters of a former overcoat and was bracing himself against the cold winds with a heavy woollen hat pulled down as far as the stitching would allow. There was no one else. Every now and then an arm would appear from beneath the coat and lift a glass bottle to the lips underneath the hat. Corantin approached the man cautiously.

"Excusez-moi monsieur. I'm sorry to trouble you. Did you see two children at this theatre earlier today?" His other hand appeared from under the coat and pulled back his woollen hat revealing two cautious eyes. They eyed Corantin up and down and having decided that he proved no threat, softened.

"I don't know anything about children mon amie. But I am glad that the racket that has been going on all day from that infernal salesman has rested and I can sit in peace. Super this, camera that...he wouldn't shut up."

Something quickened inside Corantin, who felt immediately alert. "What did he look like monsieur?"

"Fat little thing. He had this long, waxy infernal moustache. He was prattling on about some Observer... some Ob... "

"Obscura?"

"Oui. That is it."

"Merci mon amie. For your trouble." Corantin handed over his last franc to the man who immediately thrust it into his mouth and bit down on it with his good tooth. Satisfied, he put it into his pocket with cold fingers and pulled his woollen hat back over his head.

Corantin's head was spinning with this new information. Possibilities swirled in his thoughts, understanding growing into fear. He ran back to the tenement in the darkness, ran up the stairwell and down his corridor. The door to Madame Covin opened slightly as he passed.

"Any word, monsieur?"

"None I'm afraid." Corantin did not stop to elaborate and her door remained ajar in expectation but he disappeared into his apartment, firmly closing the door. Panicking, he went straight to the firebox. The loose bricks were still in place which he quickly removed by the lamplight. Reaching into the dark cavity he pulled out the small chest. Though dusty, the lock was intact and untouched. He breathed a momentary sigh of relief. There were more secrets. He pulled back the old hessian rug over the living room floor and found where the floorboards were split. He reached his fingers into the hollow and pulled up the small panel of boards that lifted as one, revealing the cavity beneath. He lifted out old garments covered in decades of dust and traffic, a leather jerkin, overcoat and cape. Beneath that was a modified blunderbuss, its barrel wider and shorter than was the standard. He reached into the overcoat and took out an old key from the pocket. At last he returned to the small chest in the furnace. The key turned in the worn lock with a click and the chest opened. It was still there. He reached in and took out the small package. Beneath the oilskin cloth, the shape of the small wooden box was still evident. Corantin carefully unwrapped it and began.

CHAPTER 8
THE TENEMENT ON RUE MONTMARTRE

The Obscura morning had passed without any real evidence of its progression. In the course of a day, the movement of the earth around the sun is slight. So slight that one would struggle to find the moment when the day moves from morning to afternoon. Yet there is *some* evidence in the sky, a change in the lengths of shadow, a softness that permeates the air as the sun gradually slides beneath the horizon. Although Phillipe had never truly been aware of the light in all of its daily forms, he became acutely aware of its absence. Halflight kept the world poised in a single moment in time and try as he might, he could not get used to the progression of time being only reflected on his clock face. They were to stay indoors, stay away from open windows and gaps in the curtains. There were eyes everywhere, or so the Cerf had told them after breakfast, before he left for his workshop in the city. He would return before nightfall. The children were in danger and had no option but to trust the old man. As Phillipe and Angelique sat alone in the low light of the cellar, they conversed only in hushed tones.

"We must find Papa." This was the only truth that Phillipe

understood. In a new world where danger was ever present there was still a sense deep down that perhaps it was yet a dream. Yes, the Cerf had shown them a kindness, and they had witnessed the violence of the wolves and Gaslampers with their own eyes. It was true that in an upside down world, where all that was certain and familiar was now uncertain and strange, one had to trust their instincts. Philipe's instincts were that Corantin would be able to fix this somehow.

"Papa is not here Phillipe. You heard the Cerf. He cannot be in both worlds. How could he also be in the Obscura? Did he stand on his head in the theatre also?" Just saying these words was beginning to take its toll once again on Angelique's emotions, and she found her voice fragile and thin, her lip quivering against her will. Her argument was compelling; it was impossible for either child to imagine their father doing a handstand in the theatre and somehow fracturing the dimension of time. A phenomenon which they had accidentally achieved. Nothing made sense anymore.

"Perhaps you are right Angel. But what if you are wrong? What if the Cerf is wrong? His understanding of our world came from people just like us, did it not? What if he doesn't yet know all there is to know? I do believe we can trust him. I do. But what if he does not have all the answers?"

"I do want to find Papa. Phillipe, it is all I want. But we don't yet know what dangers we may face out there." This was true and it already weighed heavily on Phillipe's mind. They sank into a mutual silence as each contemplated their situation. There was a heavier question lingering for Phillipe. This question had already moved beyond the recesses of his thoughts and he felt the weight of it in his heart. What if they did find Papa? What could be do? What could a typesetter do in a dark world of semi-light? A world of wolves and curfews and Icelandic darkness that crept across the continent. Then a thought dropped into his consciousness and he spoke it before he had time to weigh its value.

"What if it is him who needs us?" The question lingered in the air like a freshly sprayed fragrance, but it was suddenly inter-rupted by the sound of pounding on the front door. The room fell deathly silent. A moment. Pounding again. Without a look or a word, Angelique silently stole her way to the top of the stairs, the sound of muffled knocking ever present. The bookshelf that disguised the stairwell on which she now stood was open. She could see straight into the living room and although the curtains were drawn, she could see movement as shadows moved back and forth through the sliver of light in between. The knocking was becoming more aggressive now and a muffled voice shouted through the wall. "Enzo Greniere. We know you are in there. Open this door by order of the Maire and the Parisian prefec-ture." A growl emanated outside the door, low and dangerous. Wolves. Phillipe was instantly by his sister's side and the two pulled at the bookshelf with all of their might trying to seal the tomb in which they stood. Carefully they inched it closed as the sounds outside the door amplified. Two sharp blows and the sounds were now in the living room. Bodies moving from room to room with the sharp barks of wolves indicating where smells were strongest. It was only a matter of time. Phillipe ran to the small window perched at the ceiling height, careful to move lightly on his toes to minimise any noise. He held his breath and slowly opened the curtain. There was no movement evident in the limited vision before him. The window itself was small, but just large enough. The glass frame was hinged on either side and opened like a shutter. He turned to Angelique and gestured for a lift. She hoisted him up to the best of her ability so that he could get his head out for a proper investigation. There were no imme-diate sounds outside; all of the sounds were in the house at present. He used his arms to reach to the yard before him and wriggle himself out onto the lawn. Immediately turning to help Angelique, both became aware of an incessant barking at the bookshelf. They had been found. This was followed by the scraping sound of the bookshelf beginning to shift across the floor. Angelique could not wait for her brother's arm, she leapt to the window and skilfully pulled herself through to the halflight world outside. In that moment, the basement filled with the sound of barking wolves and muffled shouts.

They ran.

There was no thought, there was no plan. They simply ran. Trees scratched and tore at their skin and clothing and they hurtled through the outskirts of the woods, always imagining wolves pounding through the terrain right behind them. Each sibling could hear the other's breath by their side and see their shape in the periphery but there could be no turning, no pausing, just a violent and desperate escape into the semi-darkness.

Then the sounds began. The howling in the distance and the breaking of the brittle forest floor under the powerful dash of bloodthirsty paws. Suddenly Angelique was on the cobblestone road. She did not know how. Perhaps they had ran in a curve, perhaps the halflight had deceived her senses. But before them was Meudon bridge and behind them the slavering beasts and their masters. It was over. They could not outrun their pursuers on the road. As the sounds echoing through the forest quickly approached, the siblings ran to the bridge's edge. There was a small stone wall and then a drop of perhaps seventy feet to the Seine. There are few in the world who experience the hopelessness of a situation where death faces you at every turn, where every choice arouses the taste of bile in your throat and uncontrollable palpitations in your heart. But in those moments, in some, there can be sublime clarity, where inspired thoughts crystallise like the sharpening focus of a lens. In that moment, as Angelique and Phillipe both peered over the stone edge to the icy dark waters below, her head was a sum of calculations, speeds and distances and in an instant she knew. She took Phillipe's hand and there was a shared understanding. Before they were seen. Before the wild dogs came careening out of the scrub and gave them away. They took a breath.

And jumped.

Hurtling through air slowly, as though he had swallowed gravity itself and then exploding through the watery earth, Phillipe sank into its dark depths. Icy cold water raced through his nostrils and every cell of his body as he plummeted the secrets of the Seine. Impossibly deep, impossibly dark, Phillipe did not touch the earth but with empty lungs began a natural ascent. Slowly at first. But quickening as though the air itself were sucking him back to life and then gasping through the choppy surface. Sucking air desperately back into his consciousness. He was alive. Where was Angelique? He looked feverishly around him in the semi-darkness, desperately wanting to cry out, to shout her name but knowing that detection meant certain death. Waves and silence. Then breaking the surface in the distance he saw her. Gasping for air, she was across the other side of the river and she too looked frantically about her. Their eyes locked. Phillipe gestured cautiously to Angelique to make her way to him where they could hide in the shadow of the bridge's pylon. She slowly swam towards Phillipe, carefully keeping only the top of her head visible from above. Finally when she reached her brother they clasped hands - all while treading water - and made their way to the stone pylon under the bridge.

Phillipe went to speak and was immediately stopped by Angelique's finger to her lips. No sound. He understood. We wait. They waited. It felt like an eternity that they continued to tread water, holding themselves against a pylon in the darkness. The barking above soon abated and the confused shouts of Gaslampers slowly quietened to a distant murmur as they searched empty woods and farmhouses. It was not until the half-light had given way to pitch black that the children conversed in whispers, mumbling into the cover of the night.

"Are you alright, Angelique?"

"I think so. You?"

"Yes. But my legs are getting tired."

"Mine too."

"What do we do now?"

"Perhaps you are right. Perhaps we should try and find Papa."

"I should like to go home and just see if he is there...perhaps."

Angelique was silent and thoughtful for some time. She too longed for this more than anything else, although there was a small part of her that was very afraid of what they might find there. "The Seine is the safest way for us to get back to the tenements at night. We can swim under the cover of the banks and rest at the bridges if need be. We will have to take our chances when we get to the quay near the Rue Marmont."

"Agreed."

There were no more words exchanged. Both were aware of the dangers ahead of them, but neither felt that they had any choice and this was now a plan after all. The two silently and carefully stole away into the watery darkness.

❦

The water was cold. They had not noticed it at first, as fear and adrenaline had insulated them against the icy sting. But as they slowly glided through the frigid currents, the cold began to bore through their skin and bones. They kept moving. Silently, carefully, keeping close to the grassy banks and away from the light of the moon that shone above them the children carried on. Continual movement seemed to neutralise the growing chill within them. It wasn't long before the grass and reeds by the banks gave way to stonewall as they entered the city perimeter. Every so often they would pass under the archway of a bridge and rest momentarily under shadow until the cold became too much to bear and they pushed on. Around them, the stone walls climbed to flickering lamps that would cast long rays of light across the Seine. From the water it looked a veritable fairy land, but Angelique was all too aware that each ray of light brought with it the possibility of detection. The city looked so different from the water, landmarks were difficult to decipher from the low vantage point and it didn't take long before Angelique began to question her orientation and whereabouts. The last thing they needed was to become lost in the city. All around the river were small lamps moving, no doubt Gaslampers with their wolves, desperately searching for the children that had evaded them at Meudon. Finally, under the cover of an overhead bridge archway, Angelique shared her fears in a whisper.

"Phillipe, I'm no longer sure where we are. I thought this was the Point de l'Alma and that we had just passed the Champ de Mars, but I can not see the Hippodrome."

"I don't think we have passed it yet."

"It is too dark to see. I fear that we have already passed it."

"What shall we do?"

A voice above them silenced them instantly. A shout. Perhaps across the street on the bridge above. "You. Stop...Arretez." This was followed by fierce barking and a moment of silence. Phillipe stared wide eyed at Angelique in the darkness. Then the voice of a woman. Calm and resolute.

"You have no business with me Officer. I am a guest of the Maire."

"A guest of the Maire, Madame?" The muffled tone was unmistakably mocking.

"I am a guest of the Maire, who will be most concerned if I am harmed in any way." It was difficult to understand what was transpiring from the water's surface, but Angelique guessed that the woman was showing some form of proof as there was a moment of quiet inaudible conversation. A shout from one Gaslamper to another further in the distance.

"She says she's a guest. She has a permit of sorts." Then the distant shout responded urgently.

"It's her! Grab her...arretez!"

There was a snarl, a barking, a howling and a scream. In an instant a shadow plummeted from the top of the bridge to the water only several feet away from Phillipe. She sank momentarily before exploding to the surface and began swimming to the edge. There was a flurry of sound above as lanterns erratically bobbed towards the stairs and pathways to the adjacent quay. In a moment, the bridge archway where the children took refuge would be flooded with frantic lamps and investigation.

"Come!" Angelique grabbed Phillipe's hand and dragged him beneath the surface to the water's edge. There was no time for discussion, they would have to get out of the water now before the quay was swarming with Gaslampers and wolves and flee on foot...wherever they were. Upon touching the stone wall, they hauled themselves out of the water as one, and threw themselves into the dark shadows of the nearby wall before the lamps descended the stairs. The moment the lanterns and wolves arrived at the foot of the stairs, the woman hauled herself onto the dock. She was instantly lit with lanterns held aloft and froze, trapped. It was the perfect opportunity for the children to make their escape. They could slip into the darkness with all of the eyes of the Parisian docks on this poor woman. Her long auburn hair now clung to her soaking body. It had been pinned back but now loosely hung around the woman's pale face. Dressed in a fitted bodice and full skirt that dripped onto the pavers beneath her black boots, it did not look possible that she had just leaped into the waters of the Seine. In the light, her middle-aged face looked beautiful, familiar and desperate. As they looked upon this cornered woman with wolves slavering as they approached, they could not leave her. Another instinct took hold and they could not shake it. It was a brief look to one another and a shared moment of understanding.

But what could they do? In the tiniest of moments, two unrelated things caught Phillipe's eye. Several rats the size of cats near the river's edge climbed two stone bricks and scurried into a small black hole that appeared to be a water drain of sorts. He noticed an identical hole near the stairs where the Gaslampers stood. And nearby, a singular kerosine lantern sat on a small wooden wharf by a modest fishing bateaux, no doubt waiting its owner's return. These unrelated visions - though trivial - forged a possibility in Phillipe's thoughts. Without time to weigh its value he sprang into action and scurried to the wharf, grabbing the lantern quickly. Though now illuminated in the darkness in full view, he took the chance that the focus of the Gaslampers would still be on the mysterious woman. He ran back to Angelique and, unscrewing the metal cap, poured the kerosine into the mouth of the stone wall hole. He raised the glass chimney, leaning the burner into the fuel and in a burst of flames, the hole in the brickwork instantly ignited. This was followed by sounds within, high and keening. Rats. Screeching and scurrying, they poured out of the other hole at the stair base as though the Piper of Hamlin had sounded his fife. Hundreds of rats filled the dock, scampering about in their pursuit of safety. A pursuit that turned out to be folly, for in that instant the wolves fell upon them hungrily. Despite all of the wolve's training and drills, their baser instincts prevailed and the scene quickly descended into chaos. It was in this chaos that the beautiful woman, in all her soaking refinement darted into the shadows and took leave. It was also in this chaos that Phillipe scanned the docklands around him for possible exits to the streets. In the distance, just out of the street lamp light, he could make out a wooden ladder that lead from the dock to the quay above. There were no better options. As the sound of wolves resounded around the archways nearby, he touched Angelique's arm so she could see what he saw and with a nod, they ran.

The dark streets above were quiet and still, the discordant sound beneath them drifting into the distance as they advanced along the street searching for a clue to their location. They were thoroughly soaked and though constantly moving, they each shivered uncontrollably. Shapeless buildings loomed menacingly on either side, denying any chance of recognition. Until finally, hovering above the rooftops they glimpsed the spire. Like a phoenix rising from the ashes, the dome appeared beneath it of the Chapel of the Martyrs of Montmartre Abbey. The tenement block was only a few blocks from the Abbey in the hills.

Home.

Their pace quickened as they began to glimpse familiar streets and architecture. Every now and then they would hear the growl of wolves in the distance or the bobbing of lanterns at the end of the street and they would pause in the shadows and await the passing of the danger. Never before had a city so familiar and hospitable become so unfamiliar and unwelcoming. Finally after what felt like an eternity, they arrived at the tenements. There were few lanterns in Montmartre that evening, most were by the docklands searching for the missing woman. Whoever she was. A blessing nonetheless. Phillipe paused at the stairs at the front of the tenement apartments and ran his fingers along the treads. Every comfort he had known in this building was absent and he felt a chill run down his body that felt more than just the cold. Slowly and anxiously, Phillipe and Angelique entered the building. So many thousands of times they had ran up the staircase to the corridor on the first floor, but tonight they walked. Every step a labour of fatigue and fear. Surely with the lingering hope of Papa just around the corner their spirits should have lifted, yet they did not. Instead there was a discomfort that grew at the base of the stomach and reached its fingers around their windpipes making it difficult to breathe. The corridor, no longer familiar, led to the apartment door at its end. Finally standing at the door, Phillipe looked apologetically at Angelique. This had been his idea after all and it now felt like a mistake. He pushed on the heavy wooden door and it opened.

Inside, the rooms were their rooms. Angelique could navigate straight to the children's bedroom, but they were devoid of life and largely empty. Stark wooden furniture gathered the dust of abandonment and for the first time since they had stumbled into this dark unfamiliar world, Angelique felt the full weight of hopelessness. There was no Papa. There were no signs that he had ever been there. Cold and wet, she finally sat and wept. Phillipe shared her grief and overwhelming sadness, and could think of nothing to do to help. The wound on his leg, though much improved, was beginning to throb and in his grief and disappointment he was becoming acutely aware of it once again. He pushed the dull ache out of his thoughts and focused instead on Angelique. Perhaps there was something he could do. Phillipe walked over to the hearth in the living area and leaned into the firebox looking for the loose bricks. He pulled the first out and a spark ignited within him. He pulled out the second and the third, until he had opened the cavity in the side of the fireplace. He reached into the dark hole. No small chest. Nothing. Just as hope had sparked deep within him it was again extinguished. This was not their home, it was an empty apartment in a hopeless city in a hopeless world.

Phillipe looked across at Angelique sitting alone in the darkness sobbing and felt helpless once again. Perhaps a fire would help. This thought created a welcome diversion for Phillipe, who felt great relief at being able to do something practical. He scouted around the apartment and found an old steel handle from a chamber pot, the straw stuffing from an abandoned mattress and in the absence of chert stone, broke a piece of the stonework out of the firebox itself that, although not flint, felt sedimentary. He placed the straw into the firebox and began striking the stone against the handle. It took time and patience but eventually he saw the slightest spark flicker into the straw and breathed life into it carefully. Nearby he repurposed a rickety wooden chair and pulled it apart for firewood. In no time at all the flames filled the hearth and warmed the room about them. The power of a warm fire can not be underestimated and instantly both Phillipe and Angelique felt their hearts lift a little. Phillipe finally sat by his sister and put his arms around her. They were now dry and comfortable, and for the first time in what felt like days, they fell asleep by the fire in the abandoned apartment that was no longer their home.

CHAPTER 9
A SEPARATION

She had gone.

The news had finally reached the Maire by half-light dawn the following morning. A reluctant officer who had clearly drawn the short straw had cautiously knocked on the hard oak door at first light. It was a well-rehearsed knock that reflected a carefully deliberated decision. Would it be best to awake the Maire as soon as the news was confirmed or to await his awakening before troubling him with more unfortunate disclosures? It was an announcement that was neither surprising, nor unexpected to the Maire. For he had felt it beforehand.

She had gone.

There was something deep inside his knowing that felt her leave. She was a prisoner as much as a guest and a guest as much as a prisoner, although this was not the way he had wanted it to be. And now she was gone. How, was as much a mystery to him as to anyone else. She was clever. There was no doubt of that and she had a spirit and grit deep within her that resisted every offer of comfort and devotion he could propose. He had awoken in his chambers that morning in darkness with the deep sense of loss that is only known to those who have loved. The news of her departure half an hour later was merely a confirmation of what he already knew. He had hoped that with time and opportunity she would come around, perhaps find affection for him once again. But instead, she had escaped. Somehow the ungrateful wretch had found a chink in his armour.

He had arisen at the news, dressed and made his way from his bedroom towards the civic meeting chambers. Walking through the central courtyard, his attention was momentarily diverted by the industry that occupied every quarter of the space. In one corner, huge sheets of angled canvas were being stitched tightly together and glued; hands constantly pulling and stretching, testing for its durability. Another engineer was tightening a valve on a copper gas pipe against the stone wall. The gas pipe would send gas into an ignited flue where - with adjustments - it would turn from yellow to blue as the flames intensified. Here were the smartest minds in Paris. Engineers, scientists and inventors working towards a common good, furthering the progress of their city beyond the realms of previous possibility. This was the consequence of effective governing. The idea of flight was not his own. The Maire had borrowed it from another many decades ago. Another man who had grand ideas, ingenious ideas but no capacity or desire to ever make them anything more than just possibilities. It was this *other* whom the Maire had sought, and had so far failed to acquire.

The Maire pushed open the large double doors to the chambers and stood for a moment, examining the board of mediocrity before him. At the right of the large wooden table stood the head inspector, the tubby buffoon who had lost the children on their first night in the city. He stood there stroking his waxed moustache as though he were at the pinnacle of his craft, but truth would have it, he was far from successful... merely loyal. The Inspector's chief constable stood by his side, Thibault. He represented the antithesis of his superior. Where the Inspector was all bluster and incompetence, Thibault was all substance and skill.

He had served in the French Foreign Legion for near twenty years and bore the scars of experience and close encounters across his face. His gas mask was strapped to his brown leather coat, which bore the red emblem of the lens on its shoulder. Thibault could be relied upon to follow orders and would be a soldier to the end. Beside him stood Lord Gossard. He was a fossil who had been excavated from the previous government and necessarily installed. He was a piece of window dressing really, nothing more than necessary decoration and the man was happy to simply feel relevant enough to be in the room. The old man's grey hair was tied tightly at his nape. He was always dressed in elegance and refinement as a distraction and compensation for his utter incompetence. But he was harmless enough because he would do whatever he was told without question and without fuss. It appeared that his memory was fading and his faculties were dubious to say the least, his responsibilities were limited and his depth of knowledge and understanding of the goings on at the compound were at the lowest level of confidentiality. But he was popular. God knows why, but the people seemed to love him. He was a necessary step to power, and his presence - however token it was - did seem to appease the masses somewhat. Beside Gossard stood the only woman in the room. Madame Lally was to be feared. Her dowdy, matronly appearance was nothing but a charade that would lure unsuspecting victims into her confidence. To the Maire, this was her value. Her appearance was at odds with her practice, and she proved to be a very reliable informant for the current administration. She had *agents* all over the city, from washerwomen to street-walkers, and although reporting was mandatory for all citizens, hers could be relied upon to do so accurately. To think that she was a pushover would be a mistake. The Maire had witnessed her atrocities first hand and it was her quick and efficient disposal of unreliable sources that had built her a team of loyal informers. Madame Lally was checked by the physician upon every entry within the walls. It was of vital importance that she remained anonymous to the people outside the compound, and to this end she could never be masked against the disease and filth that gnawed at the city outside.

"Well?" The Maire let his question linger without qualifying it with more information so that they would all know that he was inconvenienced by merely being there. The silence loitered momentarily.

"As you are aware, Monsieur Maire, your prisoner escaped in the late hours last night and we are still trying to get to the bottom of how it happened. It appears there might be a traitor within these..."

"Prisoner?"

"I meant guest, sir... your guest." The inspector bowed his head low in deference, only raising his eyes for directional clues. "We fished her out of the river last night and had her surrounded on the dock. But she... managed to evade capture. We have of course got every officer available looking for her as we speak. If she is within the city walls she will be found."

"Every officer?"

"Well... those who are not currently employed in the search for the children, sir. But on that accord I have some good..." With that, the words were too many for the Maire and he hurled himself at the rotund inspector, pinning him to the chamber wall by his throat. The inspector wriggled and writhed, gasping for air as the other man's fingers tightened around him like a vice. Reddened and under great duress the portly ringmaster gasped out the last of his sentence,

"...NEEWWSS." He wildly tried gesticulating at the door. Neither Thibault, Lord Gossard or Madam Lally moved from their positions. They did not intervene, they did not utter any disagreement as they knew their place, and experience had taught them the value of knowing one's place in the pecking order. Finally, hearing the last word, the Maire loosened his grip while the inspector doubled over and made a great spectacle of loudly gasping for air. He was hurt, true. But he was an opportunist who would not miss his opportunity. He held up a hand, gesturing that he needed time to compose himself, he had been near death; near death mind you and his loyalty had once again gone unappreciated. The Maire, having calmed himself significantly, continued with a new form of communication.

"You let the children go. You let my guest go. You have every officer in Paris looking for them unsuccessfully and now you have good news."

"Yes, my Lord." The inspector paused to noisily gasp one last time. He looked across at Madam Lally so that she would feel the full weight of what he was about to say. " I have information. Gathered by one of my own sources. One of my own agents." He looked intensely at Lally making sure she was looking intently at him. "He is outside right now Monsieur Maire and he has only just finished briefing me about what he has witnessed with his own eyes only last..."

"Get to the point man!"

"He saw the children, sir. At Montemarte tenements late last night. They have not yet left." He paused, looking carefully around the room to gauge the jealousy of his peers. "Would you like me to arrest them, Monsieur Maire?"

"Not yet." The Maire nodded his approval to the inspector who relished the recognition. "I think they might lead us to others that we seek also. We might be able to shut down this organisation in one fell swoop. Finish the Calibrators once and for all."

"Yes sir. Then what would you have me do?"

"Follow them."

At half-light dawn, the children awoke. The previous two days had felt like a dream, although the stark surroundings of their apartment, now unfamiliar, confirmed that it was not. Angelique felt stiff from an uncomfortable night's rest and stretched on the floor while glancing at her surroundings by the half-light of day. Phillipe wandered around the rooms, inspecting them slowly, hoping that he may manufacture inspiration through concentration alone. Everything in the apartment now looked foreign. All of the warmth that he had previously associated with his home had gone and in its place were cold stone walls, empty of life. He longed for his father so very much. He felt that he should also like to cry, but noticed that Angelique appeared in better spirits and this lifted his heart a little. There was no longer any point in searching for Corantin in this world, it was now apparent that they were alone in it and needed to find a way back. Heavy black drapes hung about the windows and seemed to echo the bleakness that the children both felt on that morning.

"Did you sleep well, Phillipe?"

"I'm afraid I did not. The floors are harder than I remember in this room." This statement was met with honest laughter. This both surprised Phillipe and softened his mood a little. "How did you sleep, Angel?"

"The same. Do you think we should try and get back to the Cerf?"

Phillipe shook his head in response. "I imagine it would be still too dangerous to go back to Meudon. They will be watching the cottage for certain." Phillipe sat on the floor opposite Angelique and both sat in silent thought for a while. Finally Angelique spoke.

"I don't know how we shall find our way back. I still don't really understand how we arrived in the first place. It was as if we had tricked our brains into thinking that we were seeing the world upside down. But I don't think it is that simple." A sudden and urgent thought or realisation is often compared to a lightening bolt. Indeed, if there was an electrical phenomena that occurred in the room in that moment, then that is how Phillipe would explain the thought that sparked in his brain and the electricity it suddenly generated in the young boy.

"That's it! Perhaps it is that simple. What if we could replicate the Obscura in one of the theatres you are so familiar with. We could use these black drapes to block out light and cut a hole in one. Surely we could stand on our heads and trick our brains once again." Phillipe felt like a crazy scientist raving in the madness of his own genius, but perhaps it was not so crazy. Angelique was catching his enthusiasm and her eyes began to glint with a new light.

"Oui. Perhaps it will be that simple. We are only ten blocks from the Theatre de l'Atelier. It is a small theatre with high windows. I like this idea Phillipe. It might work. What do we need?"

"We shall take the black drapes from this apartment with us, perhaps some cord or rope if we can find it and a blade from the kitchen dresser to cut a hole for the light. But we must be careful. The Cerf said there are eyes everywhere. We will need to find a way to travel unseen." With very little ceremony the children pulled down the heavy black drapes from the windows. They found no rope but there were long sashes that tied the drapes back which would suffice. Finally, Phillipe took the blade from the dresser that he saw during his early morning investigations. His intention for this was largely to cut a hole in the drape, but in his deepest recesses he considered another possibility and shuddered at the thought.

Out on the street in half-light, the children were heavily laden with their cargo and would not escape suspicion if they simply walked down the street to the nearby theatre. A Gaslamper walked around the nearby corner with a wolf by his side. Possibly patrolling the village as routine would mandate, but there was also the chance that he was searching for something specific. Both of the children moved into the shadows aided by the fabric that they draped over themselves. Phillipe felt a fear rise deep within him. He had found the Gaslampers menacing by night-lamp and had hoped that in the half-light of day he would see them for what they were. Not demons or monsters, but simply men. However, as he peered across the road from under his cover at the patrol, there still remained something other worldly about the figure and his canid companion. Phillipe closed his eyes and prayed that he would pass without event.

He did.

For now.

Both children scanned the street cautiously looking for inspiration. It was Angelique who saw it first. At one end of the street, a grocer had three wooden hand carts that were lined up along the street. It was still early and he was setting up for the day's trading. He would walk from the handcarts to his wagon full of produce, and with full arms, place several baskets and crates in the first handcart readying himself for trade. Due to a horse trough and tethering rail that blocked direct access, he had to traipse along the verandah and walk around the corner to access his wagon.

"If you are quick Phillipe. You will be able to take one before he notices it is gone." Angelique noted Phillipe's moral hesitation. "We can return it later."

"If our darkroom doesn't work."

"Oui. If our darkroom doesn't work."

"What will you do?"

"There is another part to the plan. I will meet you back here when you get the cart." With that, she was gone. Phillipe was not sure what his sister's plan was, or to where she had darted off, but he had no choice but to trust her. He scuttled off - keeping to the shadows - and made his way to the end of the street where the grocer was working up an early morning sweat despite the chill in the air. The plan seemed simple enough. Wait until the grocer walked around to the corner to his wagon and then quickly take possession of one of the hand carts. But what had seemed foolproof two minutes earlier now seemed fraught with problems and possibilities. What if someone else saw him take the cart? What if he timed it poorly and didn't get the cart far enough away in time? The last thing they needed was a middle aged grocer chasing them down the street shouting "Arretez thief." Or what if the grocer changes his mind, forgets a crate and returns early? So many things that could go wrong raced through Phillipe's head. He calmed his nerves, waited until the grocer industriously stepped around the corner and then set to the unscrupulous repurposing. In a moment he was at the wooden handles of the handcart, quickly glancing around to see if anyone else in the street was watching. There were very few people around at that hour and they seemed far too occupied with their own undertakings to be concerned with petty theft. The cart was not heavy but the wooden carrying arms were an awkward distance for a young lad and Phillipe had to really heave to get the cart moving. It became instantly apparent that the cart had not been moved for some time and that maintaining the wheels had not been a priority in the grocer's routine, as the wheels were locked with rust and, in the effort of motion let out a loud screech, heralding the theft to all ears. Phillipe instantly froze, looking frantically around to see if anyone else had heard the mechanical alarm. But none had. Resolute, he pulled on further and with more screeching and grinding, the cart came freely and in a moment was racing behind Phillipe as he ran up the sidewalk back to the rendezvous location. Phillipe anticipated detection with every step, waiting for a shout from behind or across the street. But none came, for the grocer was hard of hearing and on this day, fortune had conspired in his favour.

When he finally hauled the cart to the agreed meeting point,

Angelique was already there. He could smell her twenty feet before he even saw her. She was grinning from ear to ear with what appeared to be manure spread over her face and neck and two large clumps in both hands. Phillipe didn't even get a chance to ask the obvious question before she smeared it into his face and arms upon arrival.

"What are you doing? This stinks!" Phillipe was both disgusted and confused.

"This Phillipe, is the plan."

"What is wrong with you?" Phillipe could not hide his sudden annoyance. It felt like such a childish prank and from Angelique of all people.

"We need to keep people away. I think this will do it. The Gaslampers are looking for two children. You climb in the cart and I will hide you with the drapes. If anyone asks, I am a muck-raker although I doubt anyone will come close enough."

"How did you?" Phillipe gestured at the dark smears on his face which emanated a rancid smell that was making his stomach turn.

"A draught horse dropped it over there by the carriage. Don't worry. No one saw. It wasn't enough to fill a cart, but it will be enough to make someone believe that it has filled the cart."

This was difficult to argue with and he had to admit, the plan was ingenious. If he could survive ten blocks with his stench under the drape they could make it. Shaking his head in reluctant admiration Phillipe climbed into the cart and pulled the drapes over himself. "Ready," came his muffled gagging voice from under the drapes. Angelique heaved and pulled the cart behind her to begin the longest ten blocks in all of Paris.

It was an uneventful beginning of the journey, as the stench as anticipated was a potent repellant for all passers by. Pedestrians would get within range of the cart, grimace and walk to the other side of the street. They were careful not to cause offence by their obvious behaviour and so avoided looking at the poor, young muckraking girl, as it was not her fault after all but merely a consequence of her station in life. This served Angelique well as it created a largely empty passageway for her route. She passed the other tenement buildings and found herself traversing a series of alleyways and side streets in an effort to avoid the main thoroughfare of the Boulevard de Lorrette. She was fairly confident that she could avoid it if she followed the parallel lane, and the most exposure she would have to its traffic would be the occasional glance across to the Boulevard when she crossed a perpendicular street. It was on such a crossing that she again glanced at the Gaslamper observed earlier, still patrolling with his wolf on the Boulevard. She immediately lowered her eyes and quietly pushed. In that moment, the cart had never seemed heavier and wheels never noisier. In her peripheral she sensed him glancing across and pausing in the street upon noticing her.

"Arretez. Garcon stop!" The muffled shout was unmistakable and Angelique froze. Should she run? The Gaslamper pulled the wolf tight on the rope and steered it towards the laneway. He advanced. Angelique breathed deeply. She stood. As the Gaslamper came closer and closer, the flaw in her plan became painfully clear. Their leather masks clearly filtered a great deal more than disease. She cursed herself that her oversight may well cost them their lives. And stood.

"Excusez-moi, I thought you were a boy. Why are you muckraking in this street? This is not a thoroughfare for horses?"

Angelique went to speak but could not find her voice. There was something about the gruff sound of the question spoken through the leather that made her faculties freeze. She hoped and prayed that Phillipe would be quiet and still and was aware of the situation. Finally finding her voice, she spoke loudly for the benefit of warning Phillipe.

"This is my first day, monsieur. I did not know." The wolf growled and the Gaslamper seemed unsatisfied.

"Why do you cover your load with drapes?"

"It is the smell, monsieur. My employer thought we would get more work if our presence were less offensive." It was a powerful and quick argument and Angelique knew it. The Gaslamper stepped closer, he had clearly not considered the stench and sniffed as if trying to ascertain the truth of the statement. Angelique noticed his eyes wince behind the goggles. The wolf growled, baring its teeth at the cart and its handler pulled hard on the rope.

"Proceed...But not here. There is no muckraking on the back streets, you need to go out to the Boulevard." It was not advice, it was a clear direction. Angelique did not want to chance her luck any further. She slowly turned the cart under the watchful eyes of her interrogator and his beast and plodded towards the main thoroughfare with no other option. Upon turning into the Boulevard a passing team of Ardennes draught horses pulling a break carriage momentarily paused. One of the horses used this opportune time to unload a great weight of manure, where it remained after the horses continued as another steaming reminder of the flaws in Angelique's plan. She turned back to see the Gaslamper still watching intently from the side street. With little other option and in a desperate bid to feign authenticity she pulled the cart alongside the waste and with no other tools picked it up in her hands and dropped it into the cart under the drapes. She watched Phillipe squirm under the fabric in revulsion. She nodded to the Gaslamper and pushed on.

If Phillipe was drowning in the acrid fumes of his unwanted new companion he uttered not a word, but stoically bore it in silence. All the while, Angelique continued to pull. Her arms were now quivering with fatigue and she had to dig deep to find the strength to finish the long expedition. They finally arrived at the side street of the theatre and turned down a quiet deserted lane.

"Only a moment longer, we are almost there."

"Thank God. I've decided I hate horses." Came his quiet voice from under the drapes. Angelique smiled despite her exhaustion.

She lowered the cart out of sight of the street and pulled the drapes off her brother who gasped like a drowning man breaking the surface. It was worse than she had hoped. Phillipe was covered in wet, fresh manure and as he climbed out of the cart he began to laugh. Angelique joined him. It was the first laugh that they had shared for as long as she could remember and it felt good.

"Are you okay, Phillipe?"

"Oui Angel. I've smelled better, but I'm okay. How about you? That was close."

"It was. Too close. But we are here now. Hopefully the theatre will be closed until tonight. Come."

Phillipe lifted the drapes from the cart and laid them over his shoulder in an attempt to hide the stains over his clothing. Perhaps people would assume they were installing the drapes. The children made their way to the front of the theatre to try the main door. Angelique was correct, the theatre was indeed closed... and locked. There the children stood, having traversed worlds, rivers, forests and cities, covered in excrement, exhausted and alone they now faced one more obstacle before them, a locked door. It appeared all the doors in this world seemed locked in one way or another. Phillipe sighed and began considering new ways to obtain entrance. Perhaps they could return at night when the theatre was open and stow away until it again closed from view. Perhaps there was a window or a side door that could be persuaded in some way... or perhaps a key. Phillipe reached his fingers deep into the pocket of his soiled trousers and felt around for what he hoped was still there. Despite negotiating worlds, rivers, forests and cities he took hold of the key that was amazingly still in his pocket.

"What is that?"

"Just keep a look out for anyone passing by will you?"

Phillipe put the key into the lock of the heavy front door. He listened carefully to the sounds it made as he turned it. With his ear to the door he slowly adjusted the key wards. The collar and pin rotated slowly and he listened for the sound of connection. Click. Angelique immediately turned at the sound and Phillipe couldn't help but grin with self pride.

"You are a marvel Phillipe Chastain. An absolute marvel." With one final glance to the street the children slipped inside the theatre foyer and closed the door.

Inside, the theatre was largely as Angelique had remembered. The windows in the foyer were high, but small, allowing very little light to penetrate the space. While the light was low, their eyes were well adjusted to the dimness of half-light and so they immediately set to work to blacken the space. The first window was at least fifteen feet from the floor, Angelique took hold of an ornate composite column and began to nimbly ascend its trunk effortlessly. Upon reaching the capital, she leaned across to a triangular pediment above the window and locked her body between the two. She gestured to Phillipe for the first drape which he endeavoured to throw up to her. After basking in the recognition of his lock picking skills, Phillipe plummeted to depths of inadequacy as he tried to throw the heavy drape to Angelique's lofty height. It was heavy and he was tired. At least that is how he consoled himself when attempt after attempt fell short of his target. Finally, defeated, he considered another tact. He rolled the drape into a tight ball and tied one of the sashes around it firmly. He now bent low and with all his strength hurled it into the air. It collided with both Angelique and the window, only narrowly avoiding hurtling to its freedom through the glass and knocking Angelique from her perilous height. But she was strong and was firmly locked in her position, and managed to take the impact of the heavy curtain without flinching. After a scowl at Phillipe below she unravelled the drape and hung it over the triangular pediment, securing it with the sash. Then, just as quickly as she had ascended, she threw herself back towards the column and shimmied down to the floor again. There was one more window yet to cover on the opposite side in perfect symmetry.

"I'm sorry about the throw Angel. I'm tired."

"That is fine Phillipe. We are both tired. Here, pass me the drape." This time she secured the drape around her waste. She considered for a moment the image of Phillipe throwing the knife to her at fifteen feet and thought better of it. "Also, the knife Phillipe." He lowered his head feeling suddenly useless and passed her the blade that he had kept in his pocket for this very purpose. Just as before she ascended the column with a drape around her waist and a blade between her teeth. Phillipe was in awe of the vision of his sister as a swashbuckling adventurer and felt pangs of jealousy deep down that he tried desperately to ignore. She swung back over the triangular pediment and with one arm undid the drape from her waste and fastened it above the window. Immediately the room fell into complete and utter darkness. Phillipe could only imagine at this point that Angelique, still secured with only one arm, took the blade from her teeth and cut a hole in the fabric before the glass window, for in that moment he saw a shaft of light, shoot like a meteor across the room and fill the back wall with illumination.

Angelique, realising new dangers of potentially falling fifteen feet if indeed, they did turn upside down, dropped without injury from the pediment to the floor to stand by Phillipe's side and keep him from harm.

"The knife?" Phillipe kept his voice level showing neither his shame nor envy. Angelique placed it into his hand and held her hand there momentarily by way of apology. This did not help and Phillipe moved his hand away quickly, pocketing the blade.

They stared at the wall. Angelique took Phillipe's hand.

Slowly like an oil painting, shapes began to form on the wall. With each moment they progressed in clarity until finally they could see the world of the street projected within the darkness of the foyer. With each moment the projection became clearer. At first they could see the shapes of buildings outside, movement across the frame. The image focused before their eyes and soon they could see the stonework around the arches across the street and the occasional pedestrian hurrying along the pavement. But it was not upside down. By some contortion of light, the image before them remained upright. How could this be? Phillipe looked to Angelique confused and nodded. The two of them knelt to the floor, placed their hands on either side of their heads and raised their legs in the air in a handstand. The blood rushed to their heads in an instant and the world projected before them continued to remain upright, correct in their vision. Was their mind playing tricks on them?

They waited.

Nothing.

Suddenly a door opened and a wash of brilliant light flooded the scene before them. Phillipe fell from his handstand, momentarily blinded by the sudden light.

"It won't work."

Angelique was now also back on her knees squinting at the lone figure before her. There was something urgent about its tone.

"You need to get up. We must go." The figure closed the door and stepped into the shaft of light, now visible for the first time. It was Renard Rouge. Her goggles were propped on her head and she was dressed in the same fitted leather coat she had worn on the first day they arrived.

"It's how we arrived here in the first place. It should work." Phillipe piped in, now confident in his identification of the stranger and a little indignant at her tone. "Well it hasn't," she continued to stare at the image on the wall as if expecting to see something. "I will not mince words. Get up, you are in danger." At this, both children rose to their feet. Phillipe was still annoyed at her disregard and insensitivity, and decided that he was keen to go to the lavatory and wash away some of the smell that was still overwhelming his senses. After all, how urgent could the danger be? They had been constantly in danger since their arrival and danger could surely wait until Phillipe had washed away some of the smell and disappointment that suddenly weighed so heavily on him.

Without a word, he started down the narrow corridor towards the dark door that he assumed was the restroom.

"Where are you going?"

"Lavatory. I shan't be a moment." Phillipe paused, finally seeking Renard's approval. She paused momentarily, fiercely concentrating on the illuminated wall. Something caught her eye. It was subtle and she gave very little away herself, but there was the slightest narrowing of her eyes as she adjusted her focus. She looked back to Phillipe and nodded mouthing the words.

"Go."

Phillipe did. He turned and with hastened steps travelled into the darkness of the corridor. In that moment heavy hands grabbed him from behind in the darkness, gripping tightly around his mouth so he could not utter a sound. He was dragged further down the corridor as he wrestled against the tightening hands that muffled his every sound. But he heard. The door to the theatre burst open at the front and what sounded like a side door simultaneously. Shouts and the dull thud of boots reverberated around the timber walls.

Renard Rouge had half expected the ambush. There had been other followers, she knew that. As she had watched Angelique and her manure cart make her way down the boulevard she was aware of other eyes that watched at least as intently as she did. She thought she might have time, just a little to get them to safety. In that instant, as she saw the subtle movement across the projection before her, she knew that they were coming in through the front door. She did not know that they were also coming in through a side door and that is where she came undone. The instant the door exploded behind her, she met the first

Gaslamper with a swift kick, hard and sharp to the side of his gas mask, knocking it completely from his head as he fell to the floor in dull silence. With eyes only narrowly adjusting to the darkness, the next two that entered met similar fates. As they stumbled through the door trying to find their footing over their fallen comrade, Renard sent two swift punches across their cheeks sending them backwards. She was only slight but fast and strong, her greatest strength was being underestimated.

Angelique watched on in terror. She did not know what to do and still kneeling on the floor, was frozen with fear. She watched Renard Rouge, explosive and fierce, meeting each assailant with unmatched skill. But a second door that had opened to the side brought in more and more Gaslampers until it was clear that she would be overwhelmed. Then came the snarl of the wolves whose eyes had no limitations in the darkness. Sensing this, in a moment of cool desperation, she drew a short pistol from within her boot. It all happened with lightening speed, but in that moment the arm of a Gaslamper came out of nowhere and took both Renard's hand and the pistol skyward. A shot was fired into the ceiling before the Gaslamper knocked the pistol from her hand and turned swiftly, knocking Renard to the ground with his elbow. She immediately rose back to her feet and launched at the assailant with a kick that cracked the green glass lenses of his mask. He momentarily stumbled back as she wasted no time to follow this with a second kick on her alternate leg. But he was fast. Too fast. Thibault whipped the broken mask from his face with one hand and with the other caught her leg mid-flight. He was faster and stronger than she expected. Deflecting her kick, he brought up his own leg and sent her careening to the floor. In a moment it was all over. She was pinned to the ground and surrounded. The wolves straining against taut ropes prevented any hope of escape. Swept up in the moment with adrenaline coursing through her body, Angelique had not noticed the strong hands that had restrained her from behind.

Thibault wiped the blood from his nose on the back of his leather glove. Now that he had unmasked and exposed himself to the air, he would need to undertake a mandatory physician's investigation before he would be permitted back in the compound. He stared at Renard Rouge and the other wiry girl. They gave very little away. "There is one more here. Find the boy." Immediately, other Gaslampers dispersed in different directions, navigating into the darkness in search of the boy. A moment later, the rotund figure of the Inspector stepped into the theatre. He slowly looked around the space, trying desperately to look worthy of his rank and post but was betrayed by an arrogant grin that spontaneously grew on his face.

"There is another, Chief Constable. A boy. Where is the boy?"

"We are searching Monsieur Inspector. If he is here, we will find him."

"Find him? How could you have lost him? He is a boy... A boy. Well done apprehending the two little girls though." His condescending tone was not lost on Thibault who bowed his head in supplication to his superior, however unwarranted his criticism was. The Gaslampers then returned to the Chief Constable having searched the theatre, stairs, lavatory and balcony.

"The boy?" queried the Inspector impatiently.

"He is gone, Monsieur Inspector."

"Into thin air?" His question lingered unanswered for indeed the boy had gone.

CHAPTER 10

THE CONFESSIONAL

If you were to walk into any Catholic Cathedral in any city in the world, chances are that if you bypassed the nave and walked down the side aisle, you would pass several small wooden cubicles on your journey. To the unsuspecting eye they would seem little more than ornate, inlaid wooden doors side by side. If you were to enter the second door you would step into a small wooden booth shrouded in darkness and sit with your back to the wall. The only light source would be an obscured woven wicker window joining the adjacent booth and you would hear a voice. The voice, hushed and reverent would be the priest in the neighbouring booth who would ask you to state your sins and transgressions. You may tell him that you didn't help an old lady across the road, or that you had stolen a cob of corn from the grocer, or taken his cart. Perhaps if no transgressions came to mind you would make something trivial up which is often the case. The priest would tell you to say twelve "Hail Marys" and sin no more and you would leave the booth absolved, cleansed, buoyant. Such is the confessional experience mandated by James in his fifth chapter, in any Cathedral, in any city in the world. That is, any city except in the Obscura Paris in 1879. For there, in Notre

Dame, the church of Saint Jean Baptiste or Saint Lambert you would find none. They had gone.

Instead, every confessional booth in the city was lined up outside the walls of the compound. At the head of the parade of booths sat a desk with a masked clerk who, with a reed pen and ink would scribe the names of good citizens that queued in a line that stretched along the Boulevard De L' Hopital to the Seine. Each Citizen in the city was required by law to attend the 'Confessional' twice weekly. Each in their turn were ushered forward by other masked assistants and guided to the next vacant booth. In each neighbouring booth sat a masked auditor, with reed at the ready to scribe and take notes as necessary. It was not a confession of your behaviour that was required but rather the behaviour of your neighbour, or your work colleague or your sister or father. Any word uttered against the Maire or his regime, any suspicious behaviour or look was to be reported on. Any music, arts, or other banned idle practice was to be disclosed. Rewards were fair and concealment harshly punished, and so the confessions flowed. Drunk Uncle Pierre was railing against the government on Bastille day, the old woman was singing in her washroom, the clockmaker keeps something under a sheet in his basement and so on and so on.

It was on such a queue that the Mason stood. Twice weekly he had stood on that same queue that would stretch down to the river and have nothing to say. He was a good, honest man and so felt compelled to comply. When pressed in the booth, he would offer something meaningful without any real substance. He had heard some singing coming from down near the Quay but could not be certain of its direction. Perhaps it was a musical pipe he heard through the night air but couldn't be sure if it was merely the wind whistling through the plumbing. He would receive nods of thanks and reassurances that he was a good citizen and would need to pay closer attention to details. There would be no punishment but also no reward and he would go back to his safe, quiet life. But today was different, for he saw what he saw and would be duly rewarded.

After the prolonged wait he arrived at the Clerk's desk and after having his name recorded, was ushered into a nearby confessional booth. The muffled voice cut through the wicker window.

"What have you to report today, good citizen?"

"Well Monsieur, I am a Mason and I do repair and restoration at Notre Dame. Usually it is replacing a brick, here and there, sometimes I climb high. Very high to attend to the upper stone work..."

"Oui." The auditor struggled to hide his impatience.

"Anyways. I was working at height on the crockets on the gable when I look down below against the western wall. I see him. I couldn't be sure at first so I lower myself on the ropes to the niche where I can see more clearly. It was him for sure. He was dripping wet, I imagine he just climbed out of the Seine. And then, just like that he was gone. I don't know where. I don't know anything except he is back. The Aigle is back."

"Are you certain, Mason?"

"Oui, Monsieur. It was him."

The auditor immediately rose to urgently leave.

"My reward, Monsieur?"

"Oui. See the clerk on your way out." But the auditor was already out the door, down the street and entering the compound. This news would be rewarded greatly indeed and would need to be delivered immediately. He would not take any chances passing his new knowledge through officers of higher rank where his involvement would be diminished to a pat on the back. This would go straight from his lips to the ears of the Maire himself.

Beneath the long line of confessional boxes that stretched down the boulevard from the compound to the quay, were the bowels of the former Hospital Dr la Salpetriere. Neither the Mason nor any other good citizen that lined the street that morning could possibly know that beneath their shuffling feet was the fruit of their labour, the effect to their cause. Every piece of information, however trivial was investigated to the best of the regime's ability and resulted in more than the occasional arrest, more than the occasional *persuasive questioning* and ultimately more than the occasional imprisonment. Only fifteen feet beneath the confessional circus sat the prisoners of the prefecture. A catacomb of hundreds of storage rooms had been appropriated to become single prisoner cells for the citizens of Paris that had turned their backs on the city that had embraced them. The Maire's officers had a gift for extracting information, and each arrest inevitably led to more. There were more prisoners than prison cells and so some would disappear without a trace. Stories, like escaping steam, would rise to the surface where they would be whispered in silent corners. Above the ground a citizen lived in terror constantly and dared not break a rule for fear of the consequences, and so, few did. Beneath the ground a citizen lived in terror constantly for consequences were something they understood all too well.

Among the prisoners that morning sat Renard Rouge and Angelique. Their cells were side by side but neither could see the other, and it was merely assumption on their part that they were neighbours at all. Angelique had sat in her cell for what had seemed like hours and most likely was and it was only in the half-light of morning that she finally found the courage to investigate who was nearby. Throughout the dark night she had heard the sounds of movement in the adjacent cell. There were sounds of industrious exercise and they lasted for several hours before all fell silent and she slept. The cell surrounding her consisted of blue-stone that had been lime-washed in a previous life. It was small and simple with a basic cot on which she sat and a metal pan in the corner. There were no windows and little light, the only entrance to her cell being a large wooden door, bolted and locked. An imperfection in one of the stones at the back of the space created a small hole and allowed a connection to the adjacent cell. She had found this by meticulously running her fingers over all of the stones in the dark when instinctively exploring her space. She deduced that it was through this hole she could hear the sounds emanating from the next cell.

"Renard Rouge. Is that you?" Her tone was cautious and her words barely a whisper.

"Oui. It is. What is your name, Mademoiselle?"

It had not occurred to Angelique that in neither encounter with her rescuer had she ever divulged her name. "I am Angelique Chastain. My brother's name is Phillipe."

"Tell me Angelique, what business does the Maire have with you? Why are you so important?"

Angelique paused for a moment. It was the same question she had been asking herself since they arrived. "That I do not know. My father Corantin is a printing press typesetter in the old world. He worked from light till dark each day and we were poor. We lived in the tenements in Montematre. There is nothing. No reason at all." She fell silent and both girls listened to the silence thoughtfully. In the distance there was the occasional sound of footsteps and rattling keys.

"And your mother?"

This question took Angelique by surprise and for a moment she felt her voice tighten and words difficult to form. "I did not know her very well. She left when I was an infant." More silence.

"What do you remember about her?"

"Well...She was a dancer. I believe she was one of the most celebrated ballerinas in Paris, perhaps in Europe. I saw photographs of her performing on some of the biggest stages in

Europe. Not from Papa though. He never kept any photographs around the house." Angelique was surprised that despite her instincts to be cautious she found herself speaking so candidly.

"No. What do *you* remember?"

"Oh. Her hair mostly. She had long, thick, auburn hair and I think I remember winding my fingers in it. But, perhaps not. I was so small, I can't really even see her face. But I can smell her sometimes. It was a sweet smell, perhaps a perfume, it was like a bouquet of flowers. It is a smell that I carry deep in my memory though I have not smelt it since she disappeared."

"Disappeared?" Renard's tone suddenly moved from concerned to tense. "I thought you said she left. Did she leave or disappear?"

"Oh. I believe she left. I don't know why I said disappeared, I meant left." Even as Angelique said these words, she wasn't sure where the idea of disappearing came from, she had never uttered the word before and she suddenly couldn't be sure if she had heard it somewhere in the past. Her thoughtful silence deepened.

"What about you, Renard Rouge? What of your family?"

Her question was met with an immediate wall. "No. I have no family to speak of. No more questions." This was immediately followed by the sound of rhythmic breathing and grunts. Angelique listened intently for some time carefully heeding the last terse direction until she could resist no more and asked one final question.

"What are you doing, Renard Rouge?" The sound momentarily stopped.

"I am getting stronger...so I can get us out of here."

No sooner had Angelique heard her response, than she heard the rattling of the bolt to Renard's cell. She heard the sound of heavy boots on the stone floor.

"Get up, Renard Rouge. Get up!" They did not wait for her response.

"Get your hands off me."

"Take her to the interview room. I have some questions she will be certain to help me with."

Angelique strained to place the familiar voice. She had heard it once before. She dug deep into her memory, trying to place the rhythm and pitch. Then it came to her. In another world, a portly salesman who had enticed them into the Obscura. That was definitely the voice. But why was he here? A rattling of the bolt to her own cell took her attention as the heavy door laboured open and an officer stood in the entry.

"Mademoiselle. If you could please accompany me. He has requested to speak to you." The officer - showing none of the hostility experienced by Renard Rouge - waited patiently for Angelique to rise and follow him outside the cell. "The Maire wishes to see you in his chambers."

❦

The hand that gripped Phillipe was firm and strong but had to contend with his wrestling and writhing and when the opportunity arose, his biting as he tried to escape its clutches. Despite the sounds of ambush around him, silence was forced upon him as the figure dragged him into the darkness of the corridor. Disorientated and afraid, he found himself navigated through several doors and a stairwell to the basement. It was not until his captor lit a match that he finally released his grip over Phillipe's mouth. His instinct was to scream but as the match was lit, he saw the face of his captor for the first time and found himself face to face with the Cerf.

"Not a word," came his curt instruction. By the light of the match the Cerf lifted a small grate at the rear of the basement. He gestured for Phillipe to come and pointed down the shaft. Phillipe thought of Angelique, who at that very moment was being restrained on the floor above and he struggled to move. The Cerf understood the dilemma and the boy's hesitation. "You can not save her by staying!" he hissed. Phillipe knew this was true and so drew a breathe before sliding into the opening and dropping several feet to the darkness below. He landed up to his thighs in cold water. The Cerf dropped behind him, pulling the grate back into place upon his descent. He too plummeted into the darkness and struck another match.

"Come, young Phillipe. Follow me, we have a journey ahead of us yet." At that he waded into the distance, a dim light navigating into the darkness. Around him, dark water swirled about his thighs, erasing evidence of his direction with every step. They travelled north for several lengths, then moved eastward before travelling north once more. Every tunnel looked the same as the previous, the small halo of blue stone in front identical with every step. Finally the Cerf stopped underneath an iron ladder that reached from the stonework to a manhole above. He clamoured out of the water to the paved walkway at the side of the sewer passage. "We wait here." Phillipe also climbed from the cold water and sat on the dry stones beside the Cerf. Phillipe had so many questions but could form none. So instead sat in momentary silence. "Are you alright?" the old man finally queried.

"I think so. What about Angelique, what will happen to her?"

"She is captured, I'm afraid."

"Will they hurt her?"

The Cerf shook his head, allaying Phillipe's deepest fears. It was true, they most likely would not hurt her, they knew she came from the other world and seemed to have another purpose for her. The same could not be said for Renard Rouge. The old man shuddered silently and tried not to think on it any longer.

"Why are they hunting us?" Phillipe had so many things he did not yet know or understand.

"I was going to ask you the same question." The Cerf paused thoughtfully. "Our paths have crossed for a very important reason young Phillipe. Do not be afraid...What is the time?" A small smile appeared on the clockmaker's face. Phillipe had no concept of what time it was and had forgotten all about the time piece that had been on his wrist since he left Meudon several days before. It was unlikely the watch would still function after leaping into the frozen waters at Meudon, swimming into Paris in the Seine and the cart journey covered in excrement. But to his surprise as he lifted it to his ear he could still hear the ticking. As he suspected, the crystal case was dark from manure. He reached into the water rushing by his feet and rubbed it onto the crystal, the Cerf leaned over with his match so Phillipe could again see the hands on the dial. "It is nearly four in the afternoon, Monsieur." But then he noticed something else. It was a detail on the watch that he had not previously noted. It was a light blue window panel that followed the curve of the case. "It is a lovely timepiece. Thank you once again, I had not noticed the light blue detail before."

"It is not just detail young squire."

This had certainly piqued the young inventor's interest. What purpose could the blue panel possibly serve? He listened intently.

"The watch will tell you when Gaslampers are nearby. The light blue panel will turn dark when they are within twenty feet."

Phillipe now leaned forward in disbelief, not sure what to make of the clockmaker's magic. "How?"

"Silica tetrahedrals. They are the light blue crystals that you can see in the panel. The masks that the Gaslampers wear use a fibre made from crocidolite asbestos to filter out disease. Airborne crocidolite reacts with the silica tetrahedrals turning them dark blue, and they are airborne mind you. I have tested the time pieces meticulously. Twenty feet is accurate." The Cerf saw the look of marvel and wonderment in his young charge's eyes and smiled at him, ruffling his hair. "It's not magic Phillipe. Just Science. All of the calibrators have them and now you do as well."

"Did you invent them yourself?"

"I did. Made every one of them."

"I hope mine never darkens." Even as Phillipe said these

words he knew that it was a lie. Secretly he keenly wanted to see the miracle on his wrist work. He also knew that if he were to ever see Angelique again it would be inevitable. It was as if the Cerf had read his mind.

"Sadly it is inevitable lad."

A knock on the metal cover several feet above the ladder stopped their conversation short. It was a short knock followed by three long ones. "Come Phillipe. It is time." The Cerf climbed the ladder and rapped a response on the iron cover, three short knocks and one long. The cover slid to the side with straining fingers and a young man peered down the hole.

"Monsier Cerf, the coast is clear but we must move quickly."

The wiry old man lifted himself out onto the street effortlessly and leaned his arm back in to hoist Phillipe out also. The street was quiet for the time of day but it would not be long before workers started to make their way home safely before curfew. The Cerf quickly shuffled Phillipe across to a shadowed wall where their young assistant waited. At no point did the young man introduce himself to Phillipe, all communication was made directly with the Cerf. Several times he glanced across and looked Phillipe up and down as if sizing him up. He made no indication if he approved or not, it was as if he wanted to merely weigh up this young boy who was causing so much trouble.

"Is the arrangement in place that we discussed, Victor?" The Cerf continued to glance about the streets making sure there was no unusual attention being garnered.

"Oui, Monsieur. When you get there ask for Father Gion. He will be expecting you. You will be safe there."

"You mean caretaker Gion. Watch your words carefully Victor. If you get arrested, we are all in danger."

"Oui, Monsieur." The young man eyed the ground. It was an easy mistake to make, but could be a very costly one in the wrong company. In the new regime, there were no priests, no holy men, their tenancy was under the title and role of caretaker and the only religion was scientific progress. "One more thing monsieur." He continued to avert the Cerf's gaze. "Renard Rouge is taken. I thought you should know."

"I assumed as such. Merci, Victor. Well done. No uniform today?"

"Too dangerous, Monsieur. I'm more likely to be seen in it." With a nod, the young man handed the Cerf several pieces of fabric and slipped once more into the shadows to disappear into the faceless pedestrians that moved about the streets. The Cerf turned to Phillipe and tied the first piece of hessian linen around his chest, taking the second piece of Parisian silk and placing it around Phillipe's head and shoulders. "There."

As the old man strolled down the Parisian streets with his arm around his little girl, no citizen would have looked twice. In the distance, several Gaslampers approached and passed with their wolves by their sides. They appeared to be looking intently for what could be assumed a misplaced boy, but did not slow or show suspicion as they passed the two. The destination was not far but every step was tense and slow, for Phillipe the sense of fear far outweighed any embarrassment he felt about his attire. Walking the few blocks past the Rue de Rivoli felt like wading through an ocean of sharks. As they finally passed the grid of symmetrical windows in the Hotel de Ville, Phillipe saw the looming towers appear across the water and he suddenly knew their objective.

Notre Dame.

In Phillipe's world one could seek the sanctuary and protection of the church and would be safe within its stone walls. Those both inside and outside the law could seek asylum within the most powerful institution in the world. When those large wooden doors closed behind them they would be impervious to the laws that governed the world outside. But what about a world where there was no church? Where there were no priests but caretakers. What kind of safety could they seek within those walls? A growing worry rose within Phillipe like heated yeast and he could not shake the uncertainty he now felt. He had only ever trusted Angelique and Papa and now both were gone. Instead he had to put his faith in the old man beside him, for deep within himself what he feared the most was that he did not have the courage or ability to save his sister. Just as the lingering darkness in his heart grew heavy, so too did the half-light of day until they finally arrived at the doors of Notre Dame at nightfall.

The caretaker cautiously opened the heavy double entrance doors signifying he was expecting their company. He still wore the soutane of a priest, thirty-three buttons running in a line from neck to feet, but there were no other vestments. No crosses, no colours, no silks and nothing linking the man before them to the world that Phillipe knew. He silently invited the two companions to enter the grand vestibule before closing the doors behind them.

"Were you followed?" The caretaker's face was nervous and tense which seemed at odds with his chosen occupation and station. The Cerf shook his head. The exchange was lost on Phillipe, who found his eyes drawn across the grand space before him. From the vestibule, the building opened up to a cavernous chamber with arched beams that met in the centre like two mighty arms protecting those beneath. In all his twelve years in the city, Phillipe had never set foot in Notre Dame. There had never been cause nor reason. And now, standing here in wonder and majesty, he felt safe. For the first time since arriving in the Obscura, he felt safe. The irony that he felt the hand of God protecting him in a building that was no longer able to house the faithful was lost on him. He felt a weight lift from his shoulders and looked up at the grown men before him, hopeful, buoyant and smiling. "I have prepared a small room at the rear of the crypt. No-one will see or come upon you there. You will be safe."

"Thankyou," was the Cerf's heartfelt response. "You have taken a great risk in protecting us and we are deeply grateful...*Father* Gion." The last words were whispered and the former man of the cloth smiled at the reference. He had not heard it for a long time.

Gion led them down the steep staircase to the crypt. The building was deathly quiet and every step echoed around a thousand corners and angles amplifying their deception for all of Paris. Finally in the crypt, he opened the small wooden door to the antechamber. The room was simple. There were no windows to the outside world, no hints of the refinery and ceremony that once adorned the space. A small wooden desk, two wooden chairs and a red velvet drape that lay abandoned in the corner was the only reminder of another time.

"Rest now messieurs. You will be safe here. There is a flask of water on the desk and a pan in the corner. I'm afraid the drape is the only thing soft enough to sleep on."

"It is more than sufficient Monsieur Gion. Merci."

With that, the former clergyman closed the wooden door. Inside the small chamber the Cerf and Phillipe collapsed on the drape. They did not hear the bolt that closed in the door lock behind them and they did not see Gion ascend the stairs to open the vestibule door for a second time that evening. They did not see the dowdy woman on the stone doorstep leaning in close to the caretaker so she did not drop a word uttered before departing with the communication seared in her memory.

CHAPTER 11
THE SOARING AIGLE

The Maire carefully took the small iron key from a chain around his neck as he rose from his wooden arm chair and made his way over to the tapestry that hung on his stone office wall. It had formerly been the fleur de lis, gold on a blue field. But the Maire had the tapestry of the three petaled lily torn down on his first day. The Royal arms of France was dead and in its place had arisen a new age of progress, an age of Science and enlightenment. In its place hung the symbol of the lens, curved lines reaching out to the circle's perimeter from the centre. This was a symbol that held value, a symbol of perspective, of technology, of advancement. He moved the heavy tapestry aside with his arm and bent down to the safe hidden behind it. Turning the key in the safe he heard the click and proceeded to open the small iron door. Of course it was still there. Safely returned after its recent use. He peeled back the leather covering to look again upon the small wooden box. So simple, yet so ingenious. It was a marvel that he owed so much to so little. He locked the safe again, content that it was still there intact and there were no tricks of fate awaiting to spoil his mood. For what a stupendous mood it was. Rarely had things gone so well. His plan was so close to fruition now he could taste it.

The first news to arrive had been the night before. It was a success marred with disappointment, for while they had managed to capture the girl and Renard Rouge, the boy had escaped them. One of the children may have sufficed for his plan but he feared he may have yet needed them both. Then, late in the night, Madame Lally had arrived with more news. Her caretaker informant had the boy and the Cerf locked in the basement of Notre Dame where they would be captured that very morning. News had arrived from the confessionals that the Aigle had been sighted and it would only be a matter of time before he would be face to face with him... and she had returned. It was the *last* news that had him shaking a little as he sat back at his desk. Not of her own volition of course, that would yet take time. But she had been found and *persuaded* to return to him. It appeared the Inspector was not the completely incompetent buffoon that the Maire had assumed him to be. But now, as the icing on the cake, he would meet the other young girl for the first time. A quiet anxiety rose within him as he played out the conversation in his head.

That same girl at that very moment was being walked through the dank, dim corridor of the compound basement. It smelled of pungent moss and decay and she could not shake the smell even as she began to ascend the stairs. In the distance she could hear the sound of footsteps coming down. Hearing the same unexpected sound, the young officer that was accompanying her took several steps ahead to investigate what the sound was. Angelique went to follow him but he had sighted the source of the sound.

"Aretez, Mademoiselle." He then stood in front of her so she could not clearly see the two figures walk past them down the stairs. But try as he might to shield the vision, her desire to see was greater, and with careful and subtle movements she caught a passing glimpse of another officer accompanying the woman from the quay. She could not mistake the beautifully embroidered gown that brushed past. She was no longer wet, and Angelique could now see her thick dark hair was in fact auburn. Try as she might to see the woman's face, the young officer kept moving and craning to prevent her getting a clear vision of the passing figure. In a moment she had passed as quickly and quietly as she had arrived.

"Who is that, Monsieur?"

"No-one, Mademoiselle." He offered a sharp look which invited no reply. No reply was given. Angelique was then marched up several flights of stairs before being brought down a long cloister corridor giving her a clear vision of the industrious activity in the compound courtyard. She desperately wanted to ask about the goings on but thought better of it. She was surprised that she was not blindfolded and had a clear vision of every step she took towards her captor. She could not be sure if this was an oversight of the officer at her side and so tried to memorise every turn and stone brick on her journey. Finally, at the large wooden doors of the office she waited quietly as the officer cautiously knocked. Hearing no response he took a deep breath and knocked louder. The doors opened with a creak and she stood face to face with the Maire.

"Please come in." He gestured to Angelique, offering a reserved, polite smile. She cautiously stepped past his gesturing arm into the office followed by the officer assigned the task of guarding the girl. He was immediately stopped by the Maire's firm hand.

"Not you."

Bowing in ascent, he stood to attention outside the door. The Maire closed the doors behind him firmly. Inside, Angelique's eyes wandered over every surface. Partly because she wanted to remember anything that could be useful later or give her a clue as to her whereabouts, and partly because she had never stood in an office so grand and it quite literally took her breath away. But despite her inward awe, outwardly she gave away nothing.

"Please sit."

She sat.

In that short moment, she noted so much. The tapestry on the back wall featured the same symbol that was worn on the coats of the officers and Gaslampers. She noted that the Maire was surprisingly awkward for a man of his stature and that although his appearance was exactly as she had expected, there was something familiar about him that she could neither place her finger on nor shake. His grey hair was oiled back firmly and his woollen suit and tweed topcoat were impeccable. His gloves were placed carefully on the edge of the desk and she noted a fastidiousness about the arrangement of the room and indeed the man himself. His face and his eyes haunted her with familiarity. "I do apologise for your discomfort last night. It was never my intention to have you here as a prisoner. Were the guards fair?" His question had an edge of danger to it and she suddenly realised that she feared this man greatly.

"They were Monsieur Maire." Angelique looked to the ground, no longer able to meet her interrogator's eyes.

"You must have many questions. I will be able to answer many of them I'm sure. But I fear that you may have already been told a great deal of misleading information." The Maire took a deep breath trying to still his shaking hands and sat behind his desk. Perhaps bringing himself down to her level would make her feel more comfortable and less fearful. "You are here under my protection. You may not realise it and again I apologise for the error made in your accomodation but you and your brother are in great danger. You have been lead to believe that it is I you need to be afraid of, but I am not your enemy Mademoiselle. It is they. The Calibrators. That woman who was with you, Renard Rouge and her band of *freedom* fighters fight against their own protection and the safety of the whole of Paris. They do not realise that they are fighting against themselves. For we are all Parisians. We are all together in this...time. Every time they kill one of my officers," the Maire brought his hand down hard on the wooden table making Angelique jump despite his better judgement, "and yes, they do kill my officers. They take away the very thing that brings stability and harmony to what has been a troubled city in a troubling time." He carefully noted the look of fear and mistrust in the young girl's eyes and tried to soften his tone accordingly. "The truth is... I'm sorry Mademoiselle Chastain, I do not know your first name."

Angelique was immediately taken aback. How did he know her surname? She had shared it with no-one. She met his eyes, feeling more vulnerable than when she first arrived. She considered responding with silence or a false name, but an instinct deep within her spoke before she had a moment to reconsider. "It is Angelique, Monsieur."

"Angelique. Such a beautiful name. The truth is Angelique, I care very deeply for your family. It is most important that you understand that. And it is by no mistake that you are here. I want you to be comfortable here...and safe. There is a new order to the world in which we live. It is coming and it will be an exciting time for Paris. We will be on the world stage you see."

"You refer to Gris Lupe, no?" The question came out without thought or intention. It was met with momentary silence.

"There is much that you will understand in time. But for now you are under my protection. I merely ask that you trust me Angelique. Do you have any questions?"

"Oui," her voice shook a little, "why should I trust you?"

He looked at her with sincere regard. He had hoped that she might see something in him that she recognised. "My dear Angelique. You see no resemblance? I am your uncle."

If Phillipe had been awake, he would have noticed the light blue crystals in his timepiece turn dark. They did not hear the silent steps down the stone stairwell. They did not hear the whispered conversation at the door, and they did not hear the troops march across the Boulevard de Palais. The haunting spectres of two hundred gas masks in the early darkness surrounding Notre Dame, all poised, stood at the ready. The Maire was taking no chances this time. Every nearby shutter was closed and door bolted, for the citizens also took no chances. The first sound that Phillipe and the Cerf heard in the growing half-light of the morning was the click of a key and the kick of a door as officers exploded into the small chamber. The Cerf, though getting on in age, was still wiry and fast, and disarmed the first two officers with lightning reflexes. He threw the first into the stone wall beside the drape where he had slept, but he froze upon hearing the sound of the clicking hammer of the lefaucheux revolver that now pointed at his head. Thibault was also taking no chances this time. The Cerf slowly raised his hands, looking at the shocked face of his young charge still laying on the drape. There was no point in resisting, he knew they were outnumbered and betrayed and he could not risk any harm coming to the young lad. Without turning, he felt the hands of another officer checking him all over for any hidden surprises. There were none. It was truly unexpected.

"You are under arrest, Monsieur. Keep your hands raised and step outside." Thibault then addressed Phillipe. "You are under our protection and for your safety must be restrained and accompany us to the compound." Phillipe slowly stood where he had slept as another officer restrained him firmly, pinning his arms tightly against any resistance. He was escorted outside the room into the crypt where, with the Cerf, they were met with a dozen more Gaslampers and the portly inspector who could not hide the smile that now emanated from his face.

"Merci, Chief Constable. I will take it from here. So boy, we meet again. You are difficult to catch. I hope you have not been harmed by this old man. This *rebel* is a very dangerous man." The inspector walked over to the Cerf whose hands were being bound behind his back with a rope. The inspector took the ends of the rope from the officer and pulled with all his strength on both ends. "Tighter, Constable. Tighter. He is a very slippery one this one." The Cerf winced as the ropes cut into his wrists and the inspector moved to within a few inches of the Cerf's face. "But you are now under our protection lad. You are safe from this dangerous criminal."

"He has not harmed me, Monsieur." Phillipe, still reeling from the shock finally found his quiet voice.

"Shhh. No need to talk now boy. We will take your full report at the compound. Take them upstairs Chief Constable and prepare them for transport."

Phillipe felt a hand upon his shoulder and found himself being shuffled towards the stairwell as officers fell in behind him. He noticed that several men took hold of the Cerf, twisting his bound arms at any sign of resistance, causing him great pain. At the top of the stairs they stepped into the nave of the grand cathedral, where more officers standing at attention formed two lines leading towards the main door. Wolves strained against their ropes at every door preventing any escape. In the corner of the nave stood the caretaker, taking his place as ambassador of the building, but the former man of the cloth could not look upon those he betrayed and so he kept his eyes fixed on the ground. As the remaining officers and the inspector ascended the stairs, they paused at the head of the formation before them, waiting for a clear signal from outside that the perimeter was secure and the transportation could begin.

Through the green glass lenses of their gasmasks, they carefully scanned the vast space they were entering. The irony was that these masks which protected the officers from the diseased world in which they stood also limited their vision. It was as though they waded through an underwater tunnel, and this paradox was not lost on the inspector. It was for this reason he did not see what the Cerf saw at first. Perched high in the cathedral rafters the figure stood like an apparition. The Cerf was experienced enough to give nothing away, but against his better judgement he squinted to be sure that what he saw before him was real. There, poised on the high beams above the nave stood the Aigle. Tall and magnificent in his brown leather coat, his telescopic goggles scanning every minuscule detail below. The old man's heart skipped a beat. What Phillipe saw first was the change in the face of his companion. It was a moment of confusion as he followed the old man's ghostly white face and looked high up in the rafters. A tear ran down Phillipe's cheek. It could not be real. There, like a bird of prey poised high in the ribs of the Cathedral was Corantin Chastain. Papa had come to save him.

In that confused moment, fear formed a tight knot within Phillipe's stomach that reached high into his throat and squeezed his air so that he could not take a breath. Instead of relief at the sight of his rescuer, he felt a deep terror. He immediately feared for the life of the typesetter and what place he could hold in a world such as this. It was also in that moment that Thibault read the fear upon the boy's face and raised his head to the rafters. The events from that moment occurred in such quick succession it was difficult to later recount them in any relevant or accurate order. But all agreed it began when Thibault raised his revolver towards his lofty assailant. The Cerf, though tied, stood several feet from the Chief Constable and threw himself at the raised arm, causing Thibault to stumble forwards and the shot to ricochet off the stone cathedral wall. Nearby, Gaslampers scattered at the sound and threw themselves upon the ground, taking cover. On the assumption that Phillipe was a young boy and a protected guest, he had been neither bound nor searched which would be seen in retrospect as a grave oversight on their part. For in that moment, Phillipe found a deep courage that was born of deep fear. Without thought or contemplation he reached into his pocket and produced his knife, which no-one saw at first. He launched himself towards the Cerf as nearby arms grabbed at him in a feeble attempt to control him. With a swift movement he cut the cords that bound the old man. High above, focused and confident despite the sound of chaos beneath him, Corantin opened his leather coat and raised his musketoon blunderbuss. He had modified the flared barrel to take much larger ammunition and had loaded the first of several glass bottles filled with rum and kerosene, a rag plugging the narrow spout. He lit the phosphorus match and let the flame travel along the rag before aiming the musketoon at the main door, and firing. The flaming bottle soared towards the door and exploded in flames, lighting both the wolf and timber archway and scattering the guards that stood there. Amidst shouts and screams he took a second bottle from his brown leather bandoleer and loaded it, again lighting it and taking aim at the sacristy door to the rear. The guards in the doorways hauled on the ropes and immediately pulled the howling wolves out of Notre Dame, seeking the protection of the stone walls back on the streets, as the second doorway burst into fire. Finally, Corantin took aim and lit up the third and final exit. Notre Dame was sealed. Sealed from the hundreds of troops that looked on helplessly beyond the blazing doors that illuminated the half light street. With only a dozen officers entombed within the cathedral walls the odds were much improved. In that confused instant, as smoke began to fill the Nave, the Cerf found his feet and the blade, which without hesitation he put to the throat of the inspector several feet behind him after ripping off the gas mask that protected him. Officers scrambling for their rifles froze.

"Drop your weapons." The old man screamed, never once taking his eyes off Thibault. The Inspector, wide eyed, sweaty and uncertain of his fate, echoed his captor's sentiments.

"You heard him. Put your rifles down and... don't do anything rash." Already the sting of smoke was making his eyes water, at least that is how he would later describe it, and the thinning air made every breath a labour. Every officer followed the order, lowering their rifles to the ground and slowly raising their hands in defence of the weeping, sweaty hostage.

"Masks off." Came the second order from the Cerf. The Gaslampers looked around uncertainly, hesitant to abandon their greatest advantage. The Cerf pressed the blade harder into the Inspector's fleshy neck.

"Do it. Do it! Masks off." Came the gasping plea from the captive. Slowly the officers removed their masks and dropped them to the ground, instantly wincing as the wall of fumes hit their eyes and nose. One officer alone, several feet away was slow to follow the order. He had only just regained his balance from the Cerf's earlier assault and while slowly removing his mask also raised his revolver and pointed it at Phillipe.

"Drop the blade." Thibault's direction was calm and his ultimatum was clear. The Cerf took a laboured breath, he had not counted on this boldness. He looked into the cold, steely eyes of Thibault and he knew what he had to do.

"Lower the pistol and I'll drop the blade," was the old man's last intervention. Thibault held his aim firmly for a moment longer, he had won. He slowly lowered his revolver. In that moment, with eyes locked in a common stalemate, neither Thibault, the Inspector, the Cerf nor Phillipe had noticed the bamboo tube that dropped from the clearstorey above. If other Gaslampers saw it fall, they did not have time to raise the alarm, for it was lit and it was full...charcoal, steel shavings and gunpowder. Corantin had prepared the firecracker himself. It was all bark and no bite, but in that moment the sound of a thousand canons exploded around them, sparks and colours filled the room in every direction, and in that cloud of colour and confusion, the Aigle descended his rope to the marble floor. He had rigged it up days before, just in case, a simple block and tackle gun pulley system. He took three whaling hooks fastened to the ends of the ropes and wasted no time. In the smoky haze he swung the three hooks to the Cerf who understood the plan well enough. The Cerf in turn fastened one of the hooks to the breeches of the Inspector who was desperately trying to scramble away in the melee. He took one for himself and thrust the third into the hand of Phillipe.

"Hold tight, lad."

Corantin took the three opposing ropes and began to pull with all his strength. Like angels in a nativity pageant, the three began to rise to the ceiling, his son, the Cerf and the Inspector who shouted in protest as his trousers tightened in impossibly uncomfortable ways. Corantin had rigged the ropes well, very little effort was required on his part to elevate the three, but the Cerf leaned across and pulled on the ropes mid-air to assist all the same. By the time the firecracker was no more than a fizzing, smouldering shell and the source of the feigned attack had become evident, the Cerf and Phillipe had their feet planted firmly on the Cathedral string course. The Inspector desperately tried to get a foothold with his flailing legs in between screams and shrieks and finally managed to lock a toe of his boot on the high stone edge. It was then that through the clearing smoulder, Thibault laid his eyes upon the Aigle once again. He raised his pistol at the figure gripping the three taut ropes barely twenty feet away and pulled back the hammer. The Cerf had a clear understanding of the Aigle's mechanics at this stage and with a mighty kick let gravity have its way with the Inspector. As Thibault squeezed his trigger and his rotund superior plummeted to the floor, Corantin, holding the remaining rope soared skyward, overbalanced by the shifting distribution of weight. The shot flew long and shattered an old baptismal font in the distance as the Inspector landed heavily on the stone floor and Corantin gained footing on the high stone lip. Phillipe looked at his father in disbelief. How could this man before him possibly be his Papa?

"Come," came Corantin's only direction as he lead them along the high stone string course past the mullion windows, towards the largest window beneath the vaulting web. Phillipe shook with fear as he placed his feet one after the other, for the height was lofty and a fall would be fatal. He imagined in another life, in another world, his Papa would be furious at him for engaging in such dangerous endeavours. He never imagined in his wildest dreams being encouraged along the narrow lip one hundred and fifteen feet above the stone floor without so much as a backward glance for his safety. But these were dangerous times and he was now in a world where his courage and skills had to be enough, for there was nothing else. He walked on and did not look down. He did not listen to the shouts, nor the sound of shots that echoed throughout the nave and ricocheted off nearby stone walls. He hastened his pace, as did his Papa and the Cerf.

The window was taller than the others and made of beautiful stained glass, glass that had weathered centuries of seasons, upheaval and war. The lead light motif depicted Moses parting the Red Sea followed by minuscule coloured glass Israelites fleeing their Egyptian captors. The artwork had been a vessel of coloured illumination for nearly two centuries. Yet these were the darkest and most desperate of times and so without choice or hesitation, Corantin parted the glass with his hobnailed boot and lead the captives out of Notre Dame. With his feet planted firmly on the slate tiles on the outside rooftop, Corantin stretched his hand back inside to assist the Cerf and Phillipe. Phillipe glanced back to the floor of the nave as the typesetter's strong arm reached towards him, and locked eyes with Thibault. Although there was now some distance between them Thibault raised his pistol. He was an excellent shot and both knew that with Phillipe momentarily stationary, it would be over with one squeeze. But there was a shared moment, perhaps of something like admiration, and the former French Legionnaire lowered his arm ever so slightly and fired at the stone lip beneath the boy's feet. As

Corantin pulled him out onto the rooftop, he threw his arms around his father and held him tightly just for a moment, feeling the gratitude of having one man save his life and another spare it. Corantin received the embrace for the briefest of moments, for the danger was ever-present and now they were outside, they fell prey to the remainder of the officers that surrounded the Cathedral.

"Where to now, comrade?" The Cerf's question inferred an awareness of immediate danger that he wanted to impart to his companions. There would be time for reunions in safety.

"East side, Enzo. I have prepared our escape there." Hearing his Papa uttering the Cerf's real name took Phillipe by surprise. It felt both odd and comforting. In a low crouch the three escapees began to work their way around the rooftop to the east. The angle was steep and the movement was slow, every step needed time and care, all the while beneath they could see movement in the street and surrounds as the officers began to move in closer, now aware that their targets were high and vulnerable. Their only saving grace was that the Seine river created a natural barrier from their assailants and the distance for rifle fire was great. Only moments later, rifle fire began to ping on tiles around them all the same.

"Quickly Phillipe. It won't be long before the sharpshooters arrive. Then we will be in trouble," Corantin cautioned, as they finally edged around to the eastern rooftop. There, on the eastern elevation, the Cerf and Phillipe saw for the first time the next step in the Aigle's plan of escape. They looked like the wings of a giant bird, all bony and webbed as they lay there on the rooftop tiles. Two sets, side by side awaiting their willing aviators to take flight. Phillipe's breath quickened and it felt as though his heart would stop, it was racing dangerously quickly. The structure was simple enough. Two long arms of French pine, light and flexible, bracing hinged ribs like the veins of a leaf. Across each structure, canvas was pulled taut and tied tightly with cord. In the centre of the wings were two canvas shoulder straps and a belt of sorts. Corantin moved quickly to the first and lay backwards against the giant arms, stretching his own arms out to hold on to two straps that had been fasted to the timber. "Come Phillipe, climb on top. I had prepared this one to take us both, the other was going to be for your sister but our circumstances have changed... Come quickly." Phillipe climbed over to the timber frame and lay on his back against his Papa. He placed his arms through the straps and reached across to hold a second set of handles. "Enzo. Can you fasten our belt?" The Cerf moved swiftly over as shots continued to echo off every surface, and fastened the belt around the two before assembling himself similarly in the other timber carcas.

"Have you used these before?" The old man queried nervously.

"No."

"Are you certain they will work?"

"No."

"Excellent." The Cerf shook his head. Nothing had changed.

The Aigle raised his body, lifting his son with him, hoisting his wings from the rooftop. The Cerf followed and stood beside him. From beneath on the street there was a pause in the volley of fire as officers squinting through the green lens of their gas masks saw the two giant birds rise up like a phoenix from the ashes. Several pulled off their masks certain that this hallucination would be remedied by their naked eyes. But there they were. Two birds with extended wings silhouetted against the half-light Parisian sky. In that moment, the Inspector and Chief Constable scurried out of the eastern Notre Dame doorway where one of the fires had been finally extinguished. Neither could believe what they saw.

Corantin stretched his neck down and kissed the top of Phillipe's head as a final moment of tenderness before both drew breath, leaned forward and stepped out into the empty sky. In fear of dying alone, the Cerf quickly followed, and in that moment both plummeted for several feet before wind and air conspired in their escape and the birds took flight.

They soared.

Gusts from below raised the aviators higher above the Seine as it raced beneath them like a shimmering serpent. All eyes below watched in disbelief as their captives, who had been tied and subdued only twenty minutes earlier lifted high above the rooftops.

The world raced past Phillipe. Air pummelled his face and stung his eyes as he felt the exhilaration and terror of uncertain flight. The sounds of wolves and gunfire evaporated into the distance as the sound of whistling air buffeted about them. Beneath him Phillipe saw familiar landmarks hovering, impossibly small like miniature toys in an unfamiliar playset. The dome of St Paul's Cathedral whipped past in the north, followed by the Bastille column as they followed the Seine along the quay d' Austerlitz, and far off in the distance beyond the perimeter of the city walls lay the lush green of the Bois de Vincennes and the Grand Lake that shimmered like a giant blue brooch. Arising further to the North East lay the Fort de Vincennes, a formidable structure that needed to be avoided at all costs. It housed a large garrison of troops loyal to the Maire that would be mobilised as soon as word reached them to search for the evading trio through the forests that surrounded the city. But right now, in that moment, the Cerf was contemplating a far more immediate problem. He shouted across the wind to the Aigle.

"How do we land?"

"I don't know," came the shouted reply, "I didn't know if they would even fly." As they passed the sentries below on the eastern city walls this new dilemma became a prime consideration. "Perhaps pull on the handles?" Corantin had rigged the wing structure on two hinges, a simple idea that emulated the movement of a bird. Surely with angled wings one could control direction and altitude... surely. He pulled on the handles, forcing the wings against the wind to flex and bow towards the ground, hoping that this would redirect the air flow towards a descent. However, like all forces of nature, the wind is a difficult mistress and though predictable on paper, presented a very fickle companion in practise. In a clap that sounded like thunder, the mighty wings collapsed under the air pressure and they fell, father and son, like a wounded fowl, plummeting to earth. Desperately Corantin tried to force the wings back open to catch the falling air, but in vein. The force was too great and his strength no match and so the great Aigle fell from the sky. Strapped tightly to his Papa, Phillipe saw the earth racing towards him at breakneck speed, the wind caught in his mouth and eyes and forced air into his lungs that he could not breath. The Lake, their only hope was too far to the east and the rich green blur beneath began to form mighty trees, conifers and tall pines, dense, vast and deadly. When all hope was lost, Phillipe closed his eyes bracing himself for the certain end.

Phillipe did not see it happen, but heard the second crack and felt the exploding thrust change his direction. The Cerf saw the error of his companion and pulled his handles only until he could feel the thrust of the wind against him. He quickly discovered that in adjusting the tension of his pull, he could steer his bird and adjust his angle. It was crude and hurried, but he set himself a course for his plummeting mate and when all hope was lost careened into it. The crack was loud as the timber frames collided, momentarily slowing the descent and pushing the failing aircrafts eastward within range of the Great Lake.

Phillipe remembered so little because it happened so quickly. But in that instant he felt the force of icy water hitting him like a steam engine, and a watery cold world embraced him slowly and began to fill his lungs. Hands slowed by the dense flood of water released the grips and fumbled for the leather belt that imprisoned them in this watery tomb. Corantin, blinded and sinking felt around his son's waist for the belt fastener, trying desperately to release the pin from the leather hole and free them from the bones that dragged them to their aqueous grave. His hands were thick and clumsy but he would persevere until his lungs were full and darkness pervaded. Finally he felt the pin shift and the belt release and from the dark depths, locked his arm around his boy and kicked with his remaining strength for the surface. The two exploded into the half-light air, gasping from their spent lungs. Corantin dragged Phillipe sideways across the water to the lake's edge and resting him upon the muddy shore leaned closely to hear the soft sound of his breath. He looked back to the silent, still lake. There was no sign of the old man. He squeezed his vision to a tight focus, skimming across the dimly lit surface looking for the slightest ripple, a bubble.

There.

Without drawing breath Corantin dived back into the lake swimming with his remaining strength to save his friend.

Phillipe rolled over in the mud, fighting against the black shroud as his vision again began to focus. Gradual consciousness brought with it moments of recognition and in the distance he saw two figures clawing their way onto the mud. It was his Papa, dragging the Cerf by his torn shirt onto firm ground. In that moment he saw Corantin lean over and breathe into the lifeless body of the old man. Nothing. He leaned over and blew once again, more firmly, desperately. There was a pause and then the Cerf's body jerked upward as he coughed and spluttered water and bile from his lungs. Corantin pushed him on his side as he continued to release the liquid that had infiltrated his body. In a moment it was over and he lay still on his side, breathing slowly and gratefully. Content that his old friend would live, Corantin then slowly walked over and picked up a large rock near a tree before wading back into the sludge, straining under the weight of his load. Further out in the lake, Phillipe could make out the floating carcasses of the wings, now buoyant on the surface with no passengers to pull them beneath. Corantin heaved the rock into the distance landing it squarely on the canvas of the first wing, before trudging back to the forest's edge and taking another. The second rock was enough. After landing on the second wing, the timber bones slowly began to sink to their subversive cover. The second set of wings were further out in the lake and required more effort and time, but the typesetter knew that their lives depended on their concealment. He therefore sank the second without complaint or pause.

By the time he was done, both Phillipe and the Cerf were back on their feet. Both were groggy and shaking from the chill but ready to move off all the same. All three were grateful to be alive.

"Can you both walk?" The question was gently firm, but resonated with the urgency that Corantin felt. The Cerf nodded in response and Phillipe seeing both eyes upon him, slowly affirmed the same. "Good. Any moment, this place will be crawling with soldiers and Gaslampers. We need to keep moving to find somewhere safe and warm." A growing mass of menacing clouds now darkened what had previously been a clear sky. The Aigle and Cerf both exchanged a hopeful look.

"What is it?" Phillipe queried, not following the thoughts of his companions. The Cerf chimed in, his voice a little foreign and husky.

"Rain, lad. It will hopefully cover our tracks through the mud and forest."

Phillipe nodded with understanding. He desperately wanted to ask Papa so many questions, there was so much he didn't understand. But now was not a time for conversation. Instead he wiped the mud from his face and followed his father and the clockmaker into the wall of forest.

CHAPTER 12
CAESAR'S CIPHER

If the new world had seemed foreign and confusing to
Angelique before, it now appeared utterly upside down,
which indeed it was. The return journey along the dank,
dark corridor was long and silent. Unlike the previous passage, she
could no longer focus on the details of her surrounds. It felt as
though the weight of her confusion closed in about her and she
could no longer note any significant specifics. Her thoughts were
in a whirl. How could the Maire be her uncle? She knew so little
about her father's brother. He had died. Drowned, she was led to
believe. More pressingly, could what he said about Renard Rouge
and the Calibrators be true? For the first time since she had been
rescued by the young revolutionary, Angelique had doubts. She
thought of her dear Papa, back in Paris in the old world, and
wondered what he would caution her to do. There was no doubt
that the Maire had sought them out. Perhaps he was trying to
protect them all along and had never intended them harm. He
appeared genuine and had conceded that she was taking in a lot of
new information and would likely need time to think about it.
This was true, and despite her best efforts, her demeanour had
betrayed her surprise. *Go and rest, we will discuss it further tomor-*

row... Her head was swirling with mistrust and for the first time since they had arrived, she felt utterly alone. Either way she had to get to Phillipe. He was in danger which ever way she looked at the situation.

She noticed the young Gaslamper leading her for the first time. His slight frame suggested he couldn't have been much older than sixteen or seventeen. His uniform coat looked large on him and made him look even younger, as though he was playing at dress up from a costume chest. He finally stopped outside a doorway several floors above where she had been previously housed.

"Your room, mademoiselle."

Angelique stopped. For the second time within that hour she had found her look of surprise difficult to suppress. She looked wide eyed at the young boy who nodded in response to her invisible question. She stepped in through the doorway and discovered it was a room. An actual room. There was a four poster bed with a large green velvet drape that hung loosely from the canopy, a timber chair that sat illuminated by a shaft of pale light emerging through a moderate window overlooking the courtyard. By the chair, was a small, round wooden table with a porcelain bowl full of fruit. It occurred to Angelique at that moment that she was famished. She could not remember the last meal she ate. The young Gaslamper stood at attention at the door.

"If everything is to your satisfaction, mademoiselle, I will return in several hours with a meal."

"Oui." Angelique could think of little more to say. She had slept so poorly in the previous evening that it was only now, surrounded by comfort that she began to feel a wave of exhaustion sweep over her. With that, the heavy timber door was closed and locked and she was again alone. She no longer had any space for thoughts, or confusion or even the fruit that looked so enticing by the window. She walked over to the bed, collapsed on it and fell fast asleep.

It was a knock several hours later that woke her. She sat upright on the soft bed in the dark trying to bring her unusual surroundings into focus. For the briefest of moments she sat confused, uncertain of where she was and what was real. Her mind was a labyrinth of ambiguous memories and she was no longer confident that she could trust it. There was a second cautious knock.

"Who is it?" The door opened clumsily, as she witnessed the young Gaslamper who had escorted her earlier trying to open the door with a candle in one hand and a plate of food in the other. He was having limited success. The sinking realisation of where she was sat heavily in the pit of her stomach, yet the spectacle before her was almost comical and she found herself smiling at the boy in the dim light.

"Forgive me, mademoiselle, these duties are outside my usual tasks. I have poor skills for opening doors with my hands full." There was a playfulness in his comment and Angelique immediately softened. The young Gaslamper carried the food to the small table beneath the window, before he attended to a small firebox that sat in a stone hearth in the southern wall. Angelique had not noticed it when she first arrived, but it appeared to have already been set with kindling and logs. The lad leaned his candle towards the light twigs and instantly she heard the crackling sound of dry timber catching light. He briefly placed a steaming plate of onion soup and bread on the small table, before turning back towards Angelique declaring his completion with a small nod.

"Merci, mademoiselle. I will be back in the morning to take your plate." He drifted back towards the door and closed it once again. She heard the sound of the bolt sliding on the other side, and with full clarity she realised that she was once again alone. The smell of French onion soup drew her hungrily to the table where she began to tear the bread, soak it in the steaming liquid and devour it. She did not even have time or inclination to pick up the silver spoon beside the bowl. It was then that she first noticed it. Beyond the crest of the porcelain, her eyes fell upon a small piece of paper with words hastily scribbled on one side. She leaned over and by the flickering firelight read it.

"1/C4

Morning. Old routine silent account.
I will get extended time inside. View victory."

Her mind was instantly in a whirl. Who was the note from? How did it get there? And most pressingly, what did it mean? Her hunger dissipated in that moment and her soup sat stagnant and cooling as her eyes poured again and again over every letter, searching, hunting for meaning. The note had to have been placed there by the boy. She read the words over and over again trying to make sense of them, trying to find meaning and purpose. She could guess that it was likely the note was from Renard Rouge, but could not be certain. Perhaps she was meant to find it in the half-light of the morning. If that were true, then it appeared that Renard had not spoken to her interrogators and would be kept imprisoned for longer but she could see light at the end of the tunnel. This generally made sense, but why would she send the note through the boy at such great risk, and what was the number at the top? Was it a date of sorts? A code perhaps? The more that Angelique thought about it, the less it made sense and the more determined she became that there was more to the message than met the eye. She pulled her chair over by the fire, basking in its warmth and forsaking her meal once and for all. Her appetite had suddenly dissipated and she found herself staring into the flames deep in thought. Phillipe would know. He was always so quick to solve puzzles and saw things others often neglected. She thought again of her brother and wondered where in the city of Paris he was. Was he in danger? She tried to imagine where he might be and shuddered as her thoughts ventured into the dark recesses of her fears. The following hour passed with words moving in and around the corridors of her mind without any sense of where they were going or where they belonged.

A whinnying sound at the window cut through Angelique's thoughts and she found herself drawn to the sound as her curiosity dictated. There was a horse and rider outside in the dim light of a lit torch. The rider had removed his gas mask within the compound, and the horse seemed agitated as the rider carefully dismounted and tried to calm the beast. Another officer joined him and they exchanged a hushed conversation. Very few words made the lofty height to the window of the compound wall and so references to "the forest" and "the search" were lost on the young girl. Finally the spooked horse was calmed and relative quiet was again restored. In that moment, a thought struck Angelique sharply. Perhaps it was a memory, perhaps it was a story, she could not tell, but the vision of the pawing and stomping horse, the foreleg muscles flexing and shining in the moonlight, reminded her of the stables back in the old world. Phillipe would go there daily and talk to the farriers and stablehands. They were not permitted to place bets on the track and would often send encrypted notes to the book keepers in a coded hand so they would not be caught and reprimanded. Phillipe had been fascinated by this practise and eventually earned the trust of a young stable hand who had shown him how to use Caesar's cipher. "C4". Angelique walked over to the fire and broke off a small splinter of charred, black wood and struggling to keep her hands steady sat back to the table, examining the small note once again.

"1/C4". Angelique instinctively circled the 1st letter of every word and re-wrote the letters underneath the message. *M.OR-SA.IWGETI.VV.* Caesar's cipher simply shifted the letters across a given number, which she assumed to likely be four letters across. She began working each letter backwards by four. *I.KNOW.ES-CAPE.RR.*

A fear rose from the pit of her stomach and rather than feel accomplishment, she felt sick. There was no question the note was from Renard Rouge now, but what could she know? How could she escape? But there was one question that weighed on her so heavily, she could barely fill her lungs with breath. Could she even trust Renard Rouge?

❧

In that same moment, deep in the forest in that same city, several miles away, the three companions sat in the darkness quietly conversing in hushed whispers. The Calibrators had hidden spaces everywhere, in every inch of the city. The Cerf knew where it was, at least where it used to be and so the fugitives had finally trudged on through the torrent of rain and stumbled upon the small wooden cover hidden by scrub and undergrowth. Even knowing where it was, he had to scratch around on his hands and knees to feel for it. This boded well for successful concealment. Finally, dusting the dirt and foliage from the timber hatch he lifted the lid and they scurried down the ladder, down the shaft into the tunnel beneath just as darkness enveloped the half light world. Carefully closing the hatch again under the undergrowth, they were sealed from the searching world above for now. *No fires.* That was the order of Corantin. They might see the smoke. Instead, finding the single lantern at the bottom of the descent, a remnant of organisation from a decade before, Corantin lit his only phosphorus match and hoped against hope that the lantern had been filled with fuel and that age had not tampered with it serving its function. It lit first attempt and the three could clearly see one another for the first time. They were wet, muddy and utterly exhausted. They traversed the tunnel for several minutes until they came to a small, dry room that had been cut into rock and earth. They slumped against the walls where they could finally rest, dry and talk. Corantin had much to explain. Phillipe sat close to his Papa, leaned his shoulder in tightly so he could feel the rise and fall of his father's breath. Corantin reached across and placed his arm around his son. An expectant silence fell upon the trio as Corantin drew his breath and tried to find the words to begin his story.

"It is difficult to know where to start." He finally began.

"Perhaps the beginning, old friend." Came the sage advice from the old man who sat expectantly. There was much the Cerf already knew, and much that he did not.

"Phillipe, there is much you don't know about your father. To you, I am a typesetter who scrapes out a living working on printing machines. I raise my children and I print. This is true. I am those things. But I have not always been those things. I have had a life in another world, at another time, before your time. Here, I was not an artisan, I was not Corantin Chastain, I was an inventor and they called me *the Aigle*. I came here much the way I believe you did. By accident.

I have always been a creator, fascinated by science and machinery and I grew up much the same as you, learning from unusual sources...the streets and vendors of Paris. My older brother Charles and I would spend hours tinkering in our father's shed. It was left to us, you see, when he was gone. He was gone when I was very young, I have very little memory of him. My mother was with us until my fifteenth year. It was then that she passed away. But in that old timber shed I found that inventing was really my passion, I had a gift for it. Charles would help of course but he never really understood things the way that I did.

In that same fifteenth year - Charles was nearly eighteen - I found an old drawing in my father's bedroom drawer. The room had not been changed since he left and now that my mother had also gone, I started to go through their personal effects. The drawing was a sketch he had made of an obscura. I had never seen anything like it. The logic confounded me and the idea captivated my imagination. For weeks I became obsessed with the idea of inverted vision and finally, with the help of Charles, procured black sheets and tape and created our own. We converted the old wooden shed into our own obscura, meticulously sealing every source of light until we finally succeeded in capturing moving vision on the wall. I wanted to see if I could trick my own brain. It was an experiment, that was all. Charles and I stood on our heads and found our world turned upside down. Literally. That is how we first came here.

It was here, in this new world that I met Enzo, whom we later called *the Deer.* We came at a time of much unrest and for the first time I found my skills were a powerful commodity. Incredibly valuable. There was a man of Icelandic birth who had taken power in Paris. His ascension to power, like his reign was one both swift and terrifying. No-one had seen it coming and within months he had turned the city against itself. He raised up an army of street urchins and cut-throats and because he was not afraid to do what others dared not, because he had no morality, nothing but ambition, he was unstoppable. He was called the wolf. Gris Loup. He overthrew the monarchy who fled to safety in Belgium. There were executions in the streets for those who stood in opposition, until there were none to oppose. None but the Cerf. Forgive me my friend, but Enzo here was young back then and strong as a stag. Several stood with him, myself included and founded the resistance, the Calibrators. Our mission was to use our expertise, our understanding of science to bring about change for the better."

Phillipe sat transfixed. Every word that emanated from his father's lips felt foreign. He could no longer recognise the type-setter in this man before him. He had never noticed how large his father was until now, how tall, how broad and how strong. He sat in silence, allowing the words to sink in and to marry with the vision before him.

"In time, Gris Loup built his mercenary army and moved on further north, conquering more cities in his wake. Gris Loup had more ambitious plans than Paris, and the small garrison he had left manning the city were quickly ousted and the city fell into political turmoil. It was here that your uncle and I differed in our views. Charles had been gathering intelligence for the resistance. That was his involvement, but only ever through me. He never trusted or communicated through anyone else. But after five long years, when the trouble had shifted from tyranny to internal bickering, I longed to return to our own world, to live a normal life, and he had wanted to stay, to make a go of it in this world. In the end, it came down to the flip of a coin. The head of Louis would take us home, his tail would have us stay. We flipped the franc. Heads. Home. But now the problem was how? We tried to replicate the way we had arrived, but the world of the Obscura does not invert, ever and so it appeared Charles would have his way. Until the night I created this."

Corantin reached into the pocket of his leather coat and produced a small piece of oiled leather tied tightly with a strap. He untied the leather covering to reveal a small wooden box which he cradled carefully in his hand. There appeared to be a series of mirrors at various angles within the timber shell, with two circular eye holes cut on the other side.

"What is it?" Phillipe finally found his voice.

"It is called a lux periscope. You strap it over your eyes, stand on your head and the world will invert, regardless of your location. That is how we came home. I only ever made two of these. They brought us both home and then I locked them away for safety. You know where they were locked Phillipe. You almost discovered them. They had sat there, sealed in the chest for over twenty years. It was not long after our return to Paris that I met your mother. Well, Charles and I both met her on the same evening at the theatre and we all became very close, but your mother and I had fallen desperately in love and we married in the spring. Over the following years, a sadness came over your uncle. There was a darkness that had always possessed him, but had grown and consumed him since we had returned. It was therefore not a shock when the gendarmerie informed me he had drowned in the Seine. I blamed my ambition that had brought us to the Obscura in the first place and so that was its end. No more inventing, no more wanting. Just simple contentment. Your mother also struggled in a similar way years later, when you and Angelique were young, but that is another story."

"How did you know we were here?" There were still far too many pieces of the puzzle for Phillipe and his mind was swirling in new confusion.

"I didn't initially. There was one other thing I have to explain. It was an incident. Odd and out of place. Several years after Charles passed away, I had just started working at the printing press as an apprentice typesetter. I had just finished work for the day and was closing up the shop as I had been instructed to do, when a short, stout man approached me near the door. He had a long waxed moustache and I had never seen him before, but he seemed to know me. He had a manner of familiarity that caught me off guard. He began by discussing the weather, and other idle pursuits. But then finally when I had grown a little impatient with the conversation and turned to take my leave, he muttered something about a watchful eye and I distinctly heard the words *Gris Loup*. It startled me and I asked him to repeat himself. He became suddenly flustered and disappeared into the street. That was the end. It was odd and out of place until last week. I searched for you both all over Paris when you disappeared. I went to the Gendarmerie, I enlisted the neighbours, but it wasn't until I spoke to a vagrant outside the Vanguard theatre and he described a portly salesman that had been discussing an Obscura, that I understood. I later found it was the Inspector that captured you in Notre Dame. He is one and the same."

Phillipe nodded in understanding. His Papa was correct in his assertions, indeed it had been the Inspector who had lured them into the Vanguard theatre that day.

"But there is one other thing. It is this that I fear the most. When I went to the chest in the apartment firebox to retrieve the lux periscopes. There was only one of them there. I have no idea where and how the other has gone."

They fell into a silence for some time. There was much to contemplate. The Cerf knew much of the story already. He was there in the beginning. He had been present in all of the revolutions past and present, but he did not know about the Inspector traversing the worlds. This was a dangerous progression. It implied a much greater purpose to the entrapment of the children. Of course it was clear that the real goal was Corantin himself. But now that he understood the lengths they would undergo to get to the Aigle, he suddenly had grave fears for Renard Rouge. Corantin had not met her, she had not been born when he was last in this world. Angelique would be shown mercy in the compound because she remained an important playing piece, but the same could not be said for his granddaughter, Renard Rouge. He silently buried the fear as he had learned to do so well. Phillipe suddenly shifted and stood in the small chamber. The Cerf looked up, fearful that his emotions had betrayed him and had been detected. Corantin was instantly alert.

"What is it son?"

Phillipe was staring at his watch. "It's dark blue. They are here."

CHAPTER 13
THE GIRL WHO KNEW TOO MUCH

The night passed in fitful sleep. Angelique tossed and turned on the bed, as the darkness pounded relentlessly in her thoughts. She saw wolves. Their eyes approached in the darkness before she heard the slavering low guttural growl. In the centre was a fox. It appeared so small and helpless as the pack inched towards it. It made not a sound, but she imagined that it could also foresee being torn apart limb from limb by these savage beasts. In a moment they were upon the fox in a frenzy of squeals and howls. Then one by one, she watched them fall. Torn, savaged, blinded and quivering. There in the centre, bloodied and heaving, stood the fox, the flesh of the last wolf still hanging from its jaw. In that instant, Angelique felt a deep primal dread and she did not know which she should fear. She ran. She screamed Phillipe's name. She screamed for Corantin. But they did not hear her, for the wolves were upon them as well.

A quiet knock at the door awoke Angelique and she sat up in the half light, beads of sweat running down her face despite the crisp, cold air. The fire had long extinguished and in the dim light she remembered where she was. It all came flooding back to her and she remembered the words. And she felt a sense welling deep inside her that whatever may come, she would be enough. She rose. Wiped the sweat from her brow on her bed sheet and beckoned her visitor to enter.

It was again the young Gaslamper from the previous night. He stepped inside and gathered the half empty bowl and utensils. It appeared a pretence as he then stood awkwardly, as if awaiting something, not certain if he had been understood.

"Was your meal adequate mademoiselle?"

"Why are you here?"

The question was bold and took the young lad by surprise. He had been treading very cautiously up until this point. He took a breath. "My name is Victor. I am a friend. I can help you." He looked across to the small piece of paper still sitting on the table. "You have found the message?"

"Oui."

"It is not destroyed?"

"No." She stepped close to Victor, fearful that long corridors may have large ears. "How do I know that this is not a trap?"

"Mademoiselle, I brought the message directly from Renard Rouge herself."

"Oui. But how do I know I can trust even *her*?"

Victor understood. He walked to the door and looked cautiously down the corridor. "Come." He locked the door behind Angelique and lead her down the corridor back to the stairwell where they descended once more to the basement floor. The damp, acrid stench immediately struck her and brought back all of the memories of the previous night. The only light emanated from the occasional lit torch. On either side as she passed, moans and intermittent dull shuffling sounded behind dark doors and walls. She felt fear. She couldn't shake it. Finally Victor stopped outside a door. He looked to Angelique before knocking and sliding open the small door window. He hissed words cautiously through the opening. "Renard. Quickly, you have a visitor." Victor looked to Angelique, gesturing to her to be quick before he moved aside so that she could come forth. There was again a dull shuffling behind the door. Angelique peered through the small square hole in the door into the darkness until a face appeared before her. It was unrecognisable. One eye was completely swollen closed, the second a small slit that a wary glassy eye peered through. The swelling was a deep purple, a colour that was reflected across her entire face in degrees of darkness. Her nose and lips were also swollen with a dark, bloodied line marking the nose's ridge. Dried blood was crusted in lines and cuts all over the surface like dry river beds in an alien topography. It was only Renard's long red hair that was recognisable and Angelique felt her voice catch in her throat unexpectedly.

"What has happened to you?"

Renard spoke in a quiet gravelly voice. Her words were no more than wisps of air that escaped her swollen mouth. "Questions. That is all. It is not the first time I have not answered questions."

"How could they do this to you?"

"I am fine."

Victor touched Angelique's shoulder gently. "We must go. I'm sorry. We can not be seen here." Angelique saw the danger in his eyes and looked back into the cell one last time. Renard saw that her comrade was about to leave.

"I know," the freedom fighter hissed from the darkness.

Angelique had already started to move away and lurched back to the window for one last moment. "What do you know?"

"I know why you are here."

With that, Victor had his hand upon Angelique's shoulder and ushered her back towards the corridor. The two moved in urgent silence back up the two flights of stairs before a sound at the landing had them freeze. Victor instinctively put his hand over Angelique's mouth and held her in silence. He was acutely aware of the risk he had already taken and was not certain Angelique shared his understanding. The sounds echoed in the corridor above. They were the hobnailed footsteps of another officer. Hopefully passing. They waited for what felt an eternity until the steps disappeared into the distance. Victor released his hand and looked into Angelique's wide eyes. "I am sorry. I must get you back to your room." She nodded in silent consent. The two cautiously peered down the corridor at the top of the stairs. It appeared empty and they hastened their way to the door. Victor pulled out his iron key ring and though his hands were unsteady, opened the door as quickly as he could and ushered Angelique back inside. He felt the weight lift immediately. "Are you satisfied, mademoiselle?"

"Oui." Her thoughts were still two floors below with the swollen face of her friend. "I am satisfied."

"Private. You *are* here." A sharp voice echoed behind Victor, who had the wherewithal to place his hands upon the used crockery before turning to face his questioner.

"Oui Captain. I was just collecting mademoiselle's crockery."

"I just walked past here Private. The door was closed."

"Oh that Captain. While I was collecting the plates, the girl had a slight spell and fell upon the door. She did not eat enough last night and is still quite weak... she will rest in her bed. All is well, Monsieur." The Captain leaned into the room and glanced at the young girl. She did look somewhat pale and frail. He looked back to Victor, then back to the girl.

"You are wanted elsewhere Private. You are to report to the Quartermaster immediately. Next time you are given a task, see to it you complete it in a satisfactory time." With that, Victor faced his superior clicking his heals in subordination before the door was slammed closed. Angelique sat back upon her bed. She could trust Renard Rouge. Anyone who could do that to her, hurt her in that way, could never be believed, never be trusted. She was now consumed with a new thought. Angelique was protected, for whatever reason, she had privileges that Renard did not, it would therefore be up to her to devise a plan. She took the small note in her hand and walked over to the window, looking out at every detail in the half light. She would be enough. Perhaps the fox of her dreams was not Renard Rouge after all. She felt empowered by this thought and in that moment saw herself in a very different light. Angelique the fearless warrior, silent, cunning and powerful, would be the instrument of escape. She tore the note in half, scrunched it up tightly and swallowed it.

৩

He immediately extinguished the lantern and darkness fell upon them like a black cloak. With that darkness came the kind of silence where senses become finely tuned, where the scratching of a mouse or the movement of a slater across the stone floor crystallises sharply like a lens finding its focus. Corantin knew that any light would expose them and they needed time for their eyes to adjust. This would be their only advantage. Phillipe, in the silent darkness became aware of the wound on his leg for the first time in many days. Perhaps it was the sound above of low growls, or his heightened senses in that moment, but he could feel it itch under his trouser and he imagined that it must be in the final stages of healing. The three sat crouched low behind the wall in the chamber in the pitch darkness. Phillipe had hoped his eyes might start to adjust, that he might begin to see some limited vision, a shape perhaps, a figure clambering down the tunnel but there was none. Then he heard the first sound. The quiet scraping of the hatch several hundred yards further down in the darkness. The sound was barely audible, but there was a muffled whisper and then the dull clang of hands and feet on rungs. A voice from above in a projected whisper.

"Take a wolf with you. If they are down there, they are dangerous." There was more shuffling sounds and then the thud of feet hitting the ground followed by the growl of the wild dog as it instantly recognised the scent of its quarry. A lantern was struck and glowed in the distance as the wolf moved ahead of the Gaslampers, driven by the scent that had caught its nostrils. Corantin and the Cerf leaned into the darkness of the wall, listening as the sound approached, aware that any number of loyal government troops likely hovered on the earth several feet above them and that a misjudged skirmish could bring the entire Maire's force down upon them.

The wolf was the first around the corner. It needed no light in the darkness, its yellow eyes saw all. Phillipe sat motionless as the slavering beast caught sight of him and silently lowered itself on its front legs preparing for the attack. The only sound was a drop in the pitch of its guttural growl. Phillipe froze in fear, sensing Corantin must be near, must be aware of his danger. Hoping against all hope that he was not alone in the darkness in that moment. It was then he felt his father's body step in front of his own, the rest was all sound. The wolf launched itself at Corantin like a coiled spring with speed and accuracy terrifying to behold. In that instant, two hands shot out of the darkness and took the beast by the neck. The hands were strong, fast and sure, and without a sound the Cerf had twisted the neck of the wolf and silenced it forever. The ferocity and skill took Phillipe's breath away. His eyes had now adjusted to the darkness and he saw the imposing frame of Corantin step aside to reveal the lifeless shape at the Cerf's feet. There was almost no sound. Nothing more than a slight whine and then a snapping sound. That was all. But it was enough to hasten the steps of the lantern in the distance. In a moment, the light rounded the corner and the first green lenses of the Gaslamper quickly followed. Corantin reached straight for the canvas mask before realisation would take hold and gripping it with both hands brought the fellows head down upon his knee. There was a brief moment of struggle, but with two swift blows from his right hand he broke the green glass lens and silenced the officer behind it. He was still heaving with the effort when the second officer that had also rounded the corner caught him across the brow with his wooden nightstick. It was a strong blow and took Corantin by surprise. He fell to the ground as nausea and a throbbing fog began to take hold. The officer struck again and again. Corantin raised himself and moved in close, grappling with his assailant trying to prevent any further strikes. To Phillipe it was a moment of sheer panic, of tangled bodies, blood and desperation. He did not see the moment when the Cerf leaned into the frey and removed the Chamelot-Delvigne service revolver from the officer's holster. The first moment anyone was aware of the old man's guile was the click of the hammer being drawn back as the muzzle pressed into the cheek of the Gaslamper. He stopped immediately and without resistance dropped the baton to the ground. Slowly he stood, the revolver still pressed firmly against him. His movements were slow and careful, he understood his position immediately and had also caught sight of his partner motionless on the ground and the dead wolf. Corantin lay heaving on the ground. Blood coursed from a cut across his forehead and although struggling to find clarity, he smiled. He marvelled and he smiled. There was life in the old stag yet.

The Cerf's words were slow and clear and whispered. "Take off your uniform."

"What?"

"Take off your uniform...now."

"Monsieur, you can not be serious."

The Gaslamper raised his eyes to gaze upon the Cerf and he understood immediately. He looked towards the tunnel, still considering his options. He could certainly warn the others, raise the alarm. But he would be dead. He took a deep breath and began to unbutton his coat and blouse. Finally with the captive standing in his long undergarments, the Cerf gestured that he turn around. Slowly turning back towards the boy, the naked Gaslamper never saw it coming. The strike of the revolver handle was swift and accurate and he collapsed silently in an unconscious heap upon the floor. The old man took no time and began to undress himself. "You will need to do the same," he eyeballed Corantin who nodded in understanding and also began to undress.

"What about me?" Phillipe hesitantly questioned as Corantin finally pulled the officer's leather coat on and buttoned it to his neck.

"There is no uniform for you, son. You will be our captive, the most important piece in the plan. But for now you must stay here with Enzo. I have a small job to do first."

"You're not going out there?" The Cerf weighed in with concern.

"I must. In ten minutes there will be more. Don't worry. I will put them off the scent." He pulled the mask off the lifeless body on the floor and checked the barrel of his service revolver. "I shouldn't be long. If anything happens and I am not back by midnight, go and get more help. You won't be able to do it alone."

The old man nodded in assent. Pulling the mask over his head, the Aigle moved back down the tunnel towards the ladder to embark on his second risky venture of the day. He arrived at the ladder and could see shadowed shapes peering down from above. "What have you found?" Came a muffled voice from the surface.

"Dead end. The tunnel has collapsed. You go on and we'll join you soon."

"No. Our orders are to push on through the forest. Help him out lads," the voice directed. Corantin felt a rise of panic as he began to step slowly up the ladder. Strong arms reached down and pulled him out of the hole into the darkness of the night air. "Where is Louis?" came the pointed question from the Gaslamper only several feet away. Corantin shook his head and squatted low trying to perform his best toiletting gesture. He was afraid that within close proximity they would recognise the voice of an imposter. Several of the officers around him laughed. "What is wrong with that man? Can he not keep it in? Come. We will push on. Louis can catch up when he is done." There was no invitation in the phrase, no waiting for a reply. The Gaslampers fanned out and continued their search through the dark woodland. Corantin fell into the formation, taking special care to move furthest out on the flank hanging a little behind. The irony was not lost on him as he began the arduous search for himself.

⁂

She could not be sure if it was the sounds of distant shouts outside her window, or the orange glow that pulsed in the night's darkness, perhaps it was the smell of smoke that wafted into the room and reminded her of a different time, but Angelique rose to investigate. She had been lost in confused thoughts. For hours she had sat, replaying every moment with Renard Rouge, trying to work out how the pieces fitted together. She had thought back to her meeting with the Maire and tried to remember what she knew about her uncle. He had drowned, so she had been led to believe. Her father never spoke of his older brother, he seemed a phantom of another lifetime. As she thought about it, she began to see the resemblance with her Papa, the same mannerisms, the same careful placement of words, full of thought and intention. It was difficult to imagine that he was the force behind the violence done to Renard, how could such a man be the brother of her father, his blood coursing through her very veins.

At the window she looked out into the darkness of the night, but it was neither still nor silent. In the distance beyond the stone walls of the compound she could see the enormous fire. It rose like a grotesque pyramid with the silhouette of hundreds of figures surrounding it, their shadows moving in impossible lengths against the stone wall and pavement. As she peered into the flames she could start to recognise the fuel that stoked the inferno. Books. Thousands of books. She could see Gaslampers directing citizens with wheel barrows. They would park them at the perimeter and citizens would take turns to hurl them into the flames. She noticed one man standing on the edge of the bonfire with his violin. It took her attention because he stood there motionless. He was not cheering or shouting or raising his arms in frenzied celebration. He stood morose and defeated. She saw a Gaslamper converse with him and finally he raised the instrument above his head and threw it into the roaring flames. A group of men shuffled down the boulevard with a pianoforte. They had it balanced on several planks and four men at either end slowly moved it towards the blaze. A woman appeared from further down the street and ran towards them. Her shouts and wails could be heard cutting through the roar of the flames and crowd. She threw herself in front of the piano carriers forcing them to momentarily stop. The language of her body pleaded with them. It was cut short by a Gaslamper who swiftly intercepted her, followed by several other officers, all roughly moving the woman and detaining her with iron cuffs. The piano continued in its mournful procession before finally being tilted into the furnace where with splintering timber and exploding wires, it collapsed into its final cremation. The woman, now arrested, stood alone in her resistance. All around her, the crowd seemed ravenous for destruction, searching hungrily for more literature to fuel the inferno. Angelique felt an overwhelming sickness. It started in the base of her stomach and rose to her oesophagus and tasted of bile and corruption. She did not know what books they were, but she could guess. She turned away, no longer able to stand in witness to the event. She was surprised by a firm knock at the door.

"You may enter." She quietly directed. The door slowly opened and the Maire stepped over the threshold. Angelique was immediately taken aback. She had expected Victor, perhaps another guard, but her uncle standing in her doorway took her unpleasantly by surprise and her body subtly reacted accordingly.

"I do apologise, child. I was not expected. I have startled you."

"I am fine, Monsieur. I was watching the fire."

"Ah yes, the *productivity cleanse*. It can be very…spirited. Please call me Oncle. We are strangers no more."

"Oui…Oncle."

"I trust that you have had time to rest… and perhaps a chance to feel a little more comfortable with your surroundings?"

"Oui, Oncle."

"Good. Good. This," the Maire stretched out his arms wide gesturing to the room in which he now stood, "this is not in keeping with my intentions for you. I want to show you something." He revealed a deep green felt coat that had been draped over his shoulders and stretched it out towards Angelique. "Put this on Angelique, I want you to have nice things." Angelique tried to mask her momentary hesitation by finally smiling as she accepted the coat and pulled it over her shoulders. It was indeed a fine coat, a finer coat than Angelique had ever seen in her life. It felt smooth on her neck and arms, the satin lining caressing her skin and she found herself silently admonishing her own enjoyment. "Come," beckoned the Maire as he stepped outside the door and elevated his arm in invitation. Angelique followed him outside, down the corridor and across the courtyard. Each sentry they passed bowed respectfully in deference and Angelique noted the odd sensation she felt each time. She hastened into closer proximity to the Maire as they reached the end of the courtyard.

"Monsieur… Oncle, what is the cleanse you mentioned earlier? The fire."

The Maire paused and turned to his niece. "Sometimes Angelique, for a society to progress, they need to change direction. They need to choose productivity over idleness. The way forward for Paris is to maximise our capabilities, to encourage our citizens to be both productive and rested. This is why we have enforced a curfew, for the safety of the people and for the benefit of rest. Idleness is the devil's pursuit. Have you heard that child? What you witnessed was the cry of the people. They want the city to move forward. They want to be lead into a bright, bold, progressive future and they no longer want to be held back by idle pursuits. By destroying the idle, unproductive tools of the past, they are choosing to move forward and to make this city glorious once again." He let his last words linger in the silence of the courtyard. His eyes were alive with passion and he locked them with hers, making certain that she caught hold of the fire that he felt within. "I apologise child, I get swept away at times. Come." They proceeded to climb the stairs past the office chambers where they had met the previous day and followed the long corridor to its natural end where two elaborate grand doors stood like ornamental guards preventing access to the throne room. The Maire smiled and opened the doors.

The grandeur within the parlour before her took Angelique completely by surprise. Within the bluestone industrial exterior of the compound lay this extravagant chamber of opulence. The walls were plastered and decorated with beautiful ornate wallpaper, which ran down to marble floor tiles where grey rivers and veins rans through the glossy white. Chandeliers dropped from the ceiling with racks upon racks of candles that threw light into every corner of the room. Lush velvet couches sat in the centre, surrounding a small elaborate table. Her eyes were drawn into the exquisite minutiae, from golden roped tassels and bold, garish cushions to the ornate carvings on the chaise lounge. The Maire stood aside allowing his niece to drink in the surroundings, for her eyes to feed on all that money and power could buy. It truly was magnificent and a small grin crept across his face, softening his stern demeanour. She loved it. He knew.

"Do you like it?"

"Oui, Oncle." Angelique spoke softly and carefully, giving nothing away.

"This is my drawing room. One of many rooms of course. This is where I live," he paused for a moment letting every word plumb the depths of her comprehension. He slowly walked over to the chaise lounge and sat facing Angelique before gently patting the seat beside him in offering. Angelique did not feel she was in a position to refuse and so made her way across the room and sat beside her uncle. He sat poised for a moment as if he was trying to pull his words out of the air. "Angelique, this is also where you could live. All of you. What do you think of that?"

"All of us?" Angelique was instantly confused and shifted her weight on the cushion. She still was not sure how much her uncle knew, nor if she could trust him. She did not offer any more information.

"Your brother of course," he offered. *So he did know about Phillipe.* He carefully shifted in his seat so he could look Angelique in the eyes. He gently took her hands again choosing his words as though they were crystal glasses perched upon the highest shelf. "Angelique, what would you say if I told you that I could bring your father *here* to be with you also?"

A single tear ran down her face. "You could do that?"

"It has already begun."

CHAPTER 14
BLOODLINES

It was ten past midnight before he finally made the decision. The boy was understandably upset, but the agreement was clear. The two had sat in near silence awaiting the return of the Aigle, fearing any sound could give them away. The Gaslampers had been known to listen to the ground with wooden stethoscopes that had been confiscated from the Necker-Enfants Malades Hospital. He had seen them do this with his own eyes, leaning low to the ground with the device to their ears. "Come lad. He will catch us up." The old man struck a match, picked up the leather wrapped lux periscope and magnification goggles that the Aigle had left behind with his clothing and a discreet blade that he had left with his own. He took the remaining clothing and stuffed it tightly into a small crevice in the rock wall before covering it with nearby stones. He knew too well that if the clothing was detected, their ruse would be over. The bodies were more difficult to hide. He dragged both of them into the darkest corner of the chamber in the hope that first light might not penetrate that far.

Phillipe found it difficult to stifle his emotions. The knot in his stomach had grown by the minute, until his time piece finally clocked over the midnight hour. He felt like he might vomit. Something bad must have happened. It must have. Everything inside him wanted to stay. Wanted to give his Papa just a few more minutes, perhaps even venture a little into the woods in the chance that Phillipe could help him in a time of need. But what could he do? He watched the Cerf drag the bodies across the chamber and lean them against the wall. He imagined one of them - lifeless and silent - was Corantin and he shuddered.

"Get up son. We need to move on." The directive was clear and the voice was urgent. Phillipe slowly rose, although he felt his shaking legs may not carry him. They did. Step by step he followed the Cerf into the darkness, back towards the city, away from his Papa. His eyes had partially adjusted to the darkness over the hours and he could make out the occasional support beam holding up the structure and the packed earth as he passed them. He trudged on into the darkness for what felt like hours, the silhouetted figure of the Cerf pushing forward several feet in front. He suddenly stopped. Silently and swiftly, the old man moved back to Phillipe and gestured for silence with a finger on his lips. He pushed Phillipe down low with his back to the tunnel wall and crouched into the same position on the opposite side. They waited. Sure enough, a figure silently moved towards them the way they had come. It was a Gaslamper. Phillipe could make out the shape of the leather coat in the darkness. He held his breath as the figure was almost upon them. As the figure passed, the old man launched to his feet like a striking snake, pulling the blade from his boot to their pursuer's throat.

"It's me." Came the strained voice, the steel blade pressing hard against his vocal chords. "It's Corantin." The Cerf sheathed his blade and turned his friend to face him.

"It's dangerous to sneak up on someone," the old man replied with a grin. Phillipe threw his arms around his father for the second time that day. He had now lost him twice and had no intention of the pattern continuing.

"I'm fine, son. I'm fine." His voice was still a whisper. "I'm sorry it took so long. I had hoped they'd go on without me but they insisted I continue with them. I figured I would keep a wide distance and sneak back as soon as I could. It just took a lot longer than I hoped, one of the younger Gaslampers kept wanting a conversation. But they are far away now. We will be safe for a time."

"I'm glad you made it back old friend." It was a rare moment of sentiment from the old man.

"As am I. Come. We need to press on if we are to be back in the city any time soon."

"Oh and I picked these up for you also." The Cerf reached into his pocket and pulled out the small leather wrapped cube and the goggles and handed them to the Aigle. Corantin placed the goggles in his pocket and turned to Phillipe handing him the small bundle of leather.

"I want you to take care of this Phillipe. If anything should happen to me you are to use it as you know you should. In time I will build two more." The boy carefully placed the object in his pocket understanding the full weight of the trust placed in him.

The walk felt infinitely easier to Phillipe all of a sudden. The disappearance of his stomach knot had brought with it an entirely new disposition, he felt buoyant and hopeful and at times walked in front of the others to demonstrate his new found courage. The news that the Gaslampers were searching far into the woods made him feel much safer and also resulted in quiet conversation which proved a welcome relief.

"What do you know of this Maire?" Corantin finally asked the Cerf.

"Very little in actuality. Few people do. You likely know as much as I do. But he came after the drought. He came after Gris Loup and almost as soon as he rose to power he disappeared behind the stone curtain of the compound. The Hospital Dr la Selpetriere. Since then it has been the Gaslampers that do his work and those infernal dogs of theirs. The wolves. Some say that he is doing the work of Gris Loup. Some say. I don't know. These are dangerous times." The old man fell silent despite having more to say. He had thought again about his granddaughter in that place. He knew about the persuasive techniques, about the torture. He knew about it all too well.

⚜

If she was compromised before, she now felt utterly torn. She needed more time. That is what she told her uncle, but truth be told, her mind was made up that instant, she just needed more time to convince herself of that fact. Angelique returned to her quarters; wandering as if in a daze with no recollection of her return journey. There were no guards, there were no watching eyes, she now felt trusted. The only thing waiting for her when she returned to the same spartan room was a note. It sat again on the small wooden table and it caught her eye instantly. The embers of a previously raging fire glowed quietly outside her window. It had been a tumultuous evening. She had seen Renard Rouge battered beyond recognition, she had decided that she would be the instrument of escape and swallowed the evidence of it, she had seen a frenzy of citizens burning books and she had been told that he could bring her father to her. *He* had the power to unite them once again. She had felt a great balloon of certainty that had swelled within her puncture and deflate. She felt a captive once again. She had now seen the possibility of what had seemed impossible, seeing her father once again. What could she conceivably do? And now there was another note. She felt a tight knot form beneath her diaphragm and it made her breathing conscious and laboured. Trying to calm her shaking hands, she sat at the table and read the note.

1/C3

> *"His victory fades daily, standing hopeful.*
> *Paris lives, Gaslampers quickly lose with help.*
> *Finally having occupiers out."*

It was clever. Very clever. Angelique saw the genius in the rambling, incoherent sentiments of a captive. If ever the letter was intercepted, there was nothing there but the delirious delusions of a rebel. She took her pencil and circled the first letter of each word. HVFDSH. PLGQLWH. FHOO. She counted each letter back three steps and wrote the words out beneath. ESCAPE. MIDNITE. CELL. In that moment, her breathing had almost stopped. It had come to this. She tore the note into tiny pieces and began to place them into her mouth. She felt a deep fatigue wash over her body as she grasped at the choices before her. This was her chance to escape. To find Phillipe somehow. But what if Phillipe was brought to her? What if she could be united with her Papa again? She felt as though she bore the burden of a decision that was far beyond her capability, beyond her strength. But as she listened to the still, silent voice of her conscience, she knew. She understood in that instant that while there was hope that Phillipe and her father would be brought there, she could never leave. As she swallowed the last shred of paper, she slowly rose. She did not know the time, but feared by the darkness that now consumed her solitary room that it may well be near midnight. She owed Renard and Victor an explanation, she knew that at least.

Without another thought, she left the room. Although inwardly she felt a confinement within the prison walls she had never completely understood before, outwardly she was aware she was a valued guest and as such did not fear watchful eyes of which there were none. She made her way out into the darkness of the corridor and down the spiral stairs once again. On the lowest basement floor, she silently crept down the darkest passageway, past the cells where an occasional cough or shuffle would emanate. In the distance she could make out the shape of a Gaslamper standing outside Renard Rouge's cell. As she neared she was both relieved and anxious to make out the face of Victor. He turned to her smiling for the first time.

"You came, mademoiselle."

"Oui. But there is something I must tell you." She waited until she was only inches away as her words would need to be whispered. "I can not join you." She now heard movement in the cell as Renard Rouge moved to the cell door window, having overheard her fellow captive's declaration.

"What do you mean?" Came Renard's voice, still gravelly from in the cell. Her eyes peered at Angelique through the cell door, now eying her up and down.

"I'm sorry. I will help in anyway that I can. But I can not leave here at the moment."

"But you must leave. You are in danger here. What about your brother?" Renard could not believe what she was hearing.

"It is because of my brother. And my Papa. He will bring them both here. He said he would and I can't risk leaving."

"What do you mean he will bring them both here? Why would he? Angelique you can not trust this murderer."

"Perhaps you are right, but I can not take the chance."

"Why should you trust the Maire?" Renard's voice was rising to a crescendo of exasperation.

"Because he is my uncle."

A silence fell upon the trio. Renard's eyes were wide in disbelief until the moment when she understood that it was true. She looked to the ground of her cell no longer able to look Angelique in the face.

"Very well then." Victor finally found his voice. He had been silent in this transaction, deferring to his superior in the cell to change the girl's mind. But now he understood, as did his superior that it was useless. As long as she did not interfere within the next thirty minutes they would be beyond the gate. Victor passed one of the uniforms he held under his arm through the cell door window. "We will leave in thirty minutes if you change your mind. If you do not then I will return this uniform to the storehouse on the way." He could not leave a uniform hidden lest it would be discovered before their plan had been fully enacted. It was simple, though risky and there would be no second chances. Once in the courtyard they would be able to don their gas masks and all would be clear, but getting through the first checkpoint unmasked was his only concern. He had rummaged through the barber's rubbish in the city and extracted hair that he thought would be a reasonable match, especially in the dark. The most obvious way to turn two girls into boys would be with beards. Now there would only be one and the risk would be halved.

Angelique was uncertain what to say to Renard and stood in silence waiting for the words to come. But they did not. Renard Rouge had reclined into the shadows, and she felt that the only thing left to do was to leave. Victor mustered a small apologetic smile to her as she finally nodded to him and turned.

"Wait." Renard's hoarse voice stopped Angelique in her tracks. "There is one other thing." Angelique moved towards the prison door window once again, squinting into the shadows. "I have written you a note..." Her voice paused, trailing another idea as if there was more she wanted to say but could not find the words. "You are to read it only when you leave the compound. Promise me you will only read it when you are safe from the compound." The white paper of the letter was thrust through the gap in the bars of the door window.

"I promise." She reached out and took the note, carefully placing it in the inside pocket of her coat. "I'm sorry Renard," she blurted, turned on her heels and walked back down the dark passage. The only sounds she could hear were the clip of her shoes on the stone and the pounding of her heart and head. It was done. She had crossed the Rubicon. Oblivious to her journey, her legs carried her up the steep stairwell out of the darkness, into the relative light of the administration corridor. Perhaps there was still time. She still had thirty minutes before they would leave. Surely if she spoke to her uncle again and asked him about his plan, about what he knew and what he was going to do, then she would be certain. She would be able to see it in the expression on his face, in the movement of his hands, in the confidence in his voice, she would see the truth. The notion of confronting the Maire with her honest need for confirmation seemed both proper and appropriate. The further she travelled towards his quarters, the more certain she became. And yet, she began to shake with the weight of her doubts and felt her face redden with anxiety at the prospect of being wrong. She was so consumed in her thoughts that she did not realise the moment when she rounded the corner on the eastern wing corridor and collided violently with a gentleman travelling in the opposite direction. She was knocked to the ground.

He was an older gentleman, distinguished in his refined long suit jacket and tailored trousers. The tie that held his long grey hair at the nape of his neck had broken in the collision and his hair fell loosely about his face. A concerned face at that, for it was not every day that a gentleman would knock a young girl off her feet during the course of his perambulation. He was shocked and a little shaken himself, but still on his feet and though his heart had skipped a beat and now thumped in his chest, the fact remained that he was still standing. He reached out his hand in earnest apology to the young child.

"Mademoiselle. Excusez-moi. I am deeply sorry. I was not looking where I was going... Are you alright?"

"Oui, Monsieur. I think so." She was dazed and could taste the metallic sting of blood on her tongue but she was alright. She tried to stand and shook a little on her legs.

"Take my arm, mademoiselle. Please, come and sit." The gentleman led her further down the corridor to a hardwood bench against the stone wall and gently set her down propping her against himself as he sat beside her. "Are you sure you are alright? How many fingers am I holding up."

Angelique began to smile, for it was clear that he was not holding up any fingers. "None Monsieur. It is my belief you are trying to trick me."

"Well spotted young lady, well spotted. I am Lord Gossard. I am afraid I am like a freight wagon when I am walking. Truth be told, I am not used to seeing young ladies in the midst of these chambers. I will be more careful in the future. Tell me where were you heading in such a hurry, mademoiselle?"

"I was... nothing, Monsieur."

"Albert. Call me Albert, child."

"I'm not sure, Albert. It has been a difficult day."

Lord Gossard nodded thoughtfully. He knew enough to understand where a conversation was safest to end. "Here is what I shall do. I will escort you to wherever you need to get to safely. Then I shall take my leave. But if I can help you in any way, large or small, you tell one of the officers that you need to see Albert Gossard and they shall fetch me." He smiled and scratched his nose. "Come to think of it they won't know who Albert Gossard is, but you tell them that you are the friend of Lord Gossard and they will jolly well do what you tell them." He smiled. Angelique smiled also. Lord Gossard helped her slowly to her feet.

"If you would return me to my room please Albert." Just as her journey had lost its momentum, so had her quest for an immediate answer. She had suddenly lost the desire to see her uncle and was no longer certain of her ability to see the truth in him. She would not leave. She would simply trust her own instincts and wait. Lord Gossard gently escorted her back down the corridor towards her quarters. Gentility was his quality. On the surface he appeared senile and ornamental, he was often the running joke around the compound administration, a relic from a political landscape of long ago. But he had lived through much successive power, he saw everything. He said little and understood much. This was his true quality. He delivered Angelique to her door and bowed once more in final apology. Satisfied that she was now safe and well, he continued on, his mind a deep labyrinth of questions.

Angelique closed her door and walked over to the window, gazing out onto the moonlit courtyard. At the high stone walls on the compound perimeter, two Gaslampers stood at the entrance. They stood as sentries guarding the arched iron gate securing the courtyard. Occasionally an officer would move across the court-yard as they changed guards and exchanged messages and orders but all was still and quiet. Officers in the courtyard could often be seen pulling on their gas masks as they left the compound through the front gates after a rudimentary inspection by the sentries. There was a strict policy of masks on outside and masks off inside that Angelique had observed. She continued to wait anxiously, watching every movement through the window in anticipation, but they did not come. She suddenly feared the worst and imagined Renard, her beard in tatters being roughly detained by the guards and beaten. Again. She listened for shouts in the night air, listening for any evidence of detection, but she heard none. Then, she saw.

Two officers, much smaller than any she had seen previously made their way across the courtyard. It was difficult to tell in the moonlight, but she caught a glimpse of the beard and knew. Clear of the interior compound checks, they pulled on their gas masks ready for the final checkpoint. They confidently strode across the yard and stopped at the iron gates by the order of the sentries. Angelique felt her heart in her throat and realised she had not breathed for some time. They were paused at the gates too long. There was something wrong. For a time they were locked in conversation, one sentry shouted to another guard. All the while, the two imposters stood boldly and impossibly calm. The first sentry moved and Angelique felt like she might scream. He heaved at the iron gate and finally opened it for his fellow officers. It was then, as bold as brass that Victor and Renard Rouge marched out into the freedom of Paris.

⁂

The dawn of half-light in the city of Paris was as beautiful as it was mysterious. Like a city locked beneath a cloud, grey light would drift across the boulevards as the sun rose on the distant pastures and fields. There it would linger, casting feeble light across the buildings throughout the day, like a lantern whose canvas wick fluttered in the moments before it was extinguished. It was as though a shadowed fog crept across the city, shielding the dwellers within from a sunlight that would never rise. It was in this shadowed world that the small grate on the Boulevard de La Gare shifted in the shadows of the surrounding buildings, and three figures cautiously climbed out into the street before closing the grate and scrambling into the relative safety of the laneway. No one saw them. At least as much as they could ascertain, for their caution was great and their movement was fast. In a city full of eyes, they would accept visibility, but not detection. Corantin noted a grocer further down the street setting up his wares in an old wooden cart, but he seemed far too occupied with his task at hand to look beyond the great pile of aubergine balanced in the cart to any movement further down the boulevard. Even if they had been sighted climbing out of the sewers, it was not unusual to see Gaslamper patrols emerging from the most unusual of locations. What was unusual on this occasion was the boy that they accompanied. Corantin was all too aware that after the fire in Notre Dame the previous day and rumours of prisoners flying out of the city like birds into the forests beyond, citizens would be on high alert and keenly observing anything unusual. In the safety of the laneway, all three looked out onto the boulevard, eyes searching for any unusual observances. Very few people were out at this early hour and with the street mostly empty and quiet, Corantin and Enzo finally concluded that they were undetected and therefore safe. For now.

Corantin reached out his hand to the Cerf who immediately understood. He reached into his pocket and withdrew the telescopic goggles and placed them into the Aigle's hand. From the edge of the lane, they could see the compound in the distance. Corantin lifted his gas mask and pulled the goggles over his eyes focusing on the great stone wall that lined the street. It looked like there were only two sentries standing beyond the great iron gate and beyond that two more at the entrance to the compound building itself. He had no doubt there would be many more in the adjacent garrison, but as long as they did not draw any alarm or unnecessary attention, they could hopefully get into the building with minimal fuss. He would need to keep a close eye on the movement of the guards throughout the day and would need something up his sleeve if the situation were to turn sour. He took the goggles off and handed them back to Enzo.

"Enzo, I want you to stay here for a few hours and try to keep an eye on the movement of the guards. I will take Phillipe with me for now. We should be back before nightfall. If things go wrong, we will need a last resort. Try to stay out of sight, my friend."

"Where are you going?"

"To build a last resort." With that he patted his old companion on the back, gestured to Phillipe to follow him, and they both slipped into the shadows of the buildings. He had lost his son once and had no intention of losing him again. To build his device he would require some parts that had been stored many years ago. He was no longer certain they would still be there and be in good working order, but he had no choice. Phillipe followed his father beneath the shadows of the buildings into the cover of the trees surrounding the Place d' Italie. They walked calmly and purposefully. He was careful to keep a little distance to minimise any suspicion that might be aroused in seeing a young boy in the custody of a Gaslamper, but not so much distance that he would lose him altogether. They traveled along the Boulevard St Jaques towards the old Observatory. Corantin strode confidently, his masked head scanning the streets, keeping the order under his watchful eye. Most people kept a safe distance from the Gaslampers at all times, this he knew. Phillipe also kept a nervous eye on the streets and laneways they passed. The only thing unusual about the Gaslamper before him was the absence of a wolf. He had not yet seen a patrol without one, and he felt uncomfortable that other's suspicions may be aroused. Greater than this though, was the fear of other patrols. It was risky and they both knew it. But as they finally turned the corner to the Boulevard Arago and slipped down a narrow lane beside the observatory, both breathed a sigh of relief, for they had somehow made the journey undetected.

The Observatory itself was an imposing sandstone building both opulent and grand. A high wrought iron fence marked the perimeter of the grounds and gave the structure a formidable and impregnable presence. Guard houses stood at intervals around the fence line and officers stood at the doors to each. This structure that had once been the scientific wonder of Paris was now closed to the public. It was now the sole property of the government and another symbol of its commitment to scientific progress. This now meant one thing to Corantin. Access would be both difficult and dangerous, for in the bowels of this complex, hidden from the knowledge of all but a few, rested a small stone room. It was in that silent room in decades past that the Aigle had made his own scientific progressions.

Corantin crouched low in the laneway and gestured for Phillipe to come closer. He carefully lifted his mask so that his words would be clear and understood. "I need you to do something for me, Phillipe." His voice was careful and even. "Three blocks from here past the Cemetery Du Sud, you will find the stables of Montparnasse." Phillipe nodded, he knew them well back in the old city. "I need a horse's harness. But listen carefully. I need the loin strap and breeching, the belly band and the tug, but not the shaft. Leave the shaft."

"What about you?" Came the boy's cautious question.

"When you return, I will be standing right there." He pointed to a guardhouse on the eastern side of the iron fence where a Gaslamper stood in the sandstone entry. Phillipe looked to his father in genuine concern, who gave a subtle wink in response, pulled down his gas mask and rose to his feet. As Phillipe scurried along the shadow of the building, he could see his father making his way towards the guardhouse across the street. He could feel his heart in his throat once again.

The journey to the stables was non-eventful. As Phillipe made his way through the cemetery he was drawn to the headstones and found himself stopping more than once to read the inscriptions and reflect. There was not a name that he recognised. He had spent much time in this very cemetery in the old world and knew some of the headstones and layout intimately. But it felt so very different. The shadows were darker and longer and despite the emptiness of the grounds he felt the ever watchful presence of something. He moved as quickly as he could through the grounds and could not shake the sensation that he was being observed. He also could not shake the realisation that the lost lives that populated the soil on which he scurried were not lives from his home city, but an alien city, a world where he felt utterly lost. He was relieved when he could finally smell the pungent stench of fresh manure and hay. It was a familiar smell and brought unexpected comfort. He made his way past the timber fences until he came upon the stone coach houses at the perimeter of the property. It was now mid-morning and the stables were bustling with activity. Carriages were being cleaned as horses were being fitted with harnesses and sliding shafts. Muckrakers shovelled manure into barrows and wheeled them to the next location of deployment. Phillipe had learned back in the old world that confidence was a key that could open any door in the city and so he arrived with purpose. He offered the farrier a wink and "bonjour" as he strode past, the farrier barely raising an eye let alone suspicion. His attire was already that of the working class, there was in fact no location better suited to his appearance than the livery stables. He strode straight up to the tall blue double doors of the carriage houses so confidently that a stablehand nearby rushed up and opened the doors for him, a courtesy that would befall a fellow worker. "Merci." Inside, Phillipe knew exactly what he was after. He found the loin strap and breeching hanging on a large iron nail and on another wall, the belly band and the tug. He gathered the leather and slung it over his shoulder before walking boldly back through the double doors into the morning half-light. He walked past the carriages and rounded the corner.

"Hey!" A shout came from behind him. He froze. "Boy." He slowly turned to see an older strapper whose eye he had caught despite his bold facade. "You can't take that harness." Phillipe was speechless. "You don't have the shafts. Go and get the shafts." The strapper then proceeded to mumble to himself about the difficulty of getting good help. Phillipe swallowed allowing his heart to drop out of his throat and obediently returned to the stable to collect the shafts as instructed. He made a point on his return journey to walk past the strapper with an apologetic look which was met with a nod from his superior. Phillipe promptly rounded the corner until he was out of sight and dropped the shafts behind the stone stables. With the straps still over his shoulder his made his way swiftly back the way he had came.

He arrived back in the laneway within the hour and looked across at the guardhouse from the shadows. A Gaslamper stood on guard in the doorway and a terrifying thought occurred to Phillipe. It was difficult to tell at this distance, but it was possible that the Gaslamper in the doorway was his father. It was equally possible that it was not. The only way for him to know in all certainty was to get closer, however this brought with it a clear and present risk of detection. He really had no choice. He lowered himself closer to the ground and set off traversing from one tree in the distance to another. Each time he would pause in the shadow until he was confident that the Gaslamper had not seen him and he set off again, inching closer and closer.

Corantin stood in the doorway of the guardhouse. He had been waiting for Phillipe for the best part of an hour when he finally saw him arrive at the corner of the building. Even through the green glass lens of his face mask he could see the boy and the horse's tack he had draped over his shoulder. What he could not understand was what on earth his son was doing. In the distance the lad appeared to crouch low and shuffle along like a seawater crab to the first tree between them. Did he not realise that he was visible to all of Paris? Corantin was growing impatient, he only had three hours until the next guard would be there to relieve him and at the rate Phillipe was going, he would still be bouncing back and forth until the changing of the guard. He decided he would try and get the boy's attention. He slowly raised his arm and pointed at the boy hoping not to draw too much attention from others in the street.

Phillipe had been seen. Good heavens, the Gaslamper had seen him. Phillipe was less certain than ever that it was Corantin as the officer raised his arm and pointed, clearly implying he wanted Phillipe to identify himself. He stood behind the tree frozen with panic. It was over. He was found. But then...nothing. There was no shout and no alarms. Perhaps the guard had not seen him after all, perhaps he was just stretching. Phillipe decided he would try and get closer again to establish once and for all if it was Corantin who had not yet seen him.

Corantin watched in bewilderment as Phillipe again raised himself up from behind the tree and shuffled across to the next hedge about fifteen feet away. It was as if the boy thought he was invisible to the ever watchful eyes of Paris, he could be lighting bamboo firecrackers and draw less attention. He waited for a moment after his son disappeared behind the nearby hedge to see if he would surface again. Finally realising Phillipe clearly did not know it was him, he lifted his mask above his mouth and hissed towards the hedge. "It's me...Corantin." It was a calculated risk and paid dividends. Only a moment later, the lad's head appeared above the hedge and satisfied that it was indeed his Papa, he made one last shuffle into the guard house. "What were you doing?" Corantin was grateful that the gas mask hid his smile, but the laughter in his voice betrayed him.

"I thought you were a Gaslamper. At least, I couldn't be sure."

"But I pointed at you!"

"I thought you were stretching."

Corantin ruffled his son's hair. He had done well. Every piece of the harness he had requested was draped over his son's shoulder. "We have three hours till we are discovered. We must hurry." Phillipe followed his father down a timber ladder to the stone floor below. He had wondered what had happened to the guard on duty and had assumed that Corantin had arrived in his uniform and relieved him. But as he stepped onto the stone floor he saw the officer bound and gagged leaning against a wall. His head was lolling to the side as he moved in and out of consciousness.

"What happened, Papa?"

"I tried to relieve him, but he wouldn't have it. He wanted identification I didn't have. He'll be quiet enough until we are done. It's the next guard I'm more concerned about. Come." Phillipe followed Corantin down a narrow stone passage past the first storage room. The passage was only several feet long and appeared to lead to a dead end. It was clearly a void that had been used to store several old wooden crates and rope, all of which was covered in dust and cobwebs from seasons of dormancy. With little effort, Corantin pulled the crates away from the wall revealing a small wooden door behind. It had a small latch and clasp that had been padlocked closed.

"It is locked." Phillipe proclaimed, stating the obvious.

"I have a key." Corantin reached into the pocket of his coat and suddenly froze realising in that moment that it was no longer his coat that he was wearing. *Of all the costly mistakes.* Phillipe crouched low and began to unlace his boots. He may not have the skills to approach the gatehouse undetected but he sure could pick a lock. Inside his boot he pulled out his adjustable key. He had been keeping it in his boot of late for fear that he would lose it in his pocket and had even gone so far as to dig out a small hollow in the boot sole so the implement would sit comfortably under his foot. He stepped past his father and began to work on the lock, making slight adjustments as he listened to the sounds of movement within the mechanism. The final 'click' unlatched the lock and he pulled it off grinning widely up to his Papa. Corantin shook his head in wonder. *Genius.* Both father and son locked eyes in that moment, sharing an understanding. It was only a brief moment, but in it they both saw each other and themselves. Corantin opened the door and, crouching low, entered the hidden stone chamber with Phillipe behind him.

The room was far larger than Phillipe had anticipated and was filled with pieces of metal and half finished engines that overhung wooden racks and shelves. Decades of dust lay as a thick film covering the room and its contents. Everywhere Phillipe looked, objects caught his eye. Bottles of liquid with crude paper labels, metal drums of various fluids, valves, pipes and glassware, a vast palette of coppers and greys that sent waves of excitement into the boy's imagination. At one end, numerous instruments of science were strewn recklessly over a large wooden work bench.

"What is this?" Phillipe could barely get the words out.

"This, my boy, is my laboratory. At least it was. Twenty years ago. Back in those days, one of the calibrators worked as a guard here at the observatory and granted me access every time he was on shift." Corantin began to fossick behind one of the shelves, moving canisters and half-full drums. "It should be here. Somewhere. Ahh." His body was now half inside the timber racks before he pulled out a small metal tank. It looked like the portable oxygen concentrators that Phillipe had heard of being used at the hospital in Paris, but had the discolour of age and disuse.

"Oxygen?" Phillipe asked. Corantin shook his head, having found the first ingredient, he was now searching for the second among the drums of fluid on the floor.

"Hydrogen." He finally replied. "It is pressurised hydrogen."

"What else are you looking for?"

"Petroleum."

"Petroleum?" Phillipe had never heard of it.

"I used to get it from the kerosene factory out of the city. It's a clear brown colour. You can usually smell it... This one." He lifted the drum and offered it to Phillipe with an open lid. He immediately recoiled at the smell. Corantin took another similar tank and using a small metal funnel, filled the tank with petroleum. For the next hour he tinkered with pipes and hoses, adding a valve here and connectors there. Phillipe watched in awe as the scientist who in a previous life had been a typesetter in a print factory, built a structure impossibly beautiful. He finally took the straps that Phillipe had painstakingly borrowed earlier that morning and fastened them to the tanks as two shoulder straps and a chest harness. He carefully lifted the small structure onto his back and fastened the straps. He took the long pipe that ran down the length of his arm. There were two valves on the tanks that he had already turned on and one other he had fastened on the pipe at his wrist.

"What is it?" Phillipe could barely contain his excitement.

"It is a flame sprayer. If need be, I will become a human dragon. The high pressure hydrogen will mix with the petroleum down this hose and pipe. Watch." He faced a bare stone wall at the rear of the room and slowly turned the valve at his wrist, then taking a phosphorous match from his coat on the floor, he struck it and placed the small flame in front of the arm pipe. Phillipe recoiled as the fire exploded against the back wall, feeling the intense heat against his skin. Corantin immediately turned off the valve and the fire died. He looked cautiously at his wide eyed son. "We must be careful Phillipe, this device is like a stick of dynamite. Turn the valves off at the tanks." Phillipe did as instructed. Then helped his father put his coat on over the top, carefully feeding the metal arm pipe down the sleeve. When dressed it was completely hidden. *So, they would rescue the princess after all,* thought Phillipe. The boy, the inventor and the dragon.

CHAPTER 15
THE BOY, THE INVENTOR AND THE DRAGON

It was in the final moments of half-light when Corantin and Phillipe arrived back to the shadowed laneway overlooking the compound across the street. The Cerf was crouched in the shadows waiting silently for his fellow conspirators to arrive, the telescopic goggles still perched on his head.

"Welcome back. The guards have changed twice since you left and the next guards should not arrive for two hours. Otherwise, nothing to report. How did you go?" The Cerf shifted from his crouched position in an attempt to make his discomfort less obvious. Phillipe and Corantin looked to each other and grinned.

"We have our last resort," Corantin offered. "It breathes fire." He pulled his coat back to reveal the tanks underneath. The Cerf rose from the ground and looked underneath the Aigle's leather coat, inspecting his work. A wide grin grew across his face. It was straight out of a Jules Verne novel, all valves, metal and piping. As the sun finally disappeared behind the eastern buildings all fell silent in understanding. "It is time," Corantin finally said to no one in particular. "If you can turn the valves on the tanks to the right Enzo?" The Cerf reached his hand under the coat to follow the instruction. Corantin then went through the plan one last time so that there would be no confusion once through the gates. When they were through the first guard post they would remove their gas masks, hopefully unrecognisable in the darkness. Their captive, Phillipe, would hopefully be their ticket of entry into the compound itself, but once inside they had only a short time to get to Angelique and Renard Rouge. They would then need to seperate for efficiency and only if the situation got out of control would Corantin begin flame spraying. There was much unknown and Phillipe felt as though he might be sick, but as he looked up at the firmness in the resolution of the Cerf and the Aigle he breathed deeply and stepped out of the laneway showing his readiness. In a moment, the others were at either side where they proceeded to march him up to the first compound gatehouse.

Two guards stood adjacent to one another in Sentry boxes in front of the first iron gates. The first guard stepped out of the box seeing the Gaslampers with the boy approaching. "Halt," he directed raising his hand in clear gesture. "What do we have here?"

"We have apprehended the boy," Corantin replied firmly.

"Wait here and I will get you an escort."

"No, we have direct orders from the inspector to take him straight to the Maire," Corantin responded shaking his head. A second guard in the adjacent box saw the scene unfolding and strode over to offer his assistance.

"What seems to be the problem, officers?"

"This guard says he has orders to take the boy directly to the Maire," the first officer offered uncertainly.

"The boy escaped us at Notre Dame and was apprehended by us in the city. The Inspector gave explicit orders that he be delivered by *us* directly to the Maire. Is there a problem? What is your name, officer?" Corantin's voice was firm and authoritative. The two officers looked at one another for a brief moment in silence, before the second nodded to the first. They both proceeded to lift the heavy iron latch that was across the gates and heaved them open to allow passage. The three walked into the courtyard without incident. The second guardhouse would be a different story. Corantin and Enzo removed their gas masks as was expected within the compound and hoped that the darkness would be a sufficient disguise. Two lanterns hovered in the distance marking the next checkpoint. Phillipe could feel his heart pounding in his chest so loudly that he was sure Angelique must hear it. They arrived at the next guardhouse as both sentries stepped into the lantern light blocking entry to the next gate. One of the guards lifted the lantern off the hook and held it out so that he could see the approachers more clearly.

"Halt, who goes there?"

"We have apprehended the boy the Maire has been searching for. We have instructions from the Inspector to take him directly to the Maire." Corantin then stood silently awaiting reply. The guard lifted the lantern closer to their faces, from the Aigle to the Cerf. He paused on the Cerf.

"Hey, don't I know you?"

"I have a face like every other officer in the city. It is just a face," the Cerf replied calmly. The guard was not satisfied.

"I want to see your papers, officers. Get out your papers."

Corantin looked across to his old comrade, his hand slowly raising the clip on his revolver holster. He was interrupted by a third guard that stepped out of the compound.

"What is the problem, officers?" the new guard enquired.

"These officers have been asked to provide their paperwork for identification."

"There is no need. They have the boy. They have orders to bring him in, let them. If the order has come from the Maire then who are we to question it?" The guard opened the gate, gesturing that the other guards should return to their sentry boxes. The boy, his two protectors and the silent, secret dragon walked through the final gate into the compound followed by the third guard.

"Wait," he called to them once they were clear and inside. "*You* can take the boy to the Maire," he declared pointing to Corantin, "but *you* will come with me." He looked sharply at the Cerf. "There is no need for both of you to report and we are short of an officer at the southern entrance." The Cerf looked at Corantin. He had no choice. It would now mean that they were one man down and escape would have to be through the southern gate. Corantin nodded in understanding. He put his hand on Phillipe's back and ushered him into the compound doorway as the two officers disappeared towards the south.

They stepped into the darkness of the first stone corridor. A single lantern lit the stairwell at the southern extremity and the only sound they could hear amidst the eerie silence of the passage was the clip of their own footsteps. Corantin ushered Phillipe towards the stairwell. Time was of the essence and, provided they were not interrupted by Gaslampers, they had a fighting chance. He could only guess where prisoners would be held.

Down.

They began to descend the stairwell, spiralling down into the bowels of the compound, every step bringing terror into the heart of the Typesetter, who was imagining the trauma that must have befallen his daughter in this forsaken place. The lowest floor was again empty. The only sounds were the coughs and whimpers of the incarcerated behind the heavy wooden doors. Corantin and Phillipe ran to every door, sliding the small door windows and whispering into the darkness "Angelique?" But there were no replies and finally at the end of the passage they were left with only the company of one another. "She is not here?" Corantin resigned. "Perhaps there is another floor of prisoners." The two advanced back the way they had came and began to ascend the stairs.

Angelique could not sleep. She had not yet agreed to the quarters and conditions offered by her uncle. She had again been dreaming of the fox surrounded by wolves . She was no longer afraid *for* the fox but afraid *of* the fox. She found herself running into the woods before the wolves attacked, already aware of their ignominious end. She would hear the sounds of soft feet in the brush behind her, gaining on her, and she knew that they were the same soft feet that had devoured the pack and she awoke. She thought of Lord Gossard. Albert. It was a brief encounter, but an honest one. He had offered his assistance and perhaps it was he whom she needed to confide in. Perhaps he understood her uncle better than she, and could offer counsel and advice. She had connected with him by chance the previous evening and perchance would run into him again if she went for a short stroll outside her room. She rose from her bed, dressed in her trousers and jacket, and stepped out into the corridor. There were no sounds. She made her way to the stairwell at the southern end, the very same that took her to Lord Gossard previously, but another sound stole her attention. It was faint, but audible. The sound of ascending footsteps too irregular to be the movement of government officers echoed from below. She cautiously began to descend towards the sound.

It was Phillipe that she first saw ascend the stairs beneath her. She stood, frozen and breathless as he continued to climb, oblivious to the silent apparition hovering above. She could find neither words nor sound. But a wave of overwhelming emotion swelled within her and her breath shook as she drew it in. "Phillipe!" The word was gasped rather then spoken and he looked up in that moment and saw her. He ran to her so quickly and embraced his sister that she did not immediately notice the officer by his side, his guard and his protector. It was not until the officer stood beside them and reached his arms around that she looked up into the face of her Papa. She wept whole heartedly and bitterly. All of her fear, trepidation and confusion purged itself in her sobs and she reached up and put her arms around Corantin's neck. His relief was palpable and his arms shook a little as he held his children once again. But the risk was great and so he hardened himself and placed his face close to his children's.

"We must go." He took their hands and they again descended the stairwell, the Aigle and his eaglets. They would make their way to the southern wing and find an exit. They had not reached the bottom step before the sounds of numerous heavy footsteps could be heard above. They pressed on. Despite the weight of the dragon on his back, Corantin felt weightless. They reached the ground floor and made their way inward, towards the south. The echo of the footsteps behind them now gaining pace, no longer distant. They turned a corner and made their way toward the centre courtyard, hoping against hope that their passage met no dead ends along the way. Corantin followed the corridor around a turn and stopped dead. There before him stood a wall of officers, armed and ready. Holding the children, he turned back the way they had come just as another unit of Gaslampers fell into formation and blocked their exit. He had no choice. He gently pushed the children aside and reached out his arm, exposing the pipe from within his sleeve. His dragon would breathe fire after all. He reached his trembling hand across to his arm and twisted the valve on, then drawing a match from his coat, he struck it... Nothing. He checked the valve again. The collar was definitely turned completely to the right. He lit another match. Again nothing. The officer at the front, Thibault, drew his revolver and advanced. Thibault had been waiting for this moment since Notre Dame. He knew that his day would come, and Corantin knew that he was done. There was nothing more to do. He thought about the officers already in the passage in formation and he thought back to that moment in the laneway. There was only one other reason for the failure. In that moment, the full weight of the situation took hold of Corantin, for he realised he had been betrayed.

T he Cerf stood at the chamber door. He felt ill deep in his stomach and felt as though he may vomit. His body shook but he felt no cold. It was Madame Lally who came to him in the laneway only hours before. As he had crouched in the shadows keeping a watchful eye on the gatehouse, she had been keeping a watchful eye on him. She took him by surprise. He knew her by reputation, not by sight, and her plainness and lack of notable attributes proved to be her greatest strength. It had started as a passing washer woman, nothing more. The Cerf did not feel any need to be cautious about this woman as she passed down the laneway. He had stood with his gas mask down, completing the deception that he was an officer on duty. She had approached him and whispered into his ear.

"They will kill her, you know. I know who you are." He had immediately lifted his mask to see her with his own eyes.

"Who are you?"

"A friend." In a single movement he had taken the blade from his boot and held it to the washerwoman's throat.

"What do you know?"

"Your granddaughter, Renard Rouge is held captive at the compound." Her words were choked from under the blade and the Cerf eased the pressure a little. "She has been *persuaded* already. But they will kill her unless..."

"Unless what?" The blade pressing again.

"You can stop it. The Maire has a message for you." The Cerf pulled the blade away completely, he was all ears. Madame Lally rubbed her neck and straightened her apron, looking around her in feigned caution. "You are to deliver the Aigle to the Maire and he will release your granddaughter unharmed. You don't need to do anything but get him into the compound and the Maire will do the rest."

"How do I *deliver* him?" The word felt like venom in his mouth.

"You'll think of something, I'm sure." With that, Madame Lally eyeballed the Cerf one last time before turning and walking briskly back down the laneway towards the tenements. Her work was now complete. The Cerf had fallen where he stood, bile rising in his chest as he contemplated the choice before him.

The chamber door finally opened and he looked upon the Maire for the first time face to face. He instantly recoiled at the familiarity he felt for someone he despised so greatly.

"Please come in." The direction was cordial and firm. The Cerf slowly stepped into the office chamber, the large oak door remaining open. Without waiting, the Maire walked directly to the chair behind his large wooden desk and sat. For a long moment he eyeballed the old rebel that stood alone and awkward in the centre of the room. The Cerf looked to the ground, for he could not bring himself to meet the eyes of his highbinder. The Maire finally spoke.

"So, this is the Cerf. The oldest calibrator and rebel in this city. I feel as though I am looking upon a unicorn, or the Lock Ness monster, no? Your deeds are legendary. Your name alone strikes fear into the hearts of many loyal to the government…and yet. This is it." The Maire gestured to the old man before him dismissively. "I am disappointed. Perhaps I expected too much, but you are just a little old man. It is almost comical, don't you think?" He waited for a response but received none and decided to cut to the chase. "So we have business, do we not?" The Cerf nodded without lifting his eyes.

"We have a deal," the Cerf finally found his voice, although it quivered a little with uncertainty.

"Do we indeed?"

"My granddaughter."

"Oh, you mean the *Red Fox*." He almost spat the words as he spoke. "Renard Rouge. Yes, she is spirited isn't she? At least she was."

The Cerf's eyes shot up, wide and questioning. He could already feel the presence of others that had filed in behind him. "Where is she?" His words were now certain and dangerous.

"Do you honestly think that I could let you and the Rouge girl just *walk* out of the compound? The two of you are among the most dangerous outlaws in Paris and we would simply open the gates of the city to you." A broad smile formed across the Maire's face and grew into earnest laughter.

"Where is she?" The words held all of the weight of the threat that lingered.

"She is dead. Gone. Too much persuading." The words had not yet escaped the Maire's lips before the Cerf launched himself at the dignitary before him. Strong arms gripped him on all sides and he only got as far as the desk before he could move no further, the veins throbbing in his neck with strain. But it was no use. Officers held him firmly on all sides, restraining him from any movement.

"We had a deal." The words were now spat in desperation, pleading against hope that it wasn't true. The Cerf's eyes scanned the Maire for any sign that it was not true. But there were none, for the Maire had become a master of deception and, like a gambler at the highest stakes table, he returned a stoney gaze. The Cerf slackened and sank. It was over. The betrayer had been betrayed. The Cerf did not fight. It was a fate that he understood his actions warranted, there would be no promised silver and he would be crucified upside down. But *her.* She was all he had and she was gone. He had no fight left and fell limp with compliance. Behind the surrounding officers, the Chief Inspector stepped silently into the room. This was an event that had haunted his dreams for decades and he was not about to miss out on a ringside seat.

"Take him to his cell," the Maire commanded. On his word,

the officers lifted the great stag, now frail with grief out of the chamber and into the darkness. Only the Chief Inspector remained. The Maire finally took a sharp breath. He did not love being the emissary of such a betrayal but felt he had no choice. He needed this dangerous man disarmed and he had hoped that Renard Rouge was the key. It was true that she was not in her cell anymore. She had fled in the night and he did not know where, or how. But now he had a far more pressing concern. The Cerf had indeed delivered, and he found that the moment he had been anticipating for two decades was now upon him and he was feeling unusually anxious. It was just a reunion after all; a reunion, an explanation and an offer. It was however made all the more complex by the fact that he was not at the bottom of the Seine at all but very much alive. The Inspector cleared his throat to announce his intention to speak.

"Your guest is detained with the children in the holding chamber, Monsieur."

"*Detained?* " The Maire raised his eyebrow in genuine concern. He did not want his plan to be sabotaged by heavy-handed buffoons.

"They are unharmed monsieur. The utmost care has been taken for their comfort... But there was a *device* that was removed from the man, Monsieur."

"What device?"

"It was a gas machine of sorts. I really don't know or understand what it was, but it has been locked in the storerooms until it can be inspected. He is now unarmed and placated with the presence of the children. What would you have me do?"

"Bring them here, Inspector." At that the inspector bowed in deference and turned on his heels to leave. "Oh and Inspector, well done." The Maire was in an uncommonly good mood and as the portly ringmaster left the chamber, found himself checking the safe behind the curtain one last time to confirm that the lux periscope was still present and locked, as he often had the habit of doing. Comforted in its security, he began to rehearse his speech. It would not be an easy sell but one way or another, Corantin would do his bidding. The children would serve as his surety, for their safety meant the world to their father.

⚜

Corantin stood tensely expecting the strike of a baton or the rough handling that was a consequence of surrender, but there was none. The senior officer that he recognised from the floor of Notre Dame approached cautiously with his revolver raised and as Corantin slowly lifted his hands, he proceeded to gently disarm the Aigle with no unnecessary force or violence. On his command, several officers ushered the children towards the safety of the troop while others eased Corantin to his knees and removed his leather coat before carefully lifting the gas tanks from his back. "What is it?" came the gruff query from an older officer standing at Corantin's side, to which he merely shrugged dismissively. The officer's hand shot out instinctively to strike at the offending prisoner before it was caught mid-flight by Thibault.

"Unharmed." His words were hissed at the officer in question. "Stand down. You are dismissed." With eyes burning in anger, the officer turned and followed the order. Thibault then walked over to the gas tanks and looked curiously at the valves and pipes. He called over another officer who carefully ran his fingers over the spigot, assessing any immediate danger. Corantin used the brief moment of distraction to reach into his coat pocket on the floor and remove the small leather package, dropping it inside his gas mask which he held gingerly by his side. Satisfied that the tanks had been shutoff, Thibault returned to Corantin and offered a small smile.

"I am Captain Thibault, Monsieur Chastain. You are safe and will come to no harm," his voice was firm but warm. "The Maire would like an audience with you. That is all." Corantin stood momentarily confused. How did they know his name? There was surely a trick. He stared at the Captain but could see no obvious ruse.

"I want the children with me," he stated firmly, taking a bold gamble on the situation. The Captain nodded and officers released the children who immediately ran into the arms of their father. Without a word, Corantin passed the gas mask covertly to Phillipe.

"Please." Thibault gestured to Corantin to raise his arms as he proceeded to pat down his captive's body checking for any undisclosed weapons. He found none. "Come". The Captain led Corantin and the children back down the corridor towards a chamber further to the north. Corantin noted carefully in his periphery that two officers were opening a storage door with a key as he passed. He guessed this would be the repository for the dragon's safekeeping. He memorised that it was three doors down on the northern courtyard corridor, committing detail to memory as he was in the habit of doing. It was not long before they were ushered into a small chamber where Thibault apologised once more for the necessary detainment before closing the wooden door with a final bolt. His orders had been for civility and therefore he was civil. Had his orders been to slit the intruders throats then all three would be lying in pools of their own blood. Thibault, the French Legionnaire and Captain followed orders.

Angelique again threw her arms around her father. Corantin returned the embrace but found himself scanning the walls, acutely aware of the necessity of time. He gently leaned close to her. "My Angel, we will talk in a moment, but right now I don't know how much time we have. Forgive me." Angelique nodded and took the hand of her little brother. Corantin then began to feel around the stonework walls for a loose brick, a crack or split. His fingers felt for any imperfection until he found it. On the eastern wall, he could feel the corrosion of damp. Wet, green moss formed a slimy film over part of the wall that extended to the ceiling, but the stones were firm. He reached to the very top brick and, straining on tip-toes, felt that the worn mortar structure was particularly brittle. He tried to pry the stonework loose but could not reach. Angelique, now understanding his intention walked over to the wall beside her father and gestured he stand aside. She gripped her strong fingers between the stone bricks and wedged her toes beneath them. Arm over arm, she began to climb the brick wall until, finally poised at the top she reached her hand to the brittle mortar and brushed it aside finally removing the brick. She looked down at Corantin who shook his head in disbelief. "Phillipe, the gas mask," he whispered across the room. The boy handed it to his father. He had not been searched as Corantin had hoped. He was just a boy and so passed unnoticed and unchecked. Taking the small leather box from the mask, Corantin handed it to Angelique, who planted it in the hollow of the stonework before placing the stone back, creating a seamless facade of solid antiquity. Angelique silently dropped to the ground.

"What is it, Papa?"

"Please. Sit." Corantin gestured for his children to sit beside him as he sat against the stone wall. He began to meticulously relay all that he had previously disclosed to Phillipe. As he spoke of the Aigle, the resistance and the lux periscope, Angelique sat wide-eyed and speechless. She had no words. For a long time, she sat in silence, trying to process the story laid out before her, trying to make sense of the pieces. There was one piece that she alone held and she finally spoke.

"Papa, there is something that I must tell you. It is about the Maire." She paused, looking at her father, trying to read if it was a story he already knew. He did not. She swallowed to speak when suddenly the bolt on the door rattled and the portly Chief inspector entered the room.

"Monsieur. Children." The Inspector offered a shallow bow in feigned politeness. "We meet again." A small smile turned beneath his thick moustache.

"We meet again." Corantin returned, "I shall not be hoisting you to the rafters on this occasion though." He raised his hands demonstrating they were empty. The humour was lost on the portly Inspector who found his face instantly flushed and growing red with anger. It was a silent anger and he dutifully doused its flames with politeness.

"Indeed. You have been asked to attend an audience with the Maire. If you would be so kind as to follow me... Please."

"Do we have a choice?"

"No." It was a curt response softened in its presentation. Corantin and the children rose to their feet and followed the Inspector out of the door, along a series of corridors and up several flights of stairs until they were finally standing outside the large wooden oak doors of the Maire's office chamber.

Angelique stood, still clutching her unrevealed piece of the puzzle. She needed to tell her father what she knew, but there had been no opportunity. He would certainly find out soon enough. She also could not be certain that what she had been told was in fact the truth. One way or another, she was about to find out the truth and she therefore held a tense anticipation that was not shared by Phillipe or her father.

Corantin stood expressionless before the door, a vision of stoic calm. The Inspector rapped on the door and pushed it open for the guests. He did not follow them in but rather closed the door behind them as he had been instructed. Corantin took several steps into the vast chamber before him, Phillipe and Angelique by his side. He stared at the Maire for a brief moment without emotion, his mind a whirl of confusion as he tried to clarify and grasp the figure before him. In that moment, Angelique who had not taken her eyes off Corantin since they entered, knew. She knew that what she had been told was true and was no longer able to look upon the anguish and trauma in her father's face. She looked away. He was in shock. Corantin took several steps forward and fell into a stumble as the Maire slowly rose from behind his desk. Phillipe, also witnessing the alarming transaction did not understand what to make of it.

"Corantin." The Maire finally spoke, his voice was whispered and full of emotion.

"Charles?" Corantin barely let the question escape, the word felt so painful and impossible. The Maire silently nodded as he made his way across the floor to his brother. In that moment, Phillipe could see the resemblance, and although it made no sense, he felt some joy at their reunion as Charles finally embraced his younger brother with arms full of intention. Corantin stood for a moment with his hands limply by his side until he too, slowly lifted his strong arms and returned the embrace. The two brothers, separated by twenty years, two worlds and death, stood in each others arms. That was until something rose within Corantin like a roar and grabbing his brother by the shoulders, he shoved him backwards, throwing him off balance. Charles' face instantly shifted from joy to fear as Corantin moved towards him like an enraged, wounded bull. Phillipe had never seen his father like this, he was a stranger before him and Phillipe was afraid. As Corantin picked up his older brother and threw him against the tapestry, holding him fast, Phillipe almost wondered if he should do something.

"Papa, no!" Angelique shared the same fear and as the keeper of the devastating secret, felt a degree of responsibility. Corantin heard her small voice and in that moment saw himself. He softened. A little.

As air began to return to Charles' lungs, he gasped, "I can explain." His voice was hoarse and his hands still shook from adrenaline. Phillipe had noticed so much in those few panicked seconds. He saw the confusion and anger between the two brothers and sensed their deep secrets locked in small chests hidden in dark fireboxes. He saw the Obscura emblem emblazoned on the tapestry that shook violently in the scuffle and in that violent movement he caught a glimpse of a small iron safe. More locked chests.

"You should be buried in the Seine. You had us believe for twenty years that you were dead. How could you do this?" Corantin's voice was also raw and hoarse.

"I can explain." Charles repeated, his voice still quivering a little. He looked across at the children and paused with clear intention. "May we perhaps discuss this in private."

Corantin had no intention of letting his children out of his sight again. "They can stay."

"Yes. I am very sorry that you believed me dead. I truly am. I never had any intention of hurting you and Delphine." He looked coldly at Corantin. "You know why I left. You pretend you know nothing, but you know everything." Corantin returned the cold glare confirming the implication. "I wanted for us to make a clean start," the Maire continued. "I want you here...with me. The children led you to me."

On those words, Corantin seized his brother, hauling him from the wall and hurling him to the floor with powerful force. "You dragged my children into your vile city to serve your purpose." A vicious struggle took place momentarily before Corantin overpowered his older brother and pinned him to the floor.

"Guards," came Charles' feeble plea between pained breaths. Angelique and Phillipe stood helpless as the large wooden doors hurried open and several burly Gaslampers stepped into the room. They immediately gripped Corantin firmly and hauled him away from the Maire, twisting his arms painfully to immobilise the threat. "Don't hurt him. Just...restrain him." Charles slowly stood, dusting himself off. His clothing was dishevelled and blood flowed freely from his nose. He took a moment to calm himself before he spoke. "You are making a mistake. This, you will learn. You are not my prisoner, you are my guest. But for now you will need to be contained. That is not my choice, it is yours." He turned to the children and tried to offer an apologetic smile. "I am sorry. I had been hoping our meeting would have been a far more pleasant affair. I am your uncle Charles, and you are?" He extended his hand towards the boy who stood motionless and confused before finally taking the hand.

"I am Philippe, Monsieur."

"No doubt you are an inventor as well. No?"

Phillipe looked to Corantin uncertainly and stayed silent when he saw the fire in his father's eyes. The Maire finally addressed the officers. "Take this man to his room. The children will be staying in separate quarters for now. The doors will be locked." He looked across at his brother. "Again, for now."

Corantin looked at Angelique and Phillipe and mouthed the words "*We will be alright*," through an attempted smile. Corantin's gaze then fell upon Charles. He was still trying to process the events of the last few minutes and how this stranger before him had so suddenly turned his world upside down. The guards led Corantin out of the room, leaving Phillipe, Angelique and Charles alone. The children stood uncomfortably silent, uncertain of what they should say.

"Phillipe, Angelique, I meant it when I said that I had hoped a great deal for our first meeting. I am truly glad to meet you both. I would like it very much if you would be my guests and share my quarters until your father is feeling more...comfortable." Angelique nodded, uncertain how to respond. "You understand of course that you will not be able to wander freely at this point of time... for now." Angelique again nodded. The Maire then opened the door to the Chief Inspector and nodded to him. With a slight turn of his hand, he gestured the turning of a key and the rotund inspector nodded in understanding before escorting the children out of the office. Charles watched them leave his chamber and noted how very much like her mother Angelique looked.

Charles was again alone. His nose felt bloodied and swollen

and the iron taste of blood remained in his mouth. The meeting had not gone at all as he had rehearsed and it became apparent that time had not been the healer that he had hoped for. The last time they had seen each other had ended the same way. It was the day before he had *died*. It had involved coarse words and a violence that was reminiscent of only moments ago. It had been their differences that had driven Charles away... and love. Corantin had won back then and Charles had slunk away to disappear into the Seine. But he would not lose again. This was *his* city.

CHAPTER 16
CANVAS FLIGHT

The room was much finer than anything Phillipe had ever seen before. Despite the great distress that overwhelmed him and a fear that sat coiled in his belly, he could not help but notice extravagance in every corner of the room. He sat on the bed beside Angelique and they were silent for some time. It was the first time he had been alone with her since they were attacked in the theatre a lifetime ago. "Are you alright?" His question slipped out quietly, trying not to be more than it needed to.

"Yes, Phillipe. I am just so incredibly overwhelmed with everything. I'm not sure if I am happy or sad, relieved or burdened. I just don't know what to feel... It is good to see you. I have missed you very much. I was afraid I may never see you again." Her last word bubbled with emotion and she sat there waiting for it to pass.

Phillipe did not speak straight away but put his arm around his sister. He had felt the same way about her. He took a moment before he finally asked the question he feared the most. "Did he hurt you?"

She shook her head in reply. It was true. Her uncle had been nothing but kind to her since her arrival. There was so much that she wanted to tell Phillipe, so much confusion she wanted to share, but she felt alone in the burden and remained silent. She wanted to tell him all about the frenzied bonfire in the street where piano, book and violin alike stoked the flames of hatred. She wanted to share her collision with Lord Gossard which had revealed a welcome kindness in a world lonely and terrifying. She wanted to tell him that his time with the bookies in the Royal stables had enabled her to recognise and decode the Caesar's cipher and plan her escape. She didn't tell him any of this, but Angelique then thought upon her good fortune that she did not escape with Renard and Victor in the end. Her uncle had told the truth. She had rightly trusted him, for here she sat with her brother once again and her father by some miracle also brought into this world. Perhaps in time her father *would* come around. Perhaps he had also misunderstood his brother and anger and resentment would subside...they would indeed make a powerful alliance.

"What became of Renard Rouge?" Philipe's question broke the silence and pierced Angelique's ballooning thoughts that were now taking flight.

"I do not know." Her reply was honest. She thought of the moment that she looked upon the beaten and bloated face of Renard in her cell. That vision alone drove a coach and horses through her wishful ideals. Every time she thought upon the warm demeanour and extended palm of her uncle, she was haunted by that vision. "She escaped with a guard, but I don't know what became of her."

"She escaped and you did not?" Philipe's question was full of concern. Angelique shook her head in response.

"I believed that you would come here. I was right." For a brief moment they shared a small smile. Phillipe had told Angelique earlier about how the Cerf had rescued him at the theatre and how their father had come and rescued them both at Notre Dame on giant wooden wings. He had not spoken of the Cerf since and she feared his avoidance masked a tragedy of sorts. She braced herself for the very worst news and asked the question, simply and directly. "Phillipe, where is the Cerf?"

"I do not know." It was now Phillipe's turn to be honest. "He came with us into the compound dressed as a Gaslamper, but was sent off for other duties before we were captured. I don't know if he was taken or managed to escape." Hope hung in the air at least as densely as fear. Both of their companions were last seen alive and free and so their hearts and courage lifted a little. Since they had arrived in the room Phillipe had been distracted, his thoughts had been elsewhere as though he was trying to allow an idea the time to ripen. If Angelique had been troubled by confusion and compromised allegiance, Phillipe had been troubled by a different problem. Getting home. Since Corantin had spoken to him about the lux periscope which he had looked upon with his own eyes, he had not been able to get it out of his head. There was a second periscope that had disappeared from his father's lock box. Surely it could be the only way that Charles had entered the Obscura. Corantin must have known that also. The question that had plagued Phillipe's thoughts had been *where?* Where would the Maire keep the only lux periscope in the Obscura, the very device that must have been used by the Inspector when he came to entice the children outside the old Vanguard theatre. Then he saw it. In the moment that Corantin threw his brother against the stone wall, the tapestry had come askew ever so slightly and he had caught the merest glimpse of it. The small iron safe. With a second periscope they could get two of them home and he could return for the third. He wondered if he should share his thoughts with Angelique or Papa. There would be no point in sharing hypotheticals. The only way to know would be to find out for sure, under the cover of darkness. When the time was right he would investigate alone. He carefully took his boots off as if preparing for rest and glanced down at the hollow he had carved in the inside sole. His adjustable key had perhaps been the greatest invention of his short lifetime.

❦

Half-light brought with it new hope. The dissipation of darkness brought with it a buoyancy and clarity that dimly shone through every window and crenelle. The Maire stood at the locked door of his brother. It was unrealistic for him to think that two decades of hurt and anger would dissolve in a single meeting. It would take time. He had awoken that morning at first light with the realisation of two things. Firstly that his body was no longer young, and the aggression of the previous day had taken its toll and secondly that he had indeed broken the proverbial ice. It may be a slow melting from this point, but he had broken the ice. His brother now knew that he was alive and living in the Obscura. Corantin now knew that he was forgiven and indeed needed. A plan had began to form as he straightened himself in the looking glass and dressed for the day. It would be a two-pronged attack. He needed to demonstrate that he was of worthy character and that Corantin had misunderstood him over all these years. He would firstly need to win over the children. Phillipe did not yet trust him, but the girl, Angelique, now had proof of his earnestness. He had delivered on his promise and she would be the key to the boy. As for his brother, rather than use the children to take advantage of his obvious weakness, he would play to his affections. Science and invention was Corantin's language of love and so it was with that tongue that the Maire intended to speak. He knocked firmly on the door as the guard unlocked the bolt, offering at least the guise of privacy respected.

"May I come in?" The Maire politely called through the door. He waited a moment before the door slowly began to open. Corantin stood inside the door, the dishevelled bed suggested that he had at least slept throughout the night. The Aigle had also been doing a great deal of thinking. The last moment he had spent with Charles two decades before had played over and over in his head. Every word, every movement was examined forensically for meaning and understanding until he finally concluded that he could find none. He could not understand. But there was an unsettling feeling that hovered when he was in the presence of Charles and he sensed that there was more to the man that met the eye. He could not understand how small or large the secrets were hidden beneath his mayoral chains, but he would be careful. Very, very careful. He had also thought a great deal on the Cerf. He did not know what happened to him when they parted company and a deep fear of his safety plagued his thoughts. He considered simply asking his brother of the fate of Enzo but did not want to alert anyone to his presence in the chance that he had escaped or was endeavouring to.

Charles stepped into the dimly lit room. He lifted his posture and held his head aloft in an effort to disguise the intense fear he felt being again in the presence of Corantin. The knowledge of guards outside the door gave him some comfort in his relative safety. "I am glad to see you slept."

"A little," came the curt reply.

"Corantin. I wish to be frank with you as I know I have not been in the past. I don't expect you to forgive or forget, I just ask that you listen. Please, give me a chance, however small to share some understanding with you."

There was a long silence as Corantin stared at the stonework on the floor. He finally raised his eyes to his brother and slowly nodded. He had the children to think of, and civility would buy him time and their safety. He had been a fool the previous night and would be far more careful in the future. A large smile spread across the Maire's face.

"Very good...very good. Can I offer you some breakfast?"

Corantin nodded. The truth be known, he was starving. He

could not think of the last time he ate. He needed to keep his strength up if he was going to have any chance of getting them all back home.

"Very good. I will have the servants freshly cook you some. Please take your time to dress and I will come back in an hour. There is something that I want you to see."

⚜

An hour later, breakfasted and dressed, Corantin followed his brother down the long stone corridor, the echo of their footsteps being the only sound resonating in the silence. It occurred to Corantin that it was the same corridor where they had been captured the previous evening. He noted the third door to the left as he passed it, mentally building a map in his mind should the opportunity arise for the inventor to be reunited with his dragon. Charles did not speak. He knew that words were cheap and feared that he was not expert enough to communicate any form of an olive branch... yet. The courtyard should speak for itself.

Finally arriving at the end of the corridor he stood by a large wooden door that led to the courtyard and waited for Corantin to join him. With a swift, confident movement, he pushed open the heavy door and the Aigle stepped into the inventing engine room for the first time. Much can be said of expectations, what one imagines in their head before the curtains on reality are drawn. In itself it is an elastic concept that can be estimated, overestimated or underestimated... but there was not an expectation that could have formed in Corantin's thoughts that would have prepared him for the courtyard space into which he stepped. Despite his better judgement, he could feel his eyes darting from one spectacle to the next, he felt his mouth open ever so slightly and he knew that his wonder had betrayed him. It was beyond anything he could ever have imagined. Engines of every kind were being primed and oiled. Scientists in lab coats moved about the enormous space weighing objects, recording notes and engaging in heated debates over theories and evidence. In one corner he saw large wooden wings like those of a bird being polished and framed. In another he saw a huge engine of sorts transmitting a static sound that was occasionally interrupted by a garbled voice that crackled through the machine. It was then that he saw another scientist speaking into a device at the other end of the courtyard and realised that it was indeed his voice that was being transmitted through the air. He felt like he was witnessing a magic show of sorts, because everywhere he looked he found himself marvelling at impossible illusions. Then, in the centre, he rested his eyes on the *piece de resistance*. Large teardrops of canvas had been sewn into an enormous balloon as big as a building. It was like Faraday's experiment he had read about where seventy years previously he had made a rubber balloon take flight. But this was large enough to take a man, perhaps several. There was an engine beneath the balloon where a scientist worked with large metal funnels and valves attached to a tank within a great wicker basket. It was indeed an experiment of flight.

"May I speak with the scientist?" Corantin could not conceal his emotion.

"Of course." Charles stood grinning. He felt that it was a breakthrough greater than he could have ever anticipated. Corantin approached the giant canvas balloon and addressed the man whose greasy hands tightened a bolt with his eyes fixed firmly on the valve gauges.

"Any success?"

The man looked up, surprised at the unusual event of a question. He looked at Corantin cautiously before looking across and seeing the Maire. Satisfied that the conversation was sanctioned be responded. "A little. Did you want to see how it works?"

"Yes. I would love that."

The man finished his last turn of the bolt and stepped back

from the engine. He turned the valve on the tank and the pipes hissed under pressure, finally placing his hand on a valve at the neck of the largest pipe.

"Oxygen runs from the tank to the smaller valves where it is fed at a constant rate into the funnel. This valve will expel the oxygen at great pressure." The scientist turned the valve and a loud hiss emanated from the pipe spout. He then took a phosphorous match and lit the gas, erupting into a large cone of fire reaching several feet. As he turned the valve further, the flames grew several more feet and burned with more intensity. Corantin nodded his head and smiled as the scientist turned the flame off. "We should have the envelope stitched and reinforced by tomorrow and we will see if we can get it off the ground."

"Merci." Corantin nodded again before turning and walking back towards Charles. The enormous glass roof above the courtyard had been opened up over the front quarter that housed the balloon in anticipation. The truth was, the giant balloon may leave the ground. A little. But not enough. Corantin had felt the heat of the burner and, though intense, it was not enough for any real altitude. They were burning the wrong gas. His mind was racing as he returned to his brother whose face was flushed with joy at seeing the change.

"This, Corantin, is the engine room of tomorrow. This is where some of the brightest minds of our generation have full financial freedom to bring this city into the future for the betterment of mankind. They are good. They are great. But they are not *you*. If you could only see yourself and the children, here by my side...you would want for nothing. But this would be yours. You would have complete freedom to create as you please." He paused, letting his proposal percolate for a moment. He was acutely aware of driving his brother away by sounding too desperate. The offer had to stand on its own merit. It would take time. "There is more. There are projects that have not yet moved beyond the constraints of design that may well change civilisation as we know it."

Corantin stood, taking in his brothers words. It was true, he was impressed. Beyond his wildest imagination, he was impressed. He had followed without expectation; bitter, angry and calculating, and had now felt some of that sensation dissipate with the oxygen that fed the flames of possibility. His intention and course had not changed, but he did allow himself for a moment to consider the alternative. To imagine himself by some impossibility at the helm of this workshop, working with other great minds, propelling the unimaginable, like iron sharpening iron. In that moment he understood a little more of his brother. Despite his better judgement he found himself softening... just a little. "Merci." His gratitude was genuine. The world of science and creativity was important to Corantin, paramount, and he had been quietly starving in its absence. Charles knew all of this and had invited him into this space because he understood Corantin. It felt both thoughtful and flattering. "This is truly impressive, Charles. You have given me much to think about. It was... unexpected. This is a great deal to take in at this present time as you can imagine. I would also like to see the children."

"Of course." Charles had seen such a notable shift in his brother that this request did not seem at all unreasonable or dangerous anymore. "I can take you to them immediately. They will be very excited to see you." Perhaps there would be no need to lock the doors. Perhaps there should be a degree of trust at this point, give them the freedom to feel that they were indeed guests and not prisoners. This had gone far better than he could ever have imagined. Corantin also shared the sentiment. The morning's excursion had opened up opportunities he could never have foreseen. The balloon would indeed fly, but not in the morning. It would fly that evening, and with three passengers onboard. Out of the building and out of the Obscura.

There was a small detour first. Corantin was still dressed in the dishevelled uniform of a Gaslamper which Charles felt was both dangerous and inappropriate. If he were to feel that he was a guest in the compound, then he would need to feel that he was dressed as a man in authority and not a common guard. Charles stopped momentarily at the laundry where appropriate garments were found in the refined fabric that were becoming of the ruling class. Corantin was instructed to replace the leather coat and underclothes of an officer for the clean, linen undershirt and trousers of a gentleman. He was also given a long, tweed coat of the finest quality which he dutifully pulled on. He had no choice. The clothing did not serve his purpose, but he needed to play the part of the forgiving brother for his plan to have any chance of success.

When Corantin was finally brought into the drawing room of the Maire's own quarters, the children had already been ushered in. They embraced their father earnestly and made their way to the settee in the centre of the room, looking to Charles for permission to freely use the furniture. "Please," the Maire responded, "use the quarters as though they were your own. You are my guests... I will leave you to talk. It is wonderful to see you all together. It truly is." Charles nodded his head to Corantin, satisfied that events were taking such a wonderful turn, and took his leave, closing the heavy wooden doors behind himself. The three were alone.

"I have much to tell you, children," Corantin began. There was no time for sweet affectations, for he did not know how long they would have alone. "I think I have a way for us to get home."

"Back to Paris? Back to the old world?" Phillipe earnestly clarified.

"Oui. There is a balloon in the courtyard. It is large enough to take us all. I think I can make it fly."

"What do you mean?" Angelique was utterly confounded by this nonsensical confession and there was a part of her that was disappointed that they would be facing more danger and risk when the possibility of them staying together, happily in comfort lay before them.

"It is a giant balloon, as big as the Arc de Triomphe. It is made of canvas and can take passengers in a basket underneath. They are going to try and make it fly with oxygen in the morning. It might work, but I am sure that I can make it fly tonight. If I can get if off the ground, I can get us to safety. All of us. If I can get it high enough, fast enough...perhaps we can leave the atmosphere, the stratosphere. Perhaps if we can cheat the scientific laws of the world in which we are living we can descend into the world from which we came."

"I think there is another way." Phillipe was quiet and cautious. There was something that he could not put his finger on, but could not trust. He felt as though he needed to be careful with the information as though it were a stick of dynamite in his hand sweating and dangerous. "I think I know where the second *box* may be." The word was both general enough to be ambiguous, but specific enough that Corantin instantly caught his drift. "If it is where I think it is. I am sure that I can get it."

"I don't want you to take any risks." Corantin's voice was even and certain.

"Oui. No risks." Angelique was still caught between two worlds and feeling lost in the shifting sands beneath her feet.

"If we have two *boxes,* we can return," Phillipe's eyes moved to Angelique so his intention and plan was crystal clear, "and I will return with them for you Papa."

"No. You will not return. There will be no returning. Let's see what we can find, but there will be no returning." Corantin reached out and drew both of his children close to him. "I don't want to let either of you out of my sight again." A silence fell on the three and Phillipe found himself relieved. Relieved that he did not have to reveal any more about his suspicions, and relieved when the conversation then meandered into the minutiae. There was so much more they had wanted to tell Corantin, about the house in the Meudon woods, leaping into the icy depths of the Seine and the beautiful woman in a dress who had done the same... but it did not feel like the time and place for stories and so they did not. Instead they found safer moments of warmth and laughter, all three finally united against all odds. When they finally arose to depart, they found Charles in the corridor outside. Glad of their warm interaction, he escorted them back to their quarters where they could continue their all important discussions about their future at the compound.

It was only when they finally left the drawing room and the large timber doors closed, that Madam Lally stepped out from behind the heavy velvet drapes that had concealed her. She had been planted at the request of her master to listen to the conversation and report back on his progress at winning them over. But the conversation she had heard was not at all the conversation expected. She did not understand the references to a box to be found, but she certainly understood the clear plan of escaping in a giant flying balloon. It was not the conversation that the Maire had anticipated, but it was indeed the conversation the Maire would hear.

⚜

It was well past nightfall when Corantin finally opened the door to his quarters slowly and carefully. He had a plan. Though the risk was great, the opportunity was small and so in the silence of the flickering darkness, Corantin, Phillipe and Angelique quietly slipped out of the room. They had decided that Corantin's plan, as uncertain as it was, presented the most robust offering. The three would make their way in dim shadows to the courtyard space, only stopping once at the storeroom for the hydrogen tank necessary for ascension. Angelique silently closed the heavy wooden door behind her, being careful to step lightly and keep low, for the only sources of light were the lanterns hanging along the corridors at head height. The only sound she could hear was the thumping of her heart in her chest and the careful shuffling of feet on the stone floor. She still felt the pangs of error. She had argued cautiously for the alternative of their cooperation with Charles but found the disagreement too great and silenced her objections accordingly. She knew she would dearly love to be home again with Phillipe and her Papa, safe in their little apartment in the tenements, but it felt a world away and an impossibly dangerous distance.

The first sound they heard behind them as they rounded the corner was the click of a half cocked hammer and cylinder roll retention pin. Corantin slowly turned at the familiar sound to see Charles standing in the light of the lanterns, officers to his flank with their pistols drawn and cocked.

"It is a very quiet excursion indeed is it not? It is almost as if you did not want to be heard."

Corantin slowly edged forward and placed himself in front of his children once again. There was nothing he could say. Their intention was obvious.

"Where would you be going at this late hour, brother? The courtyard perhaps? Aspirations of flight perchance." Charles felt an unexpected Vesuvius of rage erupting to the surface as he felt the acute ingratitude and betrayal of his guests. It was not a new betrayal. It was an old one. Dressed in the pretence of reconciliation, this trojan horse had disarmed him momentarily. But he was not disarmed for long. As the old wound rose to the surface he found himself stepping towards Corantin until his face touched that of his brother's. Corantin could feel the breath of his brother's anger and veins in his neck rising like ropes that would once again confine. Charles gripped Corantin's collar and, despite his better judgement, drove his younger brother against the stone wall. The two grappled momentarily as officers stood uncertain with cocked pistols. Angelique ran between them to defend her Papa and in that moment was shoved. The hand of Charles was sure and certain as it pushed his niece against the stone wall harder than she could have expected and perhaps harder than intended, but pushed her all the same. She was surprised by how hard she hit the stone and though still conscious, she fell to the floor no longer certain of her footing. Corantin immediately went to his daughter's aid and placed his strong arm underneath her head . She was cut and bleeding, but she would live. If Charles understood betrayal, he was now not alone. The greatest pain Angelique felt in that moment, was not the cut above her head or the bruising on her arms, but that she had been wrong. Dangerously wrong. Charles drew a deep breath and raised himself back into authority. "We have all learned lessons tonight. I was wrong to have trusted any of you. It is fickle no? Trust. You were my guests. Every comfort I had available you were offered. Every freedom... and now you shall have none of those things. Officers, take each of them to separate cells in the basement block. They are not to talk. They are not going to see one another and they are sure as hell not going to fly in a balloon." At that he gave a nod and each of his officers holstered their pistols and placed heavy hands upon each of the Chastains. Angelique's struggle was silenced quickly and she gave no more resistance. Phillipe began to call out to Corantin and stopped himself. It was of no use. Within moments each were dragged down to the bowels of the compound and thrown without ceremony into, cold, dark and silent cells. There, Phillipe would sit with a key hidden deep in his shoe that would offer no value to a heavy door with an iron bar bracing and locking from the outside. He sat as did the others, in a darkness that went well beyond the lack of light. For it was a space bereft of hope, and that brought with it a darkness that reached within and drained his very heart. For at that same moment, the Maire stood with his engineers staring at the mechanics of the giant canvas balloon. They hastily unfastened the oxygen tank that connected to the hoses and valves where it would be kept with him throughout the night. He would be taking no chances. The balloon would take flight in the morning and not a moment before.

CHAPTER 17
THE IRON SAFE

Every sound in the darkness was sharp and clear. Phillipe had tried to close his eyes and rest, but his mind whirled with the memory of impossible events and visions of impossible futures. He was finally at the end of his ideas. Perhaps the morning half-light would offer new hope, but right now as he sat in the blackness, there was no hope to be had. Every shuffle and movement he made echoed and amplified around him as though the emptiness itself mocked him. He leaned against the hard wall and finally tried to empty his mind... allow his senses to focus. That was when he heard it. It was quiet at first. Barely audible, the gentle tap of cautious footsteps down the corridor. They paused outside his cell and he heard the unmistakable sound of the iron bar scraping noisily against the barrel and finally a key rattling in the lock. He stood to his feet, readying himself for anything as a fear grew and rose up from the pit of his stomach. It was then that the door opened and in the dim light he could make out the thin, gaunt frame of a man standing in the doorway.

"Young man. Come. I am a friend."

Phillipe stepped forward and could see the elderly man for the first time, his long, grey hair tied neatly at the nape of his neck.

"My name is Lord Gossard. I can not get you out of the building, but I can get you to the Aigle and your sister. They are further down the corridor. "

"Are you a Calibrator?" Phillipe had not seen this refined man before and was not certain where his trust should lie. Gossard nodded his confirmation.

"We must hurry."

Out of the cell, into the relative light of the corridor, Phillipe hurried behind the sure-footed figure before him. Within moments he could see his Papa and Angelique by the flickering lantern in the distance. He ran to them.

"Merci, Gossard," Corantin's gratitude was heartfelt. "We would have no hope without you, my old friend."

"It is I who is in your debt, Aigle. It is you in danger, not I. This regime dismisses me as old and senile. They will never suspect me because they see me as frail and ornamental."

"Yet here you are. You see and hear much, Gossard."

"I wish there was more that I could do. Forgive me, but my work here is not yet finished." With that, the Lord bowed a brief acknowledgement and smile to Angelique and disappeared into the distance. Corantin immediately crouched down next to Phillipe, his voice was low and quiet.

"We can not take the balloon anymore. It will be watched. It is too dangerous. Do you still think you can find the box?"

"Oui." Phillipe was certain. He looked over to Angelique. The blood from the cut on her forehead was dry and dark, but bruising began to swell around, as though a dark river ran through the purple ranges. Their eyes made contact and shared the same nagging fear which manifested into a question that emanated like a hidden whisper from Phillipe's lips. "What about you? There are only two boxes Papa."

"Do not worry. I have a plan. Just get that box and we will meet you at the first chamber where we were held. Angelique will get the other box from the stonework. Do you think you will be able to find your way?"

"Oui." Again he was certain. Corantin did not doubt his son's ability to navigate the dim corridors. His attention to detail was his gift, his power. Phillipe leaped forward and embraced his father and sister once more. Just in case. He then slipped into the darkness of the shadows the way he had come.

৩৯৩

If Phillipe had understood the powder keg of dangers that he navigated in the darkness, perhaps he would never have left the confines of his cell. But courage is not born of heroism, it is born from fear and necessity. It was both fear and necessity that the boy felt as he scurried along the shadows of the walls, feeling for stairs in the darkness, pausing momentarily to listen to the silent soundscape around him. A Gaslamper sat at the base of the stairs guarding the block of cells throughout the dreary night. Only Lord Gossard, the old fool, had passed him earlier and the evening had since been utterly uneventful. He had indeed drawn the short straw and made no secret of his displeasure and disinterest as he leaned against the stone wall resting his eyes as the first casualty of boredom. Phillipe kept to the shadows and did not make a sound as he passed by the Gaslamper whose indifference to his assignment rendered him a soft obstacle. He ascended the stairs without uttering a sound and found his way along the stone corridors back to the civic chambers and the office where he had first met the tyrant that turned out to be his uncle.

Upon arriving at the large wooden door, Phillipe dropped to the ground and slipped off his shoe, feeling in the darkness for the cold, hard edge of the key wedged into the sole. He took it out and began to work it into the door's lock, twisting the bow and listening carefully to the clicking of the adjustable key wards as they found the hollows in the lock. He was also listening intently for the slightest sound of habitation at the other side of the door, entering into an office occupied by the Maire was the last event he wanted to transpire. Thankfully, he heard no such indications and so when the final click of the tailpiece receiver could be heard turning the large gear on the lock, he entered the room. Slowly at first but discovering that there was no occupier present, he closed the door behind him and made his way directly to the large velvet drapes against the back wall. It was exactly as he had remembered and drawing the heavy drape, he revealed once again the sturdy iron safe that he had only seen fleetingly once before. It was just as he had suspected. Heavy, robust and seemingly impenetrable. He took his adjustable key once more and tried it in the small keyhole near the handle. It was not an easy fit, but with a little jiggling and persuasion, the key found its way completely. Again he listened with his ear to the iron door. It was difficult to hear inside as the sounds were dulled from within the heavy exterior, but he closed his eyes and allowed his hearing to sharpen. The hours he had spent in the silent, darkness of the cell had tuned his ears to the slightest vibration. With expert fingers, he gently adjusted the wards, listening as they found their way, correcting, adjusting and trialling the lengths and distances that his ears told him were correct. With each correct choice came a reward of the faintest clicking sound, but he was acutely aware that if he extended the wards too far, the key would no longer fit and he risked jamming it in the lock. Other sounds came sharply into focus, the scurrying of a mouse in the wall, the ticking of the grandfather clock near the window acting as a metronome of trepidation. Yet, despite these sounds, despite the distracting thumping of his heart in his chest, Phillipe heard the final sound of the ward clicking underneath the driver pin within the tumbler and lifting the spring above it. The small iron door swung open. There before him was a soft leather cloth covering a small wooden box just like the one Corantin had showed him. He took the box into his jacket, trying to contain the surge of excitement he suddenly felt and closed the iron door once again preparing to lock it.

But it was another key he could hear rattling in a lock, the tinkering sound of iron on iron as the handle turned on the large wooden door to the chamber. He immediately held his breath, pulled his legs in tight and made sure that he was fully concealed by the velvet drape. The heavy chamber door opened and the Maire strode into his office chamber. He struck a phosphorus match and lit the lantern on the wall, suddenly throwing a warm, flickering glow across the room before walking back over to the door muttering to himself as though he were not alone. "Strange... strange indeed. I swear I locked the door before when I left." He ran his long wiry fingers over the door lock as if to reveal some curious discrepancy. But there was none. No sign of forced entry and nothing more than the aberration of an overactive imagination fuelled by unusual events. Yet, there was something unsettling about it. Perhaps he should check the iron safe one last time. Just in case. The Maire lifted his lantern and made his way towards the velvet drapes at the back of the chamber. It was there, out of both fear and necessity that Phillipe exploded into movement. Cornered and without choice, he launched himself at his unsuspecting uncle and shoving with all his might, pushed his way through the room and out the door. In that instant, Charles did not immediately understand what hit him. He fell back, he knew that. His lantern shattered upon the stone floor and the flame licked at the edges of the drape, threatening an inferno, he also knew that. But with fire slowly climbing the fabric around him, he reached down to the iron safe and opened the unlocked door freely. It was when he saw the empty chamber inside that he fully understood. Not only had the boy escaped his incarceration, but he had stolen the most valuable object in Charles' possession... but he would not get far.

Decisions are made in many ways. Some are the results of due diligence, the result of great consideration of options and consequences. Some are made on a whim, on the flip of a coin or two clenched hands hiding behind one's back, and some are made in an instant, simply because the alternative is unthinkable, when there is no other way. It was under this pretence that Corantin decided that he would get his children home at all costs, even at the cost of his life. They had stopped at the storage room first. He had mapped the location and distance of all of the necessary procurements required for their departure. The heavy iron door was locked as expected.

"Do you have a hairpin?" he whispered to Angelique. She nodded dutifully and removed a single hairpin from her braid, handing it to her Papa. He straightened the pin and leaned in slowly, edging the pin into the key hole and jiggling it carefully while listening and feeling for the movement of the small and large cog. While Phillipe had developed great skills in the inner workings of a lock, his Papa had developed mastery. It took less than a moment for the two cogs to align, and with a sweeping, pushing motion, Corantin released the lock. He opened the door and turned to Angelique. "Did you watch what I did?" She nodded. It was true, she had watched every flick of his wrist with great curiosity. "I need you to go to the other chamber further down the corridor where we hid the lux periscope. The door may be locked so you will also need your hairpin. Get the box as quickly as possible and wait there for me. I will get there as soon as I can." A great weight formed in Angelique's stomach, a nervous energy that surged through every fibre of her body. She did not know if she could pick the locked door, certainly not alone. But she would try. She took the pin and touched her father gently on the arm, just in case, before turning and making her way back towards the chamber.

I t only felt like moments later that she arrived at the chamber door, her heart still pounding violently while an overwhelming sense of nausea rose from deep within her. Despite her heightened senses, she could not recall any moment of the journey to the chamber. She had listened for every sound, focused on every flicker of light and yet fear had worked its powerful amnesia. All of her senses were in the *here and now*. She reached for the handle and discovering the door locked, she pulled the hairpin from her pocket. Placing it in the keyhole, she began to push and swirl her wrist in the same manner that Corantin had moments earlier. Nothing. She withdrew the hairpin and straightened it once again before inserting it a second time. Again she pushed and swirled and could feel the pin bending in the mechanism but could not find any click of release. Nothing. She checked the pin, straightening it a second time. In that moment, she said a little prayer under her breath as one does when life seems to be hanging in the balance, dangling just outside of one's control. She breathed deeply and inserted the pin again. This time she did not push, but listened. She edged it closer to the tailpiece, pulling back when she felt resistance. Finally she began to make small circles with her wrist, feeling carefully for any connection and resistance until she heard the unmistakable click of the release and the door opened. She realised she had been holding her breath and concentrated on trying to calm herself as she walked into the chamber for the second time. Within moments she had shifted her feet from stone to stone and made her way to the loose brick in the top right corner, removing it with her left hand while her legs held her firmly in place. She could feel the oiled leather cloth in the space and carefully eased it safely to the ground below. Relieved at her accomplishment, she waited in the chamber.

Only moments later, industrious sounds outside the door sent a jolt of alarm through her senses. She crept to the closed door and listened warily. The sounds of scraping timber on stone and the occasional wooden crack and break led her to cautiously inch it open, enough to look. It was Corantin. He was now wearing his hydrogen tank on his back and had re-harnessed the long pipe down his arm. He had taken no chances this time and had already turned the valve on his back on himself, he was in effect a walking inferno, only checked by the small valve at his wrist and the phosphorous match in his pocket. His refined gentleman's coat was dropped unceremoniously on the stone floor, he had no more need of concealment. His occupation however, was not with the dragon on his back but with the furniture in his hands. He had grabbed whatever chairs, tables and cupboards he could find in nearby rooms and chambers and was breaking them at will and laying the timber debris across the corridor.

A barricade.

If needed, a barricade of fire.

Angelique immediately set to helping her Papa build their defence. It may not be needed if all went well, but deep down, Angelique felt the weight of an unanswered question that lingered like a phantom, hovering silently and dangerously. She did not know what would happen if Phillipe failed and what would happen to Papa if Phillipe succeeded. She finally took a breath and asked the question she had been dreading. "Papa, if Phillipe finds the box and we do make our way back home... what will happen to you."

"Do not worry about me, Angel. I will be fine."

"I will come back for you with the second box."

"No!" Corantin's voice was firm and frightening. "No, you must never come back here. Promise me, Angel. I will make my own way back. Under no circumstances will you return. Say it." A silence lingered uncomfortably. "Say it!"

"Oui. I will not return, Papa."

He reached his hand to her cheek and caressed her softly. It was not an apology, but he regretted his stern tone. Angelique pressed her face close to her Papa's and breathed deeply, her stomach was tight and her eyes stung. It was then that they saw him.

In the distance, at the end of the corridor, they saw Phillipe. He did not sneak in the shadows. He did not quietly scurry in the darkness. He ran. In fact, he ran in a way his sister had never witnessed him run before. It was not just the speed, it was not just the energy, it was the panic. For only metres behind him ran two Gaslampers in pursuit, and fast as he was, their larger and stronger legs gained on him every step. Corantin called out to his son, to be certain he knew that his father was just beyond the barricade. But what to do? Corantin turned the valve on his wrist and took the phosphorous match from his pocket, but he could not light the barricade until his son was safely behind it. He did not have time to take the dragon off his back and he was too encumbered to be effective with it. He held his breath and prayed that inspiration would come.

In that instant, it did.

The form was unknown. No-one saw it coming. But as the boy and his pursuers passed the eastern corridor, a body came from the darkness. It launched at the Gaslampers and took them to the ground with such force that they did not stir. Phillipe did not see it, and it was only when he arrived at the barricade, his heart pounding relentlessly, that he saw it in Corantin's face. He turned to see that he was pursued no more, and slowly the figure rose from the limp bodies of the officers that had been had silenced. From the shadows, the Cerf stood, still in his Gaslamper's uniform and walked towards the barricade. His breath still heaving in his chest. No one was as surprised as the Cerf when Lord Gossard had opened the door to his cell and relayed to him the snippets of intelligence that he had. In return he vowed to seek atonement and serve in any way that he could to buy his comrades their freedom.

Corantin pocketed the match and turned his wrist valve off as his old friend slowly clambered over the small wall of timber and finally stood silently in his presence. His face was bruised and swollen and a large gash above his eye extended to his ear, now dark and dried. Bruising extended down his neck into his undershirt.

"Forgive me," the old man finally uttered, his earnest eyes finally meeting Corantin. The Aigle reached his arm across to the shoulder of his oldest friend.

"Oui. I understand." And in the moment, he did. There was no explanation necessary to disclose what compromises and coercions played a part. The Cerf was here, willing and devoted and Corantin was acutely aware of the suffering and torment that he knew he had been subjected to.

"There will be many more. You don't have much time," the old man offered. Corantin turned immediately to Phillipe, who nodded to the silent question and pulled the oiled leather wrap from within his jacket.

"The Maire saw me," he offered. "He is coming."

"Quickly." Corantin ushered both children into the small chamber. "Take note of where this room is. Remember, in Paris, this is the hospital storeroom." The children both nodded. "I want you to go straight to the tenement apartments back in Paris. Oui?"

"Then I will come back for you, Papa." Phillipe quickly added.

"Perhaps." Corantin smiled at his son, his eyes were firmly on Angelique before he leaned forward and ruffled Phillipe's hair. "I will see you both soon enough. You know what to do?" They both nodded again although neither could look at their father, the weight of the moment was taking its toll. It was then that they heard the sound of boots. There were many. The echoing sound drummed dangerously throughout the corridor.

Corantin marched outside. The Cerf had already drawn the revolver he had taken from the officers still sprawled in the corridor. It was time. Corantin turned the valve on his wrist and lit the phospherous match. As he placed it in front of the mouth of the metal pipe, his arm roared into a stream of fire. With one long stroke he lit up the barricade before him. The roar of the fuelled flame was deafening, timber crackling and exploding in its wake. The Cerf looked across at the Aigle, it was a formidable fortress that he had constructed, but they both knew it was temporary and both men sensed it would be their last stand. The throng of officers on the other side was growing. It was in that moment, in his peripheral vision, that Corantin saw the great, grey beast clambering over the broken cupboard. The roar of the fire was great, but the wolf was fast. If he burned, it was only momentarily before stumbling, slavering and incensed with pain, it raced through the chamber door. Corantin saw it happen and could not do a thing as the angry, confused beast flew past him, straight into the room where his children were escaping.

In one deft movement he shut the valve off at his wrist as he could not risk setting the chamber ablaze. In a primal, urgent burst, he raced into the chamber ready to tear the wolf apart with his bare hands if necessary... but it was empty. A dry, silent heat hung in the air ominously and the children were gone, as was the wolf. A knot of realisation formed in the pit of Corantin's stomach and he stumbled back out into the corridor as the barricade, having now burned through much of the timber that fueled its flames, began to subside and topple.

"Take my coat." The Cerf had already dressed himself in the refined gentleman's coat that Corantin had discarded on the stone floor earlier. He tossed Corantin his leather Gaslamper's coat. "Take off the dragon first. Save your gas... you will need it."

Corantin instantly understood the intention of his oldest friend. He took a breath to argue but saw that it was no use. The Cerf was already readying himself to make one final dash. Corantin looked across at Enzo and caught his eye momentarily. There was nothing to say. There were no words. He smiled and mouthed the words *farewell* before taking the cylinder from his back, pulling on the jacket and leaving.

The flames before the Cerf had subsided enough that he could see the soldiers readying themselves on the other side of the barricade. He took a deep breath and climbed over the blockade before plunging himself into the troops. So stunned were the officers as this apparition parted their ranks, that they did not move, they did not stop or hinder the Aigle as he ran with all the power the old man could muster. But gathering themselves beyond that moment, they did give chase and they fired upon the fleeing figure as they had been instructed to do. The Cerf did not feel it at first. Only the exhilaration of exacting this last deed of atonement. It was not until his legs fell from beneath him that he realised the sting of the shot. He propped himself up and slowly ascended again to his feet, sounds closing in all around him. Shuffling forward he felt the sudden inability in his leg dragging behind him, willing it to propel him forward. If only to gain distance, to buy time. It was then that he felt a burst through his shoulder so powerful that it spun him.

Yet he pressed on.

Sounds and voices enveloped him and the world began to slow as though he waded through thick water that deepened as he sank into its warmth. It gently rose around him until he felt as though he might disappear below the watery surface. Breathing deeply he plunged beneath the water and all fell beautifully silent.

CHAPTER 18

HOMECOMING

I t was only moments before they dropped to the stone ceiling, immediately becoming a stone floor, that Phillipe first saw the slavering, wild beast pounding through the chamber door. He was prepared for the world to turn upside down once again, the wolf was not. It was this and perhaps only this that saved their lives. As Phillipe and Angelique hit the ground, the lux periscopes still in their hands, they heard the dull thud and howl of the wolf tumbling from the significant height of the floor, its disorientation both clear and momentary. The small room was suddenly filled with metal shelves stacked with cloths and sheets. It took only a second for both Phillipe and Angelique to understand their imminent danger and without thought or hesitation they rose from the ground and darted towards the open chamber door, Phillipe pulling a shelf over behind him as adrenaline coursed through his veins. The wolf, quickly recovering, tore after them, its legs suddenly powerful and focused.

The corridor was littered with iron beds and disused trolleys all stored in dormancy until they were to be required on the upper levels. As they ran, Phillipe pulled bed after bed across the corridor in an attempt to dissuade the pursuant beast. But each obstacle was met with only the slightest deviation in its course and the gap between the pursuer and pursued began to close. As they reached the end of the corridor, they immediately ascended the stairs, the sounds of the barking, howling wolf echoing along the stone walls. The sounds were so great that by the time Phillipe and Angelique reached the next floor, orderlies and nurses had filed into the upper corridor to investigate the source.

There are many things that a nurse could expect to see in a Parisian hospital in the nineteenth century. Those that had been present during the clashes of the Paris commune only decades before had witnessed the very worst of mankind, and brought with them a philosophy of preparedness for the unexpected.

But no one expected a wolf.

In a hospital.

Ever.

It was the girl they saw first. Her face grey and her eyes wide. Then the boy followed behind, a bellowing shout emanating from his lungs. It was then that they saw the wolf, huge and grey and impossibly there inside the Hospital Dr La Salpetriere. They watched as the boy stumbled, his legs kicking at air, trying to gain traction once again on the ground, the wolf now only several feet away. It launched itself at the boy, its jaw wide and dangerous, clamping down on the boy who thrust his arms in desperation at his assailant. If it wasn't for a small wooden box that got in the way of the jaws of the beast, the boy would have been dead. But instead the small wooden box locked the wolf's jaw as it tossed its head violently from side to side trying to shake it loose, finally crushing the box in its teeth. It was only then that a Gendarme who by chance was on his way to question a patient on that same floor, managed to get a clear shot at the beast. He took aim and with only three rounds, finally silenced the creature with his service revolver. A silence fell upon the space. The kind of silence that follows a great noise, the kind of silence that follows disbelief. It was then, in the realisation that the wolf had just devoured any hope of his father's homecoming, Phillipe began to sob. It was heartfelt and loud.

The first to come forward and put his arm around the boy was an older gentleman who sensed that he knew this lad somehow. Something familiar resonated with him beyond a child in need and as quickly as he could, he helped Phillipe to his feet and drew Angelique over to him also.

"You are shaking, boy. Are you hurt?"

Phillipe did not answer and in truth did not know. It felt to him his whole world had been crushed in the jaws of the canid. The gentleman ran his eyes over the boy looking for any obvious wound or injury and found none. The grey carcas lay several feet from the boy who could not take his eyes off the beast. He lowered himself to meet the children's eyes.

"My name is Gustave Eiffel. I am a friend. Come, let me take you from this creature. We shall get some air, oui?"

Phillipe struggled to find his breath between stifled sobs and offered no response. Angelique took her brother's hand and nodded. Monsieur Eiffel seemed kind and she immediately trusted him. She had left the Obscura world carrying the burden alone that she would never likely see her Papa again, and now Phillipe had been forced to face this same truth. Neither child offered any resistance when Gustave took them gently by the hand and led them down the corridor, past the orderlies, nurses and Gendarme. The policeman, his revolver still smoking, made a gesture to stop Gustave and the children.

"Monsieur. These children will need to stay."

The gentleman stopped and looked firmly at at the constable. "They will do no such thing. They are upset and afraid and they are free to leave."

"Monsieur. I must insist."

"Gendarme, I am a good friend of the General d'armee. If you do not step aside, I will have your badge before the day is done."

The officer looked the gentleman up and down and deciding

that the threat was perhaps not idle, bowed his head and stepped aside. Gustave led the children down the corridor, up the stairs to the main entrance, where they crossed the packed earth courtyard before walking out of the large iron gates onto the Boulevard de l'Hopital.

Both children stood on the lawn before the gatehouse in wonderment at the vision before them. In that moment, Phillipe's tears abated as he and Angelique looked out at the city of Paris as they had never appreciated it before. Gone were the graffitied walls, dark with oppression, gone were the citizens, afraid in their haste as they cowered under the ever watchful eye of the Gaslamper and wolf. The colours before them, both vivid and bold dissolved their hopelessness as a warmth began to soak into their very skin. It took a moment before Angelique realised it was in fact, the sun. The glorious sun that shone down on them in their utter despair and planted the smallest seed within of something like hope. The three stood for the longest moment on the grass before the roadway, the children swept away by the sights and sounds around them and the gentleman swept away by the two curious children suddenly in his care.

"You both must be feeling quite shocked, I can imagine," Gustave finally spoke across the silence, "I must take you to your parents. Where can I find your parents?"

Neither child responded immediately.

"Is there someone caring for you, child?"

Angelique finally spoke "Oui, Monsieur Eiffel. Our father is not at home at the moment. But we will go home and wait for him." Her last word trailed off as though it was difficult to utter.

"Of course. Where is your home, mademoiselle? Allow me to take you there."

Under normal circumstances she would have refused the offer, but somehow took comfort in the gentleman's presence. "We live in the tenement apartments in Montmartre, Monsieur."

"I shall fetch my buggy and driver and take you there,"

Gustave declared, a firm decision finally made. "It has been a most peculiar day. A most peculiar day indeed. First a giant balloon crashes outside the city and now a wolf is found inside our very hospital." He turned to collect his driver from the stables.

"What did you say?" Phillipe had finally found his voice. It was as though that one sentence had cut through all of the noise around him.

"Ah, it has been a peculiar day, young man."

"No, Monsieur. The balloon?"

"Oh. Have you not heard? All of Paris has been talking about it since early this morning. Some, great, canvas craft of flight has crashed in the fields near Pantin. It was like something out of a Jules Verne novel."

"Were there any passengers?" Angelique could not contain her excitement and Gustave found himself utterly confused by the sudden shift in the mood of the conversation.

"No, mademoiselle, there were none found that I am aware of. That is the greatest mystery of all. It is as if this colossal balloon had flown itself."

"Can you take us there?" The electricity in the conversation was palpable and Gustave found himself swept away in its current.

"Oui. Of course." It had been a secret desire of Gustave to witness this spectacle himself but had reprimanded his own voyeuristic motivations. But for the sake of these children he could surely now take a look. He hurried across to the stables to raise his driver and buggy.

❧

The hillside near Pantin was filled with spectators. Farmers, harvesters, factory workers, gentlemen and ladies had all gathered upon the hillside to witness the curiosity that unfolded before them. Some had gathered picnic blankets upon the wild grass and sat breaking bread and cheese with one another as though they were waiting for the prologue to begin. But the drama that unfolded before them was real and extraordinary and it felt as though Phillias Fogg himself may descend at any moment from the giant wicker basket that lay upturned near the shrubbery. When Gustave's buggy arrived, it was one of dozens that had stopped by the fields to join the growing number of Parisians who were gathering to witness the historic anomaly. In the distance they could see the wicker basket capsized near the shrubs. Metal debris, blackened and broken, lay strewn across the field, and several hundred feet away lay an enormous canvas cloth. The large tear-drop pieces were still stitched tightly together and billowed occasionally in the wind, but a great tear in part of the canvas prevented the cloth from lifting. The Gendarmerie were scattered throughout the field, some keeping an eye on the eager bystanders and others conversing on the grounds and taking notes.

Phillipe immediately leapt from the buggy and ran through the crowd towards the field. Angelique descended and ran after him as quickly as she could, she had also wanted to investigate, but was urgently afraid for her brother's impetuousness. Gustave did not have the chance to stop them. He understood very little of the situation but knew that they would not get far before they would be stopped by the Gendarmerie once again.

Few saw the young boy at first, each official on the field appeared to be preoccupied with doing a job of sorts. It was not until he was within several yards of the wreckage that the Gendarmerie finally raised their heads and took notice. One officer nearby scurried across and intercepted the boy, grabbing him by the shoulder as he struggled and thrashed. Within moments, several other officers arrived and tried to calm the lad down, but to no avail. He was set on getting to the wreckage and it pained them to have to hold the young boy down in such a manner. It was only when his sister arrived that he began to calm a little.

"Forgive us, Monsieurs. This is my brother. We believe that our father was the pilot of this tragic flight. Please. Did you find a...victim?" Angelique's voice shook as she searched for the last word. She was also very upset and did not fully understand what was going on. The older Gendarme addressed the young girl.

"You are mistaken, madamoiselle. There was no passenger, no pilot. We have searched every inch of this field and there was no body. This flight was unmanned. Your father is safe. You can be happy, no?"

It was true, amidst all of the debris, all of the torn canvas and metal, there was no body. Angelique had seen this same balloon in the courtyard of her uncle's compound. She had no doubt that it was her Papa. But how could she expect that he could traverse worlds on a canvas ship without expectation of tragedy. She moved over to her brother. "Merci, Monsieur. We are greatly relieved."

"Officers, let go of this lad, he is my charge and he is just a boy!" Gustave had finally arrived and immediately put his hand upon Phillipe's shoulder. The Gendarmerie released their hold and both Phillipe and Angelique embraced Gustave and held him tightly. It took him by surprise and he instantly took pity on these children and felt a great urge to protect them. "Come," he whispered, "you shall both come home with me until we can find your father. There is clearly much on your mind. Come." He took the children by the hand and made his way back to the buggy beyond the hill. Spectators had hovered on the fringe of the field to try and get a better view as the drama appeared to be unfolding, but seeing the boy no longer agitated and the incident somewhat resolved, they began to meander back to their groups, disappointed that the moment had not escalated as it had promised.

The hovering crowd had largely disappeared by the time Gustave finally led the children over the hill back to the buggy. "I am sorry you are disappointed." He finally said. "I realised I don't even know your names. I am so very sorry."

"This is Phillipe," Angelique responded, "and my name is…"

"Angelique." A voice in the distance cut through the crowd. It was a voice she as knew as well as her own, and her eyes searched desperately in the sea of people. Searching. Hunting.

Then she saw him.

He was still wearing the leather coat of a Gaslamper and stood like an apparition from another world. She screamed and in that moment, Phillipe saw his father also. They ran. They ran straight into his arms and the three embraced. The world around them dissolved into the Parisian sky and all they could see was one another as though time itself had stood still. Just for a moment. Not a word was spoken as they stood alone on the hill in Pantin. Corantin finally looked across at the buggy where the children had stood and saw his old friend Gustave Eiffel. Gustave looked across and marvelled at what a small world it was. For it was none other than Corantin Chastain.

"It is a small world indeed," the bridge engineer shouted to his old friend. He was about to walk over, for there was much he felt he should tell Corantin about the sinister events involving the man's charming young children whom he had only just met. But in that moment, he decided he would let them be. They would tell their father themselves when they were ready and he did not feel comfortable interrupting such an earnest embrace. So, with a final wave, Gustave climbed aboard his buggy and left. He would not be drafting plans for his tower today. He could not possibly think of grand mechanical designs when his imagination was so full of wolves in the city and flying airships.

Phillipe clung to his father as though he would never again let go. There was a moment when he had discovered his father was something other than his father. When he discovered the type-setter was a swashbuckling hero who could fight, soar and breathe fire. But he had only done those things to save his children.

Phillipe had been so proud in that discovery, so proud that his father was so much more than a typesetter. But suddenly, standing there he realised that he did not want or value those things anymore. He only wanted his Papa to stay. That was all. They were safe. It had felt as though safety was an impossible distance away. But now they were safe. Corantin finally spoke as he looked down upon his children.

"Let's go home."

They began the long walk to the tenements. It would be a silent walk, for though there would be many stories to be shared, now was not the time for stories. It was then, on the Pantin hillside, that Angelique saw the small torn piece of canvas, drifting across the long grass before her. She bent down and picked it up. Perhaps she would keep this small token to remind her of the Obscura in years to come. She would think upon the icy waters in Meudon, the kindness of the Cerf and the towering furnace of books in the street. She would remember Lord Gossard, Victor and of course Renard Rouge, she recalled the silhouette of them against the moon, walking out of the front gates of the compound.

The letter.

She suddenly recalled a moment that she had completely forgotten. Through the cell window she had been slipped a secret letter. Perhaps a dangerous letter. She immediately felt in her coat pocket, her hand digging deep into the satin lining for confirmation of the memory. There it was. She pulled out the letter from her pocket. As they walked, her eyes intently scanned the blotchy ink scribbled on the page.

Angelique.

I will not write this letter in code as you will not read this until we are all are safely out of the compound. I did not want to share this with you before, as I feared it would make you stay. I did not want to risk waiting to tell you in person in case something happened to me.

There was a woman who escaped the compound only days before we were taken prisoner. She was recaptured shortly after us. She didn't seem to be a prisoner as such, but more of a forced guest. I saw her once, she wore a beautiful silk gown and had long thick auburn hair. I didn't think anything of it at first. But one evening in my cell, I heard two guards further down the corridor talking about her. She was not from the Obscura. They said she came from your world many years ago. She had been a ballerina in Paris. I remember the night we were captured, you told me about your mother and that she had disappeared. I do not know if this woman could be your mother but I thought you should know. The guards also said her name was Delphine.

You cannot go back into the compound. See, my grandfather the Cerf, he knew a man named the Aigle. He has been gone for many years, but if the Cerf can find him, he will be able to help get her out.

I hope this letter finds you safely. These are dark times and we must all do what we can.

Until Freedom,

Renard Rouge.

Corantin looked across at Angelique who had been buried in a note of sorts while they walked across the field, but suddenly looked pale and upset.

"What is it, Angel?"

"Nothing, Papa. It is just a silly note I found in my pocket. I am fine."

The three continued to walk across the field. Angelique cautiously reached her hand deep into her other coat pocket to feel that it was still there. She touched the oilskin wrapping and peeled it back with her fingers to feel for the box underneath. The last one.

She would need it.

Once more.

www.ingramcontent.com/pod-product-compliance
Lightning Source LLC
Chambersburg PA
CBHW050258110726
47898CB00007B/2461